PENGUIN MODERN CLASSICS

THE SPOILS OF POYNTON

Henry James was born in 1843 in Washington Place, New York, of Scottish and Irish ancestry. His father was a prominent theologian and philosopher, and his elder brother, William, was also famous as a philosopher. He attended schools in New York and later in London, Paris, and Geneva, entering the Law School at Harvard in 1862. In 1865 he began to contribute reviews and short stories to American journals. In 1875, after two prior visits to Europe, he settled for a year in Paris, where he met Flaubert, Turgenev, and other literary figures. However, the next year he moved to London, where he became such an inveterate diner-out that in the winter of 1878–9 he confessed to accepting 107 invitations. In 1898 he left London and went to live at Lamb House, Rye, Sussex. Henry James became naturalized in 1915, was awarded the O.M., and died early in 1916.

In addition to many short stories, plays, books of criticism, autobiography, and travel, he wrote some twenty novels, the first published being *Roderick Hudson* (1875). They include *The Europeans, Washington Square, The Portrait of a Lady, The Bostonians, The Princess Casamassima, The Spoils of Poynton, The Awkward Age, The Wings of the Dove, The Ambassadors,* and *The Golden Bowl.*

HENRY JAMES

The Spoils of Poynton

❖

PENGUIN BOOKS

Penguin Books Ltd, Harmondsworth, Middlesex, England
Viking Penguin Inc., 40 West 23rd Street, New York, New York 10010, U.S.A.
Penguin Books Australia Ltd, Ringwood, Victoria, Australia
Penguin Books Canada Ltd, 2801 John Street, Markham, Ontario, Canada L3R 1B4
Penguin Books (N.Z.) Ltd, 182–190 Wairau Road, Auckland 10, New Zealand

—

First published 1897
Published in Penguin Books 1963
Reprinted 1964, 1968, 1971,
1972, 1975, 1977, 1978, 1980, 1981, 1983, 1985

—

—

Made and printed in Great Britain by
Richard Clay (The Chaucer Press) Ltd,
Bungay, Suffolk
Set in Linotype Times

CHAPTER 1

MRS GERETH had said she would go with the rest to church,
but suddenly it seemed to her that she should not be able to
wait even till church-time for relief: breakfast, at Waterbath,
was a punctual meal, and she had still nearly an hour on her
hands. Knowing the church to be near, she prepared in her
room for the little rural walk, and on her way down again,
passing through corridors and observing imbecilities of decoration, the aesthetic misery of the big commodious house, she
felt a return of the tide of last night's irritation, a renewal of
everything she could secretly suffer from ugliness and stupidity.
Why did she consent to such contacts, why did she so rashly
expose herself? She had had, heaven knew, her reasons, but
the whole experience was to be sharper than she had feared.
To get away from it and out into the air, into the presence
of sky and trees, flowers and birds was a necessity of every
nerve. The flowers at Waterbath would probably go wrong
in colour and the nightingales sing out of tune; but she
remembered to have heard the place described as possessing
those advantages that are usually spoken of as natural. There
were advantages enough it clearly didn't possess. It was hard
for her to believe that a woman could look presentable who
had been kept awake for hours by the wallpaper in her room;
yet none the less, as in her fresh widow's weeds she rustled
across the hall, she was sustained by the consciousness, which
always added to the unction of her social Sundays, that she
was, as usual, the only person in the house incapable of wear-
ing in her preparation the horrible stamp of the same excep-
tional smartness that would be conspicuous in a grocer's wife.
She would rather have perished than have looked *endimanchée*.

She was fortunately not challenged, the hall being empty
of the other women, who were engaged precisely in arraying
themselves to that dire end. Once in the grounds, she recognized that, with a site, a view that struck the note, set an ex-
ample to its inmates, Waterbath ought to have been charming.

5

How she herself, with such elements to handle, would have taken the fine hint of nature! Suddenly, at the turn of a walk, she came on a member of the party, a young lady seated on a bench in deep and lonely meditation. She had observed the girl at dinner and afterwards: she was always looking at girls with an apprehensive or speculative reference to her son. Deep in her heart was a conviction that Owen would, in spite of all her spells, marry at last a frump; and this from no evidence that she could have represented as adequate, but simply from her deep uneasiness, her belief that such a special sensibility as her own could have been inflicted on a woman only as a source of anguish. It would be her fate, her discipline, her cross, to have a frump brought hideously home to her. This girl, one of the two Vetches, had no beauty, but Mrs Gereth, scanning the dullness for a sign of life, had been straightaway able to classify such a figure as the least, for the moment, of her afflictions. Fleda Vetch was dressed with an idea, though perhaps with not much else; and that made a bond when there was none other, especially as in this case the idea was real, not imitation. Mrs Gereth had long ago generalized the truth that the temperament of the frump is amply consistent with a certain usual prettiness. There were five girls in the party, and the prettiness of this one, slim, pale, and black-haired, was less likely than that of the others ever to occasion an exchange of platitudes. The two less developed Brigstocks, daughters of the house, were in particular tiresomely 'lovely'. A second glance, this morning, at the young lady before her conveyed to Mrs Gereth the soothing assurance that she also was guiltless of looking hot and fine. They had had no talk as yet, but this was a note that would effectually introduce them if the girl should show herself in the least conscious of their community. She got up from her seat with a smile that but partly dissipated the prostration Mrs Gereth had recognized in her attitude. The elder woman drew her down again, and for a minute, as they sat together, their eyes met and sent out mutual soundings. 'Are you safe? Can I utter it?' each of them said to the other, quickly recognizing, almost proclaiming, their common need to escape. The tremendous fancy, as it came to be called, that Mrs Gereth was destined to take to Fleda Vetch virtually began with this discovery that the poor child had been moved to flight even more promptly than herself. That the poor child no less quickly perceived how far she could now go was proved by the immense friendliness with which she instantly broke out: 'Isn't it too dreadful?'

'Horrible – horrible!' cried Mrs Gereth, with a laugh, 'and it's really a comfort to be able to say it.' She had an idea, for it was her ambition, that she successfully made a secret of that awkward oddity, her proneness to be rendered unhappy by the presence of the dreadful. Her passion for the exquisite was the cause of this, but it was a passion she considered that she never advertised nor gloried in, contenting herself with letting it regulate her steps and show quietly in her life, remembering at all times that there are few things more soundless than a deep devotion. She was therefore struck with the acuteness of the little girl who had already put a finger on her hidden spring. What was dreadful now, what was horrible, was the intimate ugliness of Waterbath, and it was of that phenomenon these ladies talked while they sat in the shade and drew refreshment from the great tranquil sky, from which no blue saucers were suspended. It was an ugliness fundamental and systematic, the result of the abnormal nature of the Brigstocks, from whose composition the principle of taste had been extravagantly omitted. In the arrangement of their home some other principle, remarkably active, but uncanny and obscure, had operated instead, with consequences depressing to behold, consequences that took the form of a universal futility. The house was bad in all conscience, but it might have pased if they had only let it alone. This saving mercy was beyond them; they had smothered it with trumpery ornament and scrapbook art, with strange excrescences and bunchy draperies, with gim-cracks that might have been keepsakes for maid-servants and nondescript conveniences that might have been prizes for the blind. They had gone wildly astray over carpets and curtains; they had an infallible instinct for disaster, and were so cruelly doom-ridden that it rendered them almost tragic. Their drawing-room, Mrs Gereth lowered her voice to mention, caused her face to burn, and each of the new friends confided to the other that in her own apartment she had given way to

7

tears. There was in the elder lady's a set of comic water-colours, a family joke by a family genius, and in the younger's a souvenir from some centennial or other Exhibition, that they shudderingly alluded to. The house was perversely full of souvenirs of places even more ugly than itself and of things it would have been a pious duty to forget. The worst horror was the acres of varnish, something advertised and smelly, with which everything was smeared ; it was Fleda Vetch's conviction that the application of it, by their own hands and hilariously shoving each other, was the amusement of the Brigstocks on rainy days.

When, as criticism deepened, Fleda dropped the suggestion that some people would perhaps see something in Mona, Mrs Gereth caught her up with a groan of protest, a smothered familiar cry of 'Oh, my dear!' Mona was the eldest of the three, the one Mrs Gereth most suspected. She confided to her young friend that it was her suspicion that had brought her to Waterbath ; and this was going very far, for on the spot, as a refuge, a remedy, she had clutched at the idea that something might be done with the girl before her. It was her fancied exposure at any rate that had sharpened the shock ; made her ask herself with a terrible chill if fate could really be plotting to saddle her with a daughter-in-law brought up in such a place. She had seen Mona in her appropriate setting and she had seen Owen, handsome and heavy, dangle beside her ; but the effect of these first hours had happily not been to darken the prospect. It was clearer to her that she could never accept Mona, but it was after all by no means certain that Owen would ask her to. He had sat by somebody else at dinner, and afterwards he had talked to Mrs Firmin, who was as dreadful as all the rest, but redeemingly married. His heaviness, which in her need of expansion she freely named, had two aspects : one of them his monstrous lack of taste, the other his exaggerated prudence. If it should come to a question of carrying Mona with a high hand there would be no need to worry, for that was rarely his manner of proceeding.

Invited by her companion, who had asked if it weren't wonderful, Mrs Gereth had begun to say a word about Poynton ; but she heard a sound of voices that made her stop short. The next moment she rose to her feet, and Fleda could see that her alarm was by no means quenched. Behind the place where they had been sitting the ground dropped with a certain steepness, forming a long grassy bank, up which Owen Gereth and Mona Brigstock, dressed for church but making a familiar joke of it, were in the act of scrambling and helping each other. When they had reached the even ground Fleda was able to read the meaning of the exclamation in which Mrs Gereth had expressed her reserves on the subject of Miss Brigstock's personality. Miss Brigstock had been laughing and even romping, but the circumstances hadn't contributed the ghost of an expression to her countenance. Tall, straight, and fair, long-limbed and strangely festooned, she stood there without a look in her eye or any perceptible intention of any sort in any other feature. She belonged to the type in which speech is an unaided emission of sound and the secret of being is impenetrably and incorruptibly kept. Her expression would probably have been beautiful if she had had one, but whatever she communicated she communicated, in a manner best known to herself, without signs. This was not the case with Owen Gereth, who had plenty of them, and all very simple and immediate. Robust and artless, eminently natural, yet perfectly correct, he looked pointlessly active and pleasantly dull. Like his mother and like Fleda Vetch, but not for the same reason, this young pair had come out to take a turn before church.

The meeting of the two couples was sensibly awkward, and Fleda, who was sagacious, took the measure of the shock inflicted on Mrs Gereth. There had been intimacy – oh yes, intimacy as well as puerility – in the horse-play of which they had just had a glimpse. The party began to stroll together to the house, and Fleda had again a sense of Mrs Gereth's quick management in the way the lovers, or whatever they were, found themselves separated. She strolled behind with Mona, the mother possessing herself of her son, her exchange of remarks with whom, however, remained, as they went, suggestively inaudible. That member of the party in whose intenser consciousness we shall most profitably seek a reflection of the little drama with which we are concerned received an even livelier impression of Mrs Gereth's intervention from the fact

9

that ten minutes later, on the way to church, still another pairing had been effected. Owen walked with Fleda, and it was an amusement to the girl to feel sure that this was by his mother's direction. Fleda had other amusements as well: such as noting that Mrs Gereth was now with Mona Brigstock; such as observing that she was all affability to that young woman; such as reflecting that, masterful and clever, with a great bright spirit, she was one of those who impose themselves as an influence; such as feeling finally that Owen Gereth was absolutely beautiful and delightfully dense. This young person had even from herself wonderful secrets of delicacy and pride; but she came as near distinctness as in the consideration of such matters she had ever come at all in now surrendering herself to the idea that it was of a pleasant effect and rather remarkable to be stupid without offence – of a pleasanter effect and more remarkable indeed than to be clever and horrid. Owen Gereth at any rate, with his inches, his features, and his lapses, was neither of these latter things. She herself was prepared, if she should ever marry, to contribute all the cleverness, and she liked to think that her husband would be a force grateful for direction. She was in her small way a spirit of the same family as Mrs Gereth. On that flushed and huddled Sunday a great matter occurred; her little life became aware of a singular quickening. Her meagre past fell away from her like a garment of the wrong fashion, and as she came up to town on the Monday what she stared at in the suburban fields from the train was a future full of the things she particularly loved.

CHAPTER 2

THESE were neither more nor less than the things with which she had had time to learn from Mrs Gereth that Poynton over-flowed. Poynton, in the south of England, was this lady's established, or rather her disestablished home, having recently passed into the possession of her son.

The father of the boy, an only child, had died two years before, and in London, with his mother, Owen was occupying for May and June a house good-naturedly lent them by Colonel Gereth, their uncle and brother-in-law. His mother had laid her hand so engagingly on Fleda Vetch that in a very few days the girl knew it was possible they should suffer to-gether in Cadogan Place almost as much as they had suffered together at Waterbath. The kind colonel's house was also an ordeal, but the two women, for the ensuing month, had at least the relief of their confessions. The great drawback of Mrs Gereth's situation was that, thanks to the rare perfection of Poynton, she was condemned to wince wherever she turned. She had lived for a quarter of a century in such warm close-ness with the beautiful that, as she frankly admitted, life had become for her a kind of fool's paradise. She couldn't leave her own house without peril of exposure. She didn't say it in so many words, but Fleda could see she held that there was nothing in England really to compare to Poynton. There were places much grander and richer, but there was no such com-plete work of art, nothing that would appeal so to those who were really informed. In putting such elements into her hand fortune had given her an inestimable chance; she knew how rarely well things had gone with her and that she had tasted a happiness altogether rare.

There had been in the first place the exquisite old house itself, early Jacobean, supreme in every part: it was a provo-cation, an inspiration, a matchless canvas for the picture. Then there had been her husband's sympathy and generosity, his knowledge and love, their perfect accord and beautiful life together, twenty-six years of planning and seeking, a long, sunny harvest of taste and curiosity. Lastly, she never denied, there had been her personal gift, the genius, the passion, the patience of the collector – a patience, an almost infernal cunning, that had enabled her to do it all with a limited command of money. There wouldn't have been money enough for anyone else, she said with pride, but there had been money enough for her. They had saved on lots of things in life, and there were lots of things they hadn't had, but they had had in every corner of Europe their swing among the Jews. It was fascinating to poor Fleda, who hadn't had a penny in the world nor anything nice at home, and whose only treasure was her subtle mind, to hear this genuine English lady, fresh and fair, young in the fifties, declare with gaiety and conviction that she was herself the greatest Jew who had ever tracked a victim. Fleda, with her mother dead, hadn't so much even as a home, and her nearest chance of one was that there was some appearance her sister would become engaged to a curate whose eldest brother was supposed to have property and would perhaps allow him something. Her father paid some of her bills, but he didn't like her to live with him; and she had lately, in Paris, with several hundred other young women, spent a year in a studio, arming herself for the battle of life by a course with an impressionist painter. She was determined to work, but her impressions, or somebody's else, were as yet her only material. Mrs Gereth had told her she liked her because she had an extraordinary *flair*; but under the circumstances a *flair* was a questionable boon: in the dry places in which she had mainly moved she could have borne a chronic catarrh. She was constantly summoned to Cadogan Place, and before the month was out was kept to stay, to pay a visit of which the end, it was agreed, should have nothing to do with the beginning. She had a sense, partly exultant and partly alarmed, of having quickly become necessary to her imperious friend, who indeed gave a reason quite sufficient for it in telling her there was nobody else who understood. From Mrs Gereth there was in these days an immense deal to understand, though it might be freely summed up in the circumstance that she was wretched. She told Fleda that she couldn't completely know why till she

should have seen the things at Poynton. Fleda could perfectly grasp this connexion, which was exactly one of the
matters that, in their inner mystery, were a blank to everybody
else.

The girl had a promise that the wonderful house should be
shown her early in July, when Mrs Gereth would return to it
as to her home; but even before this initiation she put her
finger on the spot that in the poor lady's troubled soul ached
hardest. This was the misery that haunted her, the dread of the
inevitable surrender. What Fleda had to sit up to was the
confirmed appearance that Owen Gereth would marry Mona
Brigstock, marry her in his mother's teeth, and that such an act
would have incalculable bearings. They were present to Mrs
Gereth, her companion could see, with a vividness that at
moments almost ceased to be that of sanity. She would have
to give up Poynton, and give it up to a product of Waterbath
– that was the wrong that rankled, the humiliation at which
Fleda would be able adequately to shudder only when she
should know the place. She did know Waterbath, and she
despised it – she had that qualification for sympathy. Her
sympathy was intelligent, for she read deep into the matter ;
she stared, aghast, as it came home to her for the first time,
at the cruel English custom of the expropriation of the lonely
mother. Mr Gereth had apparently been a very amiable man,
but Mr Gereth had left things in a way that made the girl
marvel. The house and its contents had been treated as a single
splendid object ; everything was to go straight to his son, and
his widow was to have a maintenance and a cottage in another
county. No account whatever had been taken of her relation
to her treasures, of the passion with which she had waited for
them, worked for them, picked them over, made them worthy
of each other and the house, watched them, loved them, lived
with them. He appeared to have assumed that she would settle
questions with her son, that he could depend upon Owen's
affection. And in truth, as poor Mrs Gereth inquired, how
could he possibly have had a prevision – he who turned his
eyes instinctively from everything repulsive – of anything so
abnormal as a Waterbath Brigstock? He had been in ugly
houses enough, but had escaped that particular nightmare.

13

Nothing so perverse could have been expected to happen as that the heir to the loveliest thing in England should be inspired to hand it over to a girl so exceptionally tainted. Mrs Gereth spoke of poor Mona's taint as if to mention it were almost a violation of decency, and a person who had listened without enlightenment would have wondered of what fault the girl had been or had indeed not been guilty. But Owen had from a boy never cared, had never had the least pride or pleasure in his home.

'Well, then, if he doesn't care!' – Fleda exclaimed, with some impetuosity; stopping short, however, before she completed her sentence.

Mrs Gereth looked at her rather hard. 'If he doesn't care?'

Fleda hesitated; she had not quite had a definite idea. 'Well – he'll give them up.'

'Give what up?'

'Why, those beautiful things.'

'Give them up to whom?' Mrs Gereth more boldly stared.

'To you, of course – to enjoy, to keep for yourself.'

'And leave his house as bare as your hand? There's nothing in it that isn't precious.'

Fleda considered; her friend had taken her up with a smothered ferocity by which she was slightly disconcerted. 'I don't mean of course that he should surrender everything; but he might let you pick out the things to which you're most attached.'

'I think he would if he were free,' said Mrs Gereth.

'And do you mean, as it is, that *she*'ll prevent him?' Mona Brigstock, between these ladies, was now nothing but 'she'.

'By every means in her power.'

'But surely not because she understands and appreciates them?'

'No,' Mrs Gereth replied, 'but because they belong to the house and the house belongs to Owen. If I should wish to take anything, she would simply say, with that motionless mask: "It goes with the house." And day after day, in the face of every argument, of every consideration of generosity, she would repeat, without winking, in that voice like the squeeze of a doll's stomach: "It goes with the house – it goes with the house." In that attitude they'll shut themselves up.'

Fleda was struck, was even a little startled with the way Mrs Gereth had turned this over – had faced, if indeed only to recognize its futility, the notion of a battle with her only son. These words led her to make an inquiry which she had not thought it discreet to make before; she brought out the idea of the possibility, after all, of her friend's continuing to live at Poynton. Would they really wish to proceed to extremities? Was no good-humoured graceful compromise to be imagined or brought about. Couldn't the same roof cover them? Was it so very inconceivable that a married son should, for the rest of her days, share with so charming a mother the home she had devoted more than a score of years to making beautiful for him? Mrs Gereth hailed this question with a wan, compassionate smile; she replied that a common household, in such a case, was exactly so inconceivable that Fleda had only to glance over the fair face of the English land to see how few people had ever conceived it. It was always thought a wonder, a 'mistake', a piece of overstrained sentiment; and she confessed that she was as little capable of a flight of that sort as Owen himself. Even if they both had been capable, they would still have Mona's hatred to reckon with. Fleda's breath was sometimes taken away by the great bounds and elisions which, on Mrs Gereth's lips, the course of discussion could take. This was the first she had heard of Mona's hatred, though she certainly had not needed Mrs Gereth to tell her that in close quarters that young lady would prove secretly mulish. Later Fleda perceived indeed that perhaps almost any girl would hate a person who should be so markedly averse to having anything to do with her. Before this, however, in conversation with her young friend, Mrs Gereth furnished a more vivid motive for her despair by asking how she could possibly be expected to sit there with the new proprietors and accept – or call it, for a day, endure – the horrors they would perpetrate in the house. Fleda reasoned that they wouldn't after all smash things nor burn them up; and Mrs Gereth admitted when pushed that she didn't quite suppose they would. What she meant was that they would neglect them,

15

ignore them, leave them to clumsy servants (there wasn't an object of them all but should be handled with perfect love), and in many cases probably wish to replace them by pieces answerable to some vulgar modern notion of the convenient. Above all, she saw in advance, with dilated eyes, the abominations they would inevitably mix up with them – the maddening relics of Waterbath, the little brackets and pink vases, the sweepings of bazaars, the family photographs and illuminated texts, the 'household art' and household piety of Mona's hideous home. Wasn't it enough simply to contend that Mona would approach Poynton in the spirit of a Brigstock, and that in the spirit of a Brigstock she would deal with her acquisition? Did Fleda really see *her*, Mrs Gereth demanded, spending the remainder of her days with such a creature's elbow in her eye?

Fleda had to declare that she certainly didn't, and that Waterbath had been a warning it would be frivolous to overlook. At the same time she privately reflected that they were taking a great deal for granted, and that, inasmuch as to her knowledge Owen Gereth had positively denied his betrothal, the ground of their speculations was by no means firm. It seemed to our young lady that in a difficult position Owen conducted himself with some natural art; treating this domesticated confidant of his mother's wrongs with a simple civility that almost troubled her conscience, so deeply she felt that she might have had for him the air of siding with that lady against him. She wondered if he would ever know how little really she did this, and that she was there, since Mrs Gereth had insisted, not to betray, but essentially to confirm and protect. The fact that his mother disliked Mona Brigstock might have made him dislike the object of her preference, and it was detestable to Fleda to remember that she might have appeared to him to offer herself as an exemplary contrast. It was clear enough, however, that the happy youth had no more sense for a motive than a deaf man for a tune, a limitation by which, after all, she could gain as well as lose. He came and went very freely on the business with which London abundantly furnished him, but he found time more than once to say to her, 'It's awfully nice of you to look after poor Mummy.' As well

as his quick speech, which shyness made obscure – it was usually as desperate as a 'rush' at some violent game – his child's eyes in his man's face put it to her that, you know, this really meant a good deal for him and that he hoped she would stay on. With a person in the house who, like herself, was clever, poor Mummy was conveniently occupied; and Fleda found a beauty in the candour and even in the modesty which apparently kept him from suspecting that two such wiseheads could possibly be occupied with Owen Gereth.

CHAPTER 3

THEY went at last, the wiseheads, down to Poynton, where the palpitating girl had the full revelation. '*Now* do you know how I feel?' Mrs Gereth asked when in the wonderful hall, three minutes after their arrival, her pretty associate dropped on a seat with a soft gasp and a roll of dilated eyes. The answer came clearly enough, and in the rapture of that first walk through the house Fleda took a prodigious span. She perfectly understood how Mrs Gereth felt – she had understood but meagrely before; and the two women embraced with tears over the tightening of their bond – tears which on the younger one's part were the natural and usual sign of her submission to perfect beauty. It was not the first time she had cried for the joy of admiration, but it was the first time the mistress of Poynton, often as she had shown her house, had been present at such an exhibition. She exulted in it; it quickened her own tears; she assured her companion that such an occasion made the poor old place fresh to her again and more precious than ever. Yes, nobody had ever, that way, felt what she had achieved: people were so grossly ignorant, and everybody, even the knowing ones as they thought themselves, more or less dense. What Mrs Gereth had achieved was indeed an exquisite work; and in such an art of the treasure-hunter, in selection and comparison refined to that point, there was an element of creation, of personality. She had commended Fleda's *flair,* and Fleda now gave herself up to satiety. Preoccupations and scruples fell away from her; she had never known a greater happiness than the week she passed in this initiation.

Wandering through clear chambers where the general effect made preferences almost as impossible as if they had been shocks, pausing at open doors where vistas were long and bland, she would, even if she had not already known, have discovered for herself that Poynton was the record of a life. It was written in great syllables of colour and form, the tongues of other countries and the hands of rare artists. It was all France and Italy, with their ages composed to rest. For England you looked out of old windows – it was England that was the wide embrace. While outside, on the low terraces, she contradicted gardeners and refined on nature, Mrs Gereth left her guest to finger fondly the brasses that Louis Quinze might have thumbed, to sit with Venetian velvets just held in a loving palm, to hang over cases of enamels and pass and repass before cabinets. There were not many pictures – the panels and the stuffs were themselves the picture ; and in all the great wainscoted house there was not an inch of pasted paper. What struck Fleda most in it was the high pride of her friend's taste, a fine arrogance, a sense of style which, however amused and amusing, never compromised nor stooped. She felt indeed, as this lady had intimated to her that she would, both a respect and a compassion that she had not known before ; the vision of the coming surrender filled her with an equal pain. To give it all up, to die to it – that thought ached in her breast. She herself could imagine clinging there with a closeness separate from dignity. To have created such a place was to have had dignity enough ; when there was a question of defending it the fiercest attitude was the right one. After so intense a taking of possession she too was to give it up ; for she reflected that if Mrs Gereth's remaining there would have offered her a sort of future – stretching away in safe years on the other side of a gulf – the advent of the others could only be, by the same law, a great vague menace, the ruffling of a still water. Such were the emotions of a hungry girl whose sensibility was almost as great as her opportunities for comparison had been small. The museums had done something for her, but nature had done more.

If Owen had not come down with them nor joined them later, it was because he still found London jolly ; yet the question remained of whether the jollity of London was not merely the only name his small vocabulary yielded for the jollity of Mona Brigstock. There was indeed in his conduct another ambiguity – something that required explaining so long as his motive didn't come to the surface. If he was in love, what was the matter? And what was the matter still more

19

if he wasn't? The mystery was at last cleared up: this Fleda
gathered from the tone in which, one morning at breakfast, a
letter just opened made Mrs Gereth cry out. Her dismay was
almost a shriek: 'Why, he's bringing her down – he wants
her to see the house!' They flew, the two women, into each
other's arms and, with their heads together, soon made out that
the reason, the baffling reason why nothing had yet happened,
was that Mona didn't know, or Owen didn't, whether Poynton
would really please her. She was coming down to judge; and
could anything in the world be more like poor Owen than the
ponderous probity which had kept him from pressing her for
a reply till she should have learned whether she approved what
he had to offer her? That was a scruple it had naturally been
impossible to impute. If only they might fondly hope, Mrs
Gereth wailed, that the girl's expectations would be dashed!
There was a fine consistency, a sincerity quite affecting, in her
arguing that the better the place should happen to look and to
express the conceptions to which it owed its origin, the less
it would speak to an intelligence so primitive. How could a
Brigstock possibility understand what it was all about? How,
really, could a Brigstock logically do anything but hate it? Mrs
Gereth, even as she whisked away linen shrouds, persuaded
herself of the possibility on Mona's part of some bewildered
blankness, some collapse of admiration that would prove dis-
concerting to her swain – a hope of which Fleda at least
could see the absurdity and which gave the measure of the poor
lady's strange, almost maniacal disposition to thrust in everywhere the question of 'things', to read all behaviour in the
light of some fancied relation to them. 'Things' were of course
the sum of the world; only, for Mrs Gereth, the sum of the
world was rare French furniture and Oriental china. She could
at a stretch imagine people's not having, but she couldn't
imagine their not wanting and not missing.

The young couple were to be accompanied by Mrs Brigstock,
and with a prevision of how fiercely they would be watched
Fleda became conscious, before the party arrived, of an
amused, diplomatic pity for them. Almost as much as Mrs
Gereth's her taste was her life, but her life was somehow the
larger for it. Besides, she had another care now: there was

someone she wouldn't have liked to see humiliated even in the form of a young lady who would contribute to his never suspecting so much delicacy. When this young lady appeared Fleda tried, so far as the wish to efface herself allowed, to be mainly the person to take her about, show her the house, and cover up her ignorance. Owen's announcement had been that, as trains made it convenient, they would present themselves for luncheon and depart before dinner; but Mrs Gereth, true to her system of glaring civility, proposed and obtained an extension, a dining and spending of the night. She made her young friend wonder against what rebellion of fact she was sacrificing in advance so profusely to form. Fleda was appalled, after the first hour, by the rash innocence with which Mona had accepted the responsibility of observation, and indeed by the large levity with which, sitting there like a bored tourist in fine scenery, she exercised it. She felt in her nerves the effect of such a manner on her companion's, and it was this that made her want to entice the girl away, give her some merciful warning or some jocular cue. Mona met intense looks, however, with eyes that might have been blue beads, the only ones she had – eyes into which Fleda thought it strange Owen Gereth should have to plunge for his fate and his mother for a confession of whether Poynton was a success. She made no remark that helped to supply this light; her impression at any rate had nothing in common with the feeling that, as the beauty of the place throbbed out like music, had caused Fleda Vetch to burst into tears. She was as content to say nothing as if, Mrs Gereth afterwards exclaimed, she had been keeping her mouth shut in a railway tunnel. Mrs Gereth contrived at the end of an hour to convey to Fleda that it was plain she was brutally ignorant; but Fleda more subtly discovered that her ignorance was obscurely active.

She was not so stupid as not to see that something, though she scarcely knew what, was expected of her that she couldn't give; and the only mode her intelligence suggested of meeting the expectation was to plant her big feet and pull another way. Mrs Gereth wanted her to rise, somehow or somewhere, and was prepared to hate her if she didn't: very well, she couldn't, she wouldn't rise; she already moved at the altitude that suited

her, and was able to see that, since she was exposed to the
hatred, she might at least enjoy the calm. The smallest trouble,
for a girl with no nonsense about her, was to earn what she
incurred; so that, a dim instinct teaching her she would earn
it best by not being effusive, and combining with the conviction
that she now held Owen, and therefore the place, she had the
pleasure of her honesty as well as of her security. Didn't her
very honesty lead her to be belligerently blank about Poynton
inasmuch as it was just Poynton that was forced upon her as
a subject for effusiveness? Such subjects, to Mona Brigstock,
had an air almost of indecency, and the house became uncanny
to her through such an appeal – an appeal that, somewhere in
the twilight of her being, as Fleda was sure, she thanked heaven
she *was* the girl stiffly to draw back from. She was a person
whom pressure at a given point infallibly caused to expand
in the wrong place instead of, as it is usually administered in
the hope of doing, the right one. Her mother, to make up for
this, broke out universally, pronounced everything 'most
striking', and was visibly happy that Owen's captor should be
so far on the way to strike: but she jarred upon Mrs Gereth
by her formula of admiration, which was that anything she
looked at was 'in the style' of something else. This was to
show how much she had seen, but it only showed she had
seen nothing; everything at Poynton was in the style of Poynton, and poor Mrs Brigstock, who at least was determined to
rise, and had brought with her a trophy of her journey, a 'lady's
magazine' purchased at the station, a horrible thing with pat-
terns for antimacassars, which, as it was quite new, the first
number, and seemed so clever, she kindly offered to leave for
the house, was in the style of a vulgar old woman who wore
silver jewellery and tried to pass off a gross avidity as a sense
of the beautiful.

By the day's end it was clear to Fleda Vetch that, however
Mona judged, the day had been determinant; whether or not
she felt the charm, she felt the challenge: at an early moment
Owen Gereth would be able to tell his mother the worst.
Nevertheless, when the elder lady, at bedtime, coming in a
dressing-gown and a high fever to the younger one's room,
cried out, 'She hates it; but what will she do?' Fleda pretended

22

vagueness, played at obscurity, and assented disingenuously to the proposition that they at least had a respite. The future was dark to her, but there was a silken thread she could clutch in the gloom – she would never give Owen away. He might give himself – he even certainly would; but that was his own affair, and his blunders, his innocence, only added to the appeal he made to her. She would cover him, she would protect him, and beyond thinking her a cheerful inmate he would never guess her intention, any more than, beyond thinking her clever enough for anything, his acute mother would discover it. From this hour, with Mrs Gereth, there was a flaw in her frankness: her admirable friend continued to know everything she did; what was to remain unknown was the general motive.

From the window of her room, the next morning before breakfast, the girl saw Owen in the garden with Mona, who strolled beside him with a listening parasol, but without a visible look for the great florid picture that had been hung there by Mrs Gereth's hand. Mona kept dropping her eyes, as she walked, to catch the sheen of her patent-leather shoes, which resembled a man's and which she kicked forward a little – it gave her an odd movement – to help her see what she thought of them. When Fleda came down Mrs Gereth was in the breakfast-room; and at that moment Owen through a long window, passed in alone from the terrace and very endearingly kissed his mother. It immediately struck the girl that she was in their way, for hadn't he been borne on a wave of joy exactly to announce before the Brigstocks departed, that Mona had at last faltered out the sweet word he had been waiting for? He shook hands with his friendly violence, but Fleda contrived not to look into his face: what she liked most to see in it was not the reflection of Mona's big boot-toes. She could bear well enough that young lady herself, but she couldn't bear Owen's opinion of her. She was on the point of slipping into the garden when the movement was checked by Mrs Gereth's suddenly drawing her close, as if for the morning embrace, and then, while she kept her there with the bravery of the night's repose, breaking out: 'Well, my dear boy, what *does* your young friend there make of our odds and ends?'

'Oh, she thinks they're all right!'

Fleda immediately guessed from his tone that he had not come in to say what she supposed; there was even something in it to confirm Mrs Gereth's belief that their danger had dropped. She was sure, moreover, that his tribute to Mona's taste was a repetition of the eloquent words in which the girl had herself recorded it; she could indeed hear, with all vividness, the pretty passage between the pair. 'Don't you think it's rather jolly, the old shop?' 'Oh, it's all right!' Mona had graciously remarked; and then they had probably, with a slap on a back, run another race up or down a green bank. Fleda knew Mrs Gereth had not yet uttered a word to her son that would have shown him how much she feared; but it was impossible to feel her friend's arm round her and not become aware that this friend was now throbbing with a strange intention. Owen's reply had scarcely been of a nature to usher in a discussion of Mona's sensibilities; but Mrs Gereth went on, in a moment, with an innocence of which Fleda could measure the cold hypocrisy: 'Has she any sort of feeling for nice old things?' The question was as fresh as the morning light.

'Oh, of course she likes everything that's nice.' And Owen, who constitutionally disliked questions – an answer was almost as hateful to him as a 'trick' to a big dog – smiled kindly at Fleda and conveyed that she would understand what he meant even if his mother didn't. Fleda, however, mainly understood that Mrs Gereth, with an odd, wild laugh, held her so hard that she hurt her.

'I could give up everything without a pang, I think, to a person I could trust, I could respect.' The girl heard her voice tremble under the effort to show nothing but what she wanted to show, and felt the sincerity of her implication that the piety most real to her was to be on one's knees before one's high standard. 'The best things here, as you know, are the things your father and I collected, things all that we worked for and waited for and suffered for. Yes,' cried Mrs Gereth, with a fine freedom of fancy, 'there are things in the house that we almost starved for! They were our religion, they were our life, they were *us*! and now they're only *me* – except that they're also *you*, thank God, a little, you dear!' she continued, suddenly inflicting on Fleda a kiss apparently intended to knock her

24

into position. 'There isn't one of them I don't know and love –
yes, as one remembers and cherishes the happiest moments of
one's life. Blindfold, in the dark, with the brush of a finger, I
could tell one from another. They're living things to me; they
know me, they return the touch of my hand. But I could let
them all go, since I have to, so strangely, to another affection,
another conscience. There's a care they want, there's a sympathy that draws out their beauty. Rather than make them over
to a woman ignorant and vulgar, I think I'd deface them with
my own hands. Can't you see me, Fleda, and wouldn't you do
it yourself?' – she appealed to her companion with glittering
eyes. 'I couldn't bear the thought of such a woman here – I
couldn't. I don't know what she'd do; she'd be sure to invent some deviltry, if it should be only to bring in her own
little belongings and horrors. The world is full of cheap gim-
cracks, in this awful age, and they're thrust in at one at every
turn. They'd be thrust in here, on top of my treasures, my own.
Who would save *them* for me – I ask you who *would*?' and
she turned again to Fleda with a dry, strained smile. Her handsome, high-nosed, excited face might have been that of Don
Quixote tilting at a windmill. Drawn into the eddy of this
outpouring, the girl, scared and embarrassed, laughed off her
exposure; but only to feel herself more passionately caught
up and, as it seemed to her, thrust down the fine open mouth
(it showed such perfect teeth) with which poor Owen's slow
cerebration gaped. '*You* would, of course – only you, in all the
world, because you know, you feel, as I do myself, what's good
and true and pure.' No severity of the moral law could have
taken a higher tone in this implication of the young lady who
had not the only virtue Mrs Gereth actively esteemed. '*You*
would replace me, *you* would watch over them, *you* would
keep the place right,' she austerely pursued, 'and with you
here – yes, with you, I believe I might rest, at last, in my
grave!' She threw herself on Fleda's neck, and before Fleda,
horribly shamed, could shake her off, had burst into tears
which couldn't have been explained, but which might perhaps
have been understood.

CHAPTER 4

A WEEK later Owen Gereth came down to inform his mother
that he had settled with Mona Brigstock; but it was not at all
a joy to Fleda, conscious how much to himself it would be a
surprise, that he should find her still in the house. That dreadful
scene before breakfast had made her position false and odious;
it had been followed, after they were left alone, by a scene of
her own making with her extravagant friend. She notified Mrs
Gereth of her instant departure: she couldn't possibly remain
after being offered to Owen, that way, before his very face, as
his mother's candidate for the honour of his hand. That was
all he could have seen in such an outbreak and in the indecency
of her standing there to enjoy it. Fleda had on the prior
occasion dashed out of the room by the shortest course and in
her confusion had fallen upon Mona in the garden. She had
taken an aimless turn with her, and they had had some talk,
rendered at first difficult and almost disagreeable by Mona's
apparent suspicion that she had been sent out to spy, as Mrs
Gereth had tried to spy, into her opinions. Fleda was sagacious enough to treat these opinions as a mystery almost
awful; which had an effect so much more than reassuring that
at the end of five minutes the young lady from Waterbath
suddenly and perversely said: 'Why has she never had a winter
garden thrown out? If ever I have a place of my own I mean
to have one.' Fleda, dismayed, could see the thing – something
glazed and piped, on iron pillars, with untidy plants and cane
sofas; a shiny excrescence on the noble face of Poynton. She
remembered at Waterbath a conservatory where she had caught
a bad cold in the company of a stuffed cockatoo fastened to a
tropical bough and a waterless fountain composed of shells
stuck into some hardened paste. She asked Mona if her idea
would be to make something like this conservatory; to which
Mona replied: 'Oh no, much finer; we haven't got a winter
garden at Waterbath.' Fleda wondered if she meant to convey
that it was the only grandeur they lacked, and in a moment

Mona went on: 'But we have got a billiard-room – that I will say for us!' There was no billiard-room at Poynton, but there would evidently be one, and it would have, hung on its walls, framed at the 'Stores', caricature-portraits of celebrities, taken from a 'society-paper'.

When the two girls had gone in to breakfast it was for Fleda to see at a glance that there had been a further passage, of some high colour, between Owen and his mother; and she had turned pale in guessing to what extremity, at her expense, Mrs Gereth had found occasion to proceed. Hadn't she, after her clumsy flight, been pressed upon Owen in still clearer terms? Mrs Gereth would practically have said to him: 'If you'll take *her*, I'll move away without a sound. But if you take anyone else, anyone I'm not sure of, as I am of her – heaven help me, I'll fight to the death!' Breakfast, this morning, at Poynton, had been a meal singularly silent, in spite of the vague little cries with which Mrs Brigstock turned up the underside of plates and the knowing but alarming raps administered by her big knuckles to porcelain cups. Someone had to respond to her, and the duty assigned itself to Fleda, who, while pretending to meet her on the ground of explanation, wondered what Owen thought of a girl still indelicately anxious, after she had been grossly hurled at him, to prove by exhibitions of her fine taste that she was really what his mother pretended. This time, at any rate, their fate was sealed: Owen, as soon as he should get out of the house, would describe to Mona that lady's extra-ordinary conduct, and if anything more had been wanted to 'fetch' Mona, as he would call it, the deficiency was now made up. Mrs Gereth in fact took care of that – took care of it by the way, at the last, on the threshold, she said to the younger of her departing guests, with an irony of which the sting was wholly in the sense, not at all in the sound: 'We haven't had the talk we might have had, have we? You'll feel that I've neglected you, and you'll treasure it up against me. *Don't,* because really, you know, it has been quite an accident, and I've all sorts of information at your disposal. If you should come down again (only you won't, ever – I feel that!) I should give you plenty of time to worry it out of me. Indeed there are some things I should quite insist on your learning; not permit

27

you at all, in any settled way, *not* to learn. Yes indeed, you'd put me through, and I should put you, my dear! We should have each other to reckon with, and you would see me as I really am. I'm not a bit the vague, mooning, easy creature I dare say you think. However, if you won't come, you won't ; *n'en parlons plus*. It *is* stupid here after what you're accustomed to. We can only, all round, do what we can, eh? For heaven's sake, don't let your mother forget her precious publication, the female magazine, with the what-do-you-call-'em? – the grease-catchers. There ! '

Mrs Gereth, delivering herself from the doorstep, had tossed the periodical higher in air than was absolutely needful – tossed it towards the carriage the retreating party was about to enter. Mona, from the force of habit, the reflex action of the custom of sport, had popped out, with a little spring, a long arm and intercepted the missile as easily as she would have caused a tennis-ball to rebound from a racket. 'Good catch ! ' Owen had cried, so genuinely pleased that practically no notice was taken of his mother's impressive remarks. It was to the accompaniment of romping laughter, as Mrs Gereth afterwards said, that the carriage had rolled away ; but it was while that laughter was still in the air that Fleda Vetch, white and terrible, had turned upon her hostess with her scorching 'How *could* you? Great God, how *could* you? ' This lady's perfect blanket was from the first a sign of her serene conscience, and the fact that till indoctrinated she didn't even know what Fleda meant by resenting her late offence to every susceptibility gave our young woman a sore, scared perception that her own value in the house was just the value, as one might say, of a good agent. Mrs Gereth was generously sorry, but she was still more surprised – surprised at Fleda's not having liked to be shown off to Owen as the right sort of wife for him. Why not, in the name of wonder, if she absolutely *was* the right sort? She had admitted on explanation that she could see what her young friend meant by having been laid, as Fleda called it, at his feet ; but it struck the girl that the admission was only made to please her, and that Mrs Gereth was secretly surprised at her not being as happy to be sacrificed to the supremacy of a high standard as she was happy to sacrifice her. She had taken a tremendous fancy to her, but that was on account of the fancy – to Poynton of course – Fleda herself had taken. Wasn't this latter fancy then so great after all? Fleda felt that she could declare it to be great indeed when really for the sake of it she could forgive what she had suffered and, after reproaches and tears, asseverations and kisses, after learning that she was cared for only as a priestess of the altar and a view of her bruised dignity which left no alternative to flight, could accept the shame with the balm, consent not to depart, take refuge in the thin comfort of at least knowing the truth. The truth was simply that all Mrs Gereth's scruples were on one side and that her ruling passion had in a manner despoiled her of her humanity. On the second day, after the tide of emotion had somewhat ebbed, she said soothingly to her companion: 'But you *would*, after all, marry him, you know, darling, wouldn't you, if that girl were not there? I mean of course if he were to ask you,' Mrs Gereth had thoughtfully added.

'Marry him if he were to ask me? Most distinctly not!'

The question had not come up with this definiteness before, and Mrs Gereth was clearly more surprised than ever. She marvelled a moment. 'Not even to have Poynton?'

'Not even to have Poynton.'

'But why on earth?' Mrs Gereth's sad eyes were fixed on her.

Fleda coloured; she hesitated. 'Because he's too stupid!' Save on one other occasion, at which we shall in time arrive, little as the reader may believe it, she never came nearer to betraying to Mrs Gereth that she was in love with Owen. She found a dim amusement in reflecting that if Mona had not been there and he had not been too stupid and he verily had asked her, she might, should she have wished to keep her secret, have found it possible to pass off the motive of her action as a mere *passion* for Poynton.

Mrs Gereth evidently thought in these days of little but things hymeneal; for she broke out with sudden rapture, in the middle of the week: 'I know what they'll do: they *will* marry, but they'll go and live at Waterbath!' There was positive joy in that form of the idea, which she embroidered and developed: it seemed so much the safest thing that could happen. 'Yes, I'll have you, but I won't go *there*!' Mona would have said with a vicious nod at the southern horizon: 'we'll leave your horrid mother alone there for life.' It would be an ideal solution, this ingress the lively pair, with their spiritual need of a warmer medium, would playfully punch in the ribs of her ancestral home; for it would not only prevent recurring panic at Poynton – it would offer them, as in one of their gimcrack baskets or other vessels of ugliness, a definite daily felicity that Poynton could never give. Owen might manage his estate just as he managed it now, and Mrs Gereth would manage everything else. When, in the hall, on the unforgettable day of his return, she had heard his voice ring out like a call to a terrier, she had still, as Fleda afterwards learned, clutched frantically at the conceit that he had come, at the worst, to announce some compromise; to tell her she would have to put up with the girl, yes, but that some way would be arrived at of leaving her in personal possession. Fleda Vetch, whom from the first hour no illusion had brushed with its wing, now held her breath, went on tiptoe, wandered in outlying parts of the house and through delicate, muffled rooms, while the mother and son faced each other below. From time to time she stopped to listen; but all was so quiet she was almost frightened: she had vaguely expected a sound of contention. It lasted longer than she would have supposed, whatever it was they were doing; and when finally, from a window, she saw Owen stroll out of the house, stop and light a cigarette and then pensively lose himself in the plantations, she found other matter for trepidation in the fact that Mrs Gereth didn't immediately come rushing up into her arms. She wondered whether she oughtn't to go down to her, and measured the gravity of what had occurred by the circumstance, which she presently ascertained, that the poor lady had retired to her room and wished not to be disturbed. This admonition had been for her maid, with whom Fleda conferred as at the door of a death-chamber; but the girl, without either fatuity or resentment, judged that, since it could render Mrs Gereth indifferent even to the ministrations of disinterested attachments, the scene had been tremendous.

She was absent from luncheon, where indeed Fleda had enough to do to look Owen in the face; there would be so much to make that hateful in their common memory of the passage in which his last visit had terminated. This had been her apprehension at least; but as soon as he stood there she was constrained to wonder at the practical simplicity of the ordeal – a simplicity which was really just his own simplicity, the particular thing that, for Fleda Vetch, some other things of course aiding, made almost any direct relation with him pleasant. He had neither wit nor tact, nor inspiration: all she could say was that when they were together the alienation these charms were usually depended on to allay didn't occur. On this occasion, for instance, he did so much better than 'carry off' an awkward remembrance: he simply didn't have it. He had clean forgotten that she was the girl his mother would have fobbed off on him; he was conscious only that she was there in a manner for service – conscious of the dumb instinct that from the first had made him regard her not as complicating his intercouse with that personage, but as simplifying it. Fleda found beautiful that this theory should have survived the incident of the other day; found exquisite that whereas she was conscious, through faint reverberations, that for her kind little circle at large, whom it didn't concern, her tendency had begun to define itself as parasitical, this strong young man, who had a right to judge and even a reason to loathe her, didn't judge and didn't loathe, let her down gently, treated her as if she pleased him, and in fact evidently liked her to be just where she was. She asked herself what he did when Mona denounced her, and the only answer to the question was that perhaps Mona didn't denounce her. If Mona was inarticulate he wasn't such a fool, then, to marry her. That he was glad Fleda was there was at any rate sufficiently shown by the domestic familiarity with which he said to her: 'I must tell you I've been having an awful row with my mother. I'm engaged to be married to Miss Brigstock.'

'Ah, really?' cried Fleda, achieving a radiance of which she was secretly proud. 'How very exciting!'

'Too exciting for poor Mummy. She won't hear of it. She has been slating her fearfully. She says she's a "barbarian".'

'Why, she's lovely!' Fleda exclaimed.

'Oh, she's all right. Mother must come round.'

'Only give her time,' said Fleda. She had advanced to the threshold of the door thus thrown open to her and, without exactly crossing it, she threw in an appreciative glance. She asked Owen when his marriage would take place, and in the light of his reply read that Mrs Gereth's wretched attitude would have no influence at all on the event, absolutely fixed when he came down, and distant by only three months. He liked Fleda's seeming to be on his side, though that was a secondary matter, for what really most concerned him now was the line his mother took about Poynton, her declared unwillingness to give it up.

'Naturally I want my own house, you know,' he said, 'and my father made every arrangement for me to have it. But she may make it devilish awkward. What in the world's a fellow to do?' This it was that Owen wanted to know, and there could be no better proof of his friendliness than his air of depending on Fleda Vetch to tell him. She questioned him, they spent an hour together, and, as he gave her the scale of the concussion from which he had rebounded, she found herself saddened and frightened by the material he seemed to offer her to deal with. It *was* devilish awkward, and it was so in part because Owen had no imagination. It had lodged itself in that empty chamber that his mother hated the surrender because she hated Mona. He didn't of course understand why she hated Mona, but this belonged to an order of mysteries that never troubled him: there were lots of things, especially in people's minds, that a fellow didn't understand. Poor Owen went through life with a frank dread of people's minds: there were explanations he would have been almost as shy of receiving as of giving. There was therefore nothing that accounted for anything, though in its way it was vivid enough, in his picture to Fleda of his mother's virtual refusal to move. That was simply what it was; for didn't she refuse to move when she as good as declared that she would move only with the furniture? It was the furniture she wouldn't give up; and what was the good of Poynton without the furniture? Besides, the furniture happened to be his, just as everything else happened to be. The furniture – the words, on his lips, had somehow, for Fleda, the sound of washing-stands and copious bedding, and she could well

32

imagine the note it might have struck for Mrs Gereth. The girl, in this interview with him, spoke of the contents of the house only as 'the works of art'. It didn't, however, in the least matter to Owen what they were called; what did matter, she easily guessed, was that it had been laid upon him by Mona, been made in effect a condition of her consent, that he should hold his mother to the strictest accountability for them. Mona had already entered upon the enjoyment of her rights. She had made him feel that Mrs Gereth had been liberally provided for, and had asked him cogently what room there would be at Ricks for the innumerable treasures of the big house. Ricks, the sweet little place offered to the mistress of Poynton as the refuge of her declining years, had been left to the late Mr Gereth, a considerable time before his death, by an old maternal aunt, a good lady who had spent most of her life there. The house had in recent times been let, but it was amply furnished, it contained all the defunct aunt's possessions. Owen had lately inspected it, and he communicated to Fleda that he had quietly taken Mona to see it. It wasn't a place like Poynton – what dower-house ever was? – but it was an awfully jolly little place, and Mona had taken a tremendous fancy to it. If there were a few things at Poynton that were Mrs Gereth's peculiar property, of course she must take them away with her ; but one of the matters that became clear to Fleda was that this transfer would be immediately subject to Miss Brigstock's approval. The special business that she herself now became aware of being charged with was that of seeing Mrs Gereth safely and singly off the premises.

Her heart failed her, after Owen had returned to London, with the ugliness of this duty – with the ugliness, indeed, of the whole close conflict. She saw nothing of Mrs Gereth that day ; she spent it in roaming with sick sighs, in feeling, as she passed from room to room, that what was expected of her companion was really dreadful. It would have been better never to have had such a place than to have had it and lose it. It was odious to *her* to have to look for solutions: what a strange relation between mother and son when there was no fundamental tenderness out of which a solution would irrepressibly spring! Was it Owen who was mainly responsible for that poverty? Fleda couldn't think so when she remembered that, so far as he was concerned, Mrs Gereth would still have been welcome to have her seat by the Poynton fire. The fact that from the moment one accepted his marrying one saw no very different course for Owen to take made her all the rest of that aching day find her best relief in the mercy of not having yet to face her hostess. She dodged and dreamed and romanced away the time; instead of inventing a remedy or a compromise, instead of preparing a plan by which a scandal might be averted, she gave herself, in her sentient solitude, up to a mere fairy tale, up to the very taste of the beautiful peace with which she would have filled the air if only something might have been that could never have been.

CHAPTER 5

'I'LL give up the house if they'll let me take what I require!'
That, on the morrow, was what Mrs Gereth's stifled night had
qualified her to say, with a tragic face, at breakfast. Fleda
reflected that what she 'required' was simply every object that
surrounded them. The poor woman would have admitted this
truth and accepted the conclusion to be drawn from it, the
reduction to the absurd of her attitude, the exaltation of her
revolt. The girl's dread of scandal, of spectators and critics,
diminished the more she saw how little vulgar avidity had to
do with this rigour. It was not the crude love of possession;
it was the need to be faithful to a trust and loyal to an idea.
The idea was surely noble: it was that of the beauty Mrs
Gereth had so patiently and consummately wrought. Pale but
radiant, with her back to the wall, she rose there like a heroine
guarding a treasure. To give up the ship was to flinch from her
duty; there was something in her eyes that declared she would
die at her post. If their difference should become public the
shame would be all for the others. If Waterbath thought it
could afford to expose itself, then Waterbath was welcome to
the folly. Her fanaticism gave her a new distinction, and Fleda
perceived almost with awe that she had never carried herself
so well. She trod the place like a reigning queen or a proud
usurper; full as it was of splendid pieces, it could show in
these days no ornament so effective as its menaced mistress.

Our young lady's spirit was strangely divided; she had a
tenderness for Owen which she deeply concealed, yet it left
her occasion to marvel at the way a man was made who could
care in any relation for a creature like Mona Brigstock when
he had known in any relation a creature like Adela Gereth.
With such a mother to give him the pitch, how could he take
it so low? She wondered that she didn't despise him for this,
but there was something that kept her from it. If there had been
nothing else it would have sufficed that she really found herself
from this moment the medium of communication with him.

'He'll come back to assert himself,' Mrs Gereth had said; and the following week Owen in fact reappeared. He might merely have written, Fleda could see, but he had come in person because it was at once 'nicer' for his mother and stronger for his cause. He didn't like the row, though Mona probably did; if he hadn't a sense of beauty he had after all a sense of justice; but it was inevitable he should clearly announce at Poynton the date at which he must look to find the house vacant. 'You don't think I'm rough or hard, do you?' he asked Fleda, his impatience shining in his idle eyes as the dining-hour shines in club-windows. 'The place at Ricks stands there with open arms. And then I give her lots of time. Tell her she can remove everything that belongs to her.' Fleda recognized the elements of what the newspapers call a deadlock in the circumstance that nothing at Poynton belonged to Mrs Gereth either more or less than anything else. She must either take everything or nothing, and the girl's suggestion was that it might perhaps be an inspiration to do the latter and begin again on a clean page. What, however, was the poor woman, in that case, to begin with? What was she to do at all, on her meagre income, but make the best of the *objets d'art* of Ricks, the treasures collected by Mr Gereth's maiden aunt? She had never been near the place: for long years it had been let to strangers, and after that the foreboding that it would be her doom had kept her from the abasement of it. She had felt that she should see it soon enough, but Fleda (who was careful not to betray to her that Mona had seen it and had been gratified) knew her reasons for believing that the maiden's aunt's principles had had much in common with the principles of Waterbath. The only thing, in short, that she would ever have to do with the *objets d'art* of Ricks would be to turn them out into the road. What belonged to her at Poynton, as Owen said, would conveniently mitigate the void resulting from that demonstration.

The exchange of observations between the friends had grown very direct by the time Fleda asked Mrs Gereth whether she literally meant to shut herself up and stand a siege, or whether it was her idea to expose herself, more informally, to be dragged out of the house by constables. 'Oh, I prefer the constables and the dragging!' the heroine of Poynton had answered. 'I want to make Owen and Mona do everything that will be most publicly odious.' She gave it out that it was her one thought now to force them to a line that would dishonour them and dishonour the tradition they embodied, though Fleda was privately sure that she had visions of an alternative policy. The strange thing was that, proud and fastidious all her life, she now showed so little distaste for the world's hearing of the squabble. What had taken place in her above all was that a long resentment had ripened. She hated the effacement to which English usage reduced the widowed mother: she had discoursed of it passionately to Fleda; contrasted it with the beautiful homage paid in other countries to women in that position, women no better than herself, whom she had seen acclaimed and enthroned, whom she had known and envied; made in short as little as possible a secret of the injury, the bitterness she found in it. The great wrong Owen had done her was not his 'taking up' with Mona – that was disgusting, but it was a detail, an accidental form; it was his failure from the first to understand what it was to have a mother at all, to appreciate the beauty and sanctity of the character. She was just his mother as his nose was just his nose, and he had never had the least imagination or tenderness or gallantry about her. One's mother, gracious heaven, if one were the kind of fine young man one ought to be, the only kind Mrs Gereth cared for, was a subject for poetry, for idolatry. Hadn't she often told Fleda of her friend Madame de Jaume, the wittiest of women, but a small, black, crooked person, each of whose three boys, when absent, wrote to her every day of their lives? She had the house in Paris, she had the house in Poitou, she had more than in the lifetime of her husband (to whom, in spite of her appearance, she had afforded repeated cause for jealousy), because she had to the end of her days the supreme word about everything. It was easy to see that Mrs Gereth would have given again and again her complexion, her figure, and even perhaps the spotless virtue she had still more success-fully retained, to have been the consecrated Madame de Jaume. She wasn't, alas, and this was what she had at present a mag-nificent occasion to protest against. She was of course fully aware of Owen's concession, his willingness to let her take away with her the few things she liked best; but as yet she only declared that to meet him on this ground would be to give him a triumph, to put him impossibly in the right. 'Liked best?' There wasn't a thing in the house that she didn't like best, and what she liked better still was to be left where she was. How could Owen use such an expression without being conscious of his hypocrisy? Mrs Gereth, whose criticism was often gay, dilated with sardonic humour on the happy look a dozen objects from Poynton would wear and the charming effect they would conduce to when interspersed with the peculiar features of Ricks. What had her whole life been but an effort towards completeness and perfection? Better Waterbath at once, in its cynical unity, than the ignominy of such a mixture!

All this was of no great help to Fleda, in so far as Fleda tried to rise to her mission of finding a way out. When at the end of a fortnight Owen came down once more, it was ostensibly to tackle a farmer whose proceedings had been irregular; the girl was sure, however, that he had really come, on the instance of Mona, to see what his mother was doing. He wished to satisfy himself that she was preparing her departure, and he wished to perform a duty, distinct but not less imperative, in regard to the question of the perquisites with which she would retreat. The tension between them was now such that he had to perpetrate these offences without meeting his adversary. Mrs Gereth was as willing as himself that he should address to Fleda Vetch whatever cruel remarks he might have to make: she only pitied her poor young friend for repeated encounters with a person as to whom she perfectly understood the girl's repulsion. Fleda thought it nice of Owen not to have expected her to write to him; he wouldn't have wished any more than herself that she should have the air of spying on his mother in his interest. What made it comfortable to deal with him in this more familiar way was the sense that she understood so perfectly how poor Mrs Gereth suffered, and that she measured so adequately the sacrifice the other side did take rather monstrously for granted. She understood equally how Owen himself suffered, now that Mona had already begun to make him do things he didn't like. Vividly

Fleda apprehended how *she* would have first made him like anything she would have made him do ; anything even as disagreeable as this appearing there to state, virtually on Mona's behalf, that of course there must be a definite limit to the number of articles appropriated. She took a longish stroll with him in order to talk the matter over ; to say if she didn't think a dozen pieces, chosen absolutely at will, would be a handsome allowance ; and above all to consider the very delicate question of whether the advantage enjoyed by Mrs Gereth mightn't be left to her honour. To leave it so was what Owen wished ; but there was plainly a young lady at Waterbath to whom, on his side, he already had to render an account. He was as touching in his offhand annoyance as his mother was tragic in her intensity ; for if he couldn't help having a sense of propriety about the whole matter, so he could as little help hating it. It was for his hating it, Fleda reasoned, that she liked him so, and her insistence to his mother on the hatred perilously resembled on one or two occasions, a revelation of the liking. There were moments when, in conscience, that revelation pressed her ; inasmuch as it was just on the ground of her not liking him that Mrs Gereth trusted her so much. Mrs Gereth herself didn't in these days like him at all, and she was of course and always on Mrs Gereth's side. He ended really, while the preparations for his marriage went on, by quite a little custom of coming and going ; but on no one of these occasions would his mother receive him. He talked only with Fleda and strolled with Fleda ; and when he asked her, in regard to the great matter, if Mrs Gereth were really doing nothing, the girl usually replied: 'She pretends not to be, if I may say so ; but I think she's really thinking over what she'll take.' When her friend asked her what Owen was doing, she could have but one answer: 'He's waiting, dear lady, to see what *you* do!'

Mrs Gereth, a month after she had received her great shock, did something abrupt and extraordinary: she caught up her companion and went to have a look at Ricks. They had come to London first and taken a train from Liverpool Street, and the least of the sufferings they were armed against was that of passing the night. Fleda's admirable dressing-bag had been given her by her friend. 'Why, it's charming!' she exclaimed a few hours later, turning back again into the small prim parlour from a friendly advance to the single plate of the window. Mrs Gereth hated such windows, the one flat glass, sliding up and down, especially when they enjoyed a view of four iron pots on pedestals, painted white and containing ugly geraniums, ranged on the edge of a gravel path and doing their best to give it the air of a terrace. Fleda had instantly averted her eyes from these ornaments, but Mrs Gereth grimly gazed, wondering of course how a place in the deepest depths of Essex and three miles from a small station could contrive to look so suburban. The room was practically a shallow box, with the junction of the walls and ceiling guiltless of curve or cornice and marked merely by the little band of crimson paper glued round the top of the other paper, a turbid grey sprigged with silver flowers. This decoration was rather new and quite fresh; and there was in the centre of the ceiling a big square beam papered over in white, as to which Fleda hesitated about venturing to remark that it was rather picturesque. She recognized in time that this remark would be weak and that, throughout, she should be able to say nothing either for the mantlepieces or for the doors, of which she saw her companion become sensible with a soundless moan. On the subject of doors especially Mrs Gereth had the finest views: the thing in the world she most despised was the meanness of the single flap. From end to end, at Poynton, there were high double leaves. At Ricks the entrances to the rooms were like the holes of rabbit-hutches.

It was all, none the less, not so bad as Fleda had feared; it was faded and melancholy, whereas there had been a danger that it would be contradictious and positive, cheerful and loud. The house was crowded with objects of which the aggregation somehow made a thinness and the futility a grace; things that told her they had been gathered as slowly and as lovingly as the golden flowers of Poynton. She too, for a home, could have lived with them: they made her fond of the old maiden aunt; they made her even wonder if it didn't work more for happiness not to have tasted, as she herself had done, of knowledge. Without resources, without a stick, as she said, of her own, Fleda was moved, after all, to some secret surprise at the pretensions of a shipwrecked woman who could hold such an asylum cheap. The more she looked about the surer she felt of the character of the maiden aunt, the sense of whose dim presence urged her to pacification: the maiden aunt had been a dear; she would have adored the maiden aunt. The poor lady had had some tender little story; she had been sensitive and ignorant and exquisite: that too was a sort of origin, a sort of atmosphere for relics and rarities, though different from the sorts most prized at Poynton. Mrs Gereth had of course more than once said that one of the deepest mysteries of life was the way that, by certain natures, hideous objects could be loved; but it wasn't a question of love, now, for these; it was only a question of a certain practical patience. Perhaps some thought of that kind had stolen over Mrs Gereth when, at the end of a brooding hour, she exclaimed, taking in the house with a strenuous sigh: 'Well, something can be done with it!' Fleda had repeated to her more than once the indulgent fancy about the maiden aunt – she was so sure she had deeply suffered. 'I'm sure I hope she did!' was, however, all that Mrs Gereth had replied.

CHAPTER 6

IT was a great relief to the girl at last to perceive that the
dreadful move would really be made. What might happen if
it shouldn't had been from the first indefinite. It was absurd
to pretend that any violence was probable – a tussle, dishevel-
ment, shrieks; yet Fleda had an imagination of a drama, a
'great scene', a thing, somehow, of indignity and misery, of
wounds inflicted and received, in which indeed, though Mrs
Gereth's presence, with movements and sounds, loomed large
to her, Owen remained indistinct and on the whole unaggressive.
He wouldn't be there with a cigarette in his teeth, very handsome and insolently quiet: that was only the way he would
be in a novel, across whose interesting page some such figure,
as she half closed her eyes, seemed to her to walk. Fleda had
rather, and indeed with shame, a confused, pitying vision of
Mrs Gereth with her great scene left in a manner on her hands,
Mrs Gereth missing her effect and having to appear merely hot
and injured and in the wrong. The symptoms that she would
be spared even that spectacle resided not so much, through the
chambers of Poynton, in an air of concentration as in the hum
of buzzing alternatives. There was no common preparation,
but one day, at the turn of a corridor, she found her hostess
standing very still, with the hanging hands of an invalid and
the active eyes of an adventurer. These eyes appeared to Fleda
to meet her own with a strange, dim bravado, and there was
a silence, almost awkward, before either of the friends spoke.
The girl afterwards thought of the moment as one in which her
hostess mutely accused her of an accusation, meeting it
however, at the same time, by a kind of defiant acceptance.
Yet it was with mere melancholy candour that Mrs Gereth at
last sighingly exclaimed: 'I'm thinking over what I had better
take!' Fleda could have embraced her for this virtual promise
of a concession, the announcement that she had finally accepted
the problem of knocking together a shelter with a small salvage
of the wreck.

It was true that when after their return from Ricks they tried to lighten the ship, the great embarrassment was still immutably there, the odiousness of sacrificing the exquisite things one wouldn't take to the exquisite things one would. This immediately made the things one wouldn't take the very things one ought to, and as Mrs Gereth said, condemned one, in the whole business, to an eternal vicious circle. In such a circle, for days, she had been tormentedly moving, prowling up and down, comparing incomparables. It was for that one had to cling to them and their faces of supplication. Fleda herself could judge of these faces, so conscious of their race and their danger, and she had little enough to say when her companion asked her if the whole place, perversely fair on October afternoons, looked like a place to give up. It looked, to begin with, through some effect of season and light, larger than ever, immense, and it was filled with the hush of sorrow, which in turn was all charged with memories. Everything was in the air – every history of every find, every circumstance of every struggle. Mrs Gereth had drawn back every curtain and removed every cover; she prolonged the vistas, opened wide the whole house, gave it an appearance of awaiting a royal visit. The shimmer of wrought substances spent itself in the brightness; the old golds and brasses, old ivories and bronzes, the fresh old tapestries and deep old damasks threw out a radiance in which the poor woman saw in solution all her old loves and patiences, all her old tricks and triumphs.

Fleda had a depressed sense of not, after all, helping her much: this was lightened indeed by the fact that Mrs Gereth, letting her off easily, didn't now seem to expect it. Her sympathy, her interest, her feeling for everything for which Mrs Gereth felt, were a force that really worked to prolong the deadlock. 'I only wish I bored you and my possessions bored you,' that lady, with some humour declared; 'then you'd make short work with me, bundle me off, tell me just to pile certain things into a cart and have done.' Fleda's sharpest difficulty was in having to act up to the character of thinking Owen a brute, or at least to carry off the inconsistency of seeing him when he came down. By good fortune it was her duty, her function, as well as a protection to Mrs Gereth. She thought of

him perpetually, and her eyes had come to rejoice in his
manly magnificence more even than they rejoiced in the royal
cabinets of the red saloon. She wondered, very faintly at first,
why he came so often; but of course she knew nothing about
the business he had in hand, over which, with men red-faced
and leather-legged, he was sometimes closeted for an hour in
a room of his own that was the one monstrosity of Poynton:
all tobacco-pots and bootjacks, his mother had said – such an
array of arms of aggression and castigation that he himself
had confessed to eighteen rifles and forty whips. He was
arranging for settlements on his wife, he was doing things
that would meet the views of the Brigstocks. Considering the
house was his own, Fleda thought it nice of him to keep himself in the background while his mother remained; making his
visits, at some cost of ingenuity about trains from town, only
between meals, doing everything to let it press lightly upon
her that he was there. This was rather a stoppage to her
meeting Mrs Gereth on the ground of his being a brute; the
most she really at last could do was not to contradict her when
she repeated that he was watching – just insultingly watching.
He *was* watching, no doubt; but he watched somehow with
his head turned away. He knew that Fleda knew at present
what he wanted of her, so that it would be gross of him to
say it over and over. It existed as a confidence between them,
and made him sometimes, with his wandering stare, meet her
eyes as if a silence so pleasant could only unite them the more.
He had no great flow of speech, certainly, and at first the girl
took for granted that this was all there was to be said about
the matter. Little by little she speculated as to whether, with a
person who, like herself, could put him, after all, at a sort of
domestic ease, it was not supposable that he would have more
conversation if he were not keeping some of it back for Mona.

From the moment she suspected he might be thinking what
Mona would say to his chattering so to an underhand 'companion', who was all but paid, this young lady's repressed
emotion began to require still more repression. She grew
impatient of her situation at Poynton; she privately pronounced it false and horrid. She said to herself that she had
let Owen know that she had, to the best of her power, directed

44

his mother in the general sense he desired; that he quite understood it and that he also understood how unworthy it was of either of them to stand over the good lady with a notebook and a lash. Wasn't this practical unanimity just practical success? Fleda became aware of a sudden desire, as well as of pressing reasons, to bring her stay at Poynton to a close. She had not, on the one hand, like a minion of the law, undertaken to see Mrs Gereth down to the train and locked, in sign of her abdication, into a compartment; neither had she on the other committed herself to hold Owen indefinitely in dalliance while his mother gained time or dug a countermine. Besides, people *were* saying that she fastened like a leech on other people – people who had houses where something was to be picked up: this revelation was frankly made by her sister, now distinctly doomed to the curate and in view of whose nuptials she had almost finished, as a present, a wonderful piece of embroidery, suggested, at Poynton, by an old Spanish altar-cloth. She would have to exert herself still further for the intended recipient of this offering, turn her out for her marriage with more than that drapery. She would go up to town, in short, to dress Maggie; and their father, in lodgings at West Kensington, would stretch a point and take them in. He, to do him justice, never reproached her with profitable devotions; so far as they existed he consciously profited by them. Mrs Gereth gave her up as heroically as if she had been a great bargain, and Fleda knew that she wouldn't at present miss any visit of Owen's for Owen was shooting at Waterbath. Owen shooting was Owen lost, and there was scant sport at Poynton.

The first news she had from Mrs Gereth was news of that lady's having accomplished, in form at least, her migration. The letter was dated from Ricks, to which place she had been transported by an impulse apparently as sudden as the inspiration she had obeyed before.

Yes, I've literally come [she wrote] with a bandbox and a kitchen-maid; I've crossed the Rubicon, I've taken possession. It has been like plumping into cold water: I saw the only thing was to do it, not to stand shivering. I shall have warmed the place a little by simply being here for a week; when I come back the ice will have

45

been broken. I didn't write to you to meet me on my way through town, because I know how busy you are and because, besides, I'm too savage and odious to be fit company even for you. You'd say I really go too far, and there's no doubt whatever I do. I'm here, at any rate, just to look round once more, to see that certain things are done before I enter in force. I shall probably be at Poynton all next week. There's more room than I quite measured the other day, and a rather good set of old Worcester. But what are space and time, what's even old Worcester, to your wretched and affectionate A. G.?

The day after Fleda received this letter she had occasion to go into a big shop in Oxford Street – a journey that she achieved circuitously, first on foot and then by the aid of two omnibuses. The second of these vehicles put her down on the side of the street opposite her shop, and while, on the kerbstone, she humbly waited, with a parcel, an umbrella, and a tucked-up frock, to cross in security, she became aware that, close beside her, a hansom had pulled up short, in obedience to the brandished stick of a demonstrative occupant. This occupant was Owen Gereth, who had caught sight of her as he rattled along and who, with an exhibition of white teeth that, from under the hood of the cab, had almost flashed through the fog, now alighted to ask her if he couldn't give her a lift. On finding that her destination was only over the way he dismissed his vehicle and joined her, not only piloting her to the shop, but taking her in; with the assurance that his errands didn't matter, that it amused him to be concerned with hers. She told him she had come to buy a trimming for her sister's frock, and he expressed an hilarious interest in the purchase. His hilarity was almost always out of proportion to the case, but it struck her at present as more so than ever; especially when she had suggested that he might find it a good time to buy a garnishment of some sort for Mona. After wondering an instant whether he gave the full satiric meaning, such as it was, to this remark, Fleda dismissed the possibility as inconceivable. He stammered out that it was for *her* he would like to buy something, something 'ripping', and that she must give him the pleasure of telling him what would best please her: he couldn't have a better opportunity for making her a present – the present, in recognition

46

of all she had done for Mummy, that he had had in his head
for weeks.

Fleda had more than one small errand in the big bazaar,
and he went up and down with her, pointedly patient, pretending to be interested in questions of tape and of change.
She had now not the least hesitation in wondering what Mona
would think of such proceedings. But they were not her doing –
they were Owen's; and Owen, inconsequent and even extravagant, was unlike anything she had ever seen him before. He
broke off, he came back, he repeated questions without heeding
answers, he made vague, abrupt remarks about the resem-
blances of shopgirls and the uses of chiffon. He unduly prolonged their business together, giving Fleda a sense that he
was putting off something particular that he had to face. If
she had ever dreamed of Owen Gereth as nervous she would
have seen him with some such manner as this. But why should
he be nervous? Even at the height of the crisis his mother
hadn't made him so, and at present he was satisfied about his
mother. The one idea he stuck to was that Fleda should
mention something she would let him give her: there was
everything in the world in the wonderful place, and he made
her incongruous offers – a travelling-rug, a massive clock, a
table for breakfast in bed, and above all, in a resplendent
binding, a set of somebody's 'works'. His notion was a
testimonial, a tribute, and the 'works' would be a graceful
intimation that it was her cleverness he wished above all to
commemorate. He was immensely in earnest, but the articles
he pressed upon her betrayed a delicacy that went to her
heart: what he would really have liked, as he saw them
tumbled about, was one of the splendid stuffs for a gown –
a choice proscribed by his fear of seeming to patronize her,
to refer to her small means and her deficiencies. Fleda found
it easy to chaff him about his exaggeration of her deserts ;
she gave the just measure of them in consenting to accept a
small pin-cushion, costing sixpence, in which the letter F
was marked out with pins. A sense of loyalty to Mona was
not needed to enforce this discretion, and after that first
allusion to her she never sounded her name. She noticed on
this occasion more things in Owen Gereth than she had ever

noticed before, but what she noticed most was that he said no word of his intended. She asked herself what he had done, in so long a parenthesis, with his loyalty or at least his 'form', and then reflected that even if he had done something very good with them the situation in which such a question could come up was already a little strange. Of course he wasn't doing anything so vulgar as making love to her; but there was a kind of punctilio for a man who was engaged.

That punctilio didn't prevent Owen from remaining with her after they had left the shop, from hoping she had a lot more to do, and from pressing her to look with him, for a possible glimpse of something she might really let him give her, into the windows of other establishments. There was a moment when, under this pressure, she made up her mind that his tribute would be, if analysed, a tribute to her insignificance. But all the same he wanted her to come somewhere and have luncheon with him: what was that a tribute to? She must have counted very little if she didn't count too much for a romp in a restaurant. She had to get home with her trimming, and the most, in his company, she was amenable to was a retracing of her steps to the Marble Arch and then, after a discussion when they had reached it, a walk with him across the Park. She knew Mona would have considered that she ought to take the omnibus again; but she had now to think for Owen as well as for herself – she couldn't think for Mona. Even in the Park the autumn air was thick, and as they moved westward over the grass, which was what Owen preferred, the cool greyness made their words soft, made them at last rare and everything else dim. He wanted to stay with her – he wanted not to leave her: he had dropped into complete silence, but that was what his silence said. What was it he had postponed? What was it he wanted still to postpone? She grew a little scared as they strolled together and she thought. It was too confused to be believed, but it was as if somehow he felt differently. Fleda Vetch didn't suspect him at first of feeling differently to *her*, but only of feeling differently to Mona; yet she was not unconscious that this latter difference would have had some-thing to do with his being on the grass beside her. She had read in novels about gentlemen who on the eve of marriage, winding up the past, had surrendered themselves for the occasion to the influence of a former tie; and there was something in Owen's behaviour now, something in his very face, that suggested a resemblance to one of those gentlemen. But whom and what, in that case, would Fleda herself resemble? She wasn't a former tie, she wasn't any tie at all; she was only a deep little person for whom happiness was a kind of pearl-diving plunge. It was down at the very bottom of all that had lately happened; for all that had lately happened was that Owen Gereth had come and gone at Poynton. That was the small sum of her experience, and what it had made for her was her own affair, quite consistent with her not having dreamed it had made a tie – at least what *she* called one – for Owen. The old one, at any rate, was Mona – Mona who he had known so very much longer.

They walked far, to the south-west corner of the great Gardens, where, by the old round pond and the old red palace, when she had put out her hand to him in farewell, declaring that from the gate she must positively take a conveyance, it seemed suddenly to rise between them that this was a real separation. She was on his mother's side, she belonged to his mother's life, and his mother, in the future, would never come to Poynton. After what had passed she wouldn't even be at his wedding, and it was not possible now that Mrs Gereth should mention that ceremony to the girl, much less express a wish that the girl should be present at it. Mona, from decorum and with reference less to the bridegroom than to the bridegroom's mother, would of course not invite any such girl as Fleda. Everything therefore was ended; they would go their different ways; this was the last time they would stand face to face. They looked at each other with the fuller sense of it and, on Owen's part, with an expression of dumb trouble, the intensification of his usual appeal to any interlocutor to add the right thing to what he said. To Fleda, at this moment, it appeared that the right thing might easily be the wrong. He only said, at any rate: 'I want you to understand, you know – I want you to understand.'

What did he want her to understand? He seemed unable to bring it out, and this understanding was moreover exactly what she wished not to arrive at. Bewildered as she was, she had already taken in as much as she should know what to do with; the blood also was rushing into her face. He liked her – it was stupefying – more than he really ought: that was what was the matter with him and what he desired her to assimilate; so that she was suddenly as frightened as some thoughtless girl who finds herself the object of an overture from a married man.

'Good-bye, Mr Gereth – I *must* get on!' she declared with a cheerfulness that she felt to be an unnatural grimace. She broke away from him sharply, smiling, backing across the grass and then turning altogether and moving as fast as she could. 'Good-bye, good-bye!' she threw off again as she went, wondering if he would overtake her before she reached the gate; conscious with a red disgust that her movement was almost a run; conscious too of just the confused, handsome face with which he would look after her. She felt as if she had answered a kindness with a great flouncing snub, but at any rate she had got away, though the distance to the gate, her ugly gallop down the Broad Walk, every graceless jerk of which hurt her, seemed endless. She signed from afar to a cab on the stand in the Kensington Road and scrambled into it, glad of the encompassment of the four-wheeler that had officiously obeyed her summons and that, at the end of the twenty yards, when she had violently pulled up a glass, permitted her to recognize the fact that she was on the point of bursting into tears.

CHAPTER 7

As soon as her sister was married she went down to Mrs Gereth at Ricks – a promise to this effect having been promptly exacted and given; and her inner vision was much more fixed on the alterations there, complete now, as she understood, than on the success of her plotting and pinching for Maggie's happiness. Her imagination, in the interval, had indeed had plently to do and numerous scenes to visit; for when on the summons just mentioned it had taken a flight from West Kensington to Ricks, it had hung but an hour over the terrace of painted pots and then yielded to a current of the upper air that swept it straight off to Poynton and to Waterbath. Not a sound had reached her of any supreme clash, and Mrs Gereth had communicated next to nothing; giving out that, as was easily conceivable, she was too busy, too bitter, and too tired for vain civilities. All she had written was that she had got the new place well in hand and that Fleda would be surprised at the way it was turning out. Everything was even yet upside down; nevertheless, in the sense of having passed the threshold of Poynton for the last time, the amputation, as she called it, had been performed. Her leg had come off – she had now begun to stump along with the lovely wooden substitute; she would stump for life, and what her young friend was to come and admire was the beauty of her movement and the noise she made about the house. The reserve of Poynton and Waterbath had been matched by the austerity of Fleda's own secret, under the discipline of which she had repeated to herself a hundred times a day that she rejoiced at having cares that excluded all thought of it. She had lavished herself, in act, on Maggie and the curate, and had opposed to her father's selfishness a sweetness quite ecstatic. The young couple wondered why they had waited so long, since everything was after all so easy. She had thought of everything, even to how the 'quietness' of the wedding should be relieved by champagne and her father kept brilliant on a single bottle.

Fleda knew, in short, and liked the knowledge, that for several weeks she had appeared exemplary in every relation of life.

She had been perfectly prepared to be surprised at Ricks, for Mrs Gereth was a wonder-working wizard, with a command, when all was said, of good material; but the impression in wait for her on the threshold made her catch her breath and falter. Dusk had fallen when she arrived, and in the plain square hall, one of the few good features, the glow of a Venetian lamp just showed, on either wall, the richness of an admirable tapestry. This instant perception that the place had been dressed at the expense of Poynton was a shock: it was as if she had abruptly seen herself in the light of an accomplice. The next moment, folded in Mrs Gereth's arms, her eyes were diverted; but she had already had, in a flash, the vision of the great gaps in the other house. The two tapestries, not the largest, but those most splendidly toned by time, had been on the whole its most uplifted pride. When she could really see again she was on a sofa in the drawing-room, staring with intensity at an object soon distinct as the great Italian cabinet that, at Poynton, had been in the red saloon. Without looking, she was sure the room was occupied with other objects like it, stuffed with as many as it could hold of the trophies of her friend's struggle. By this time the very fingers of her glove, resting on the seat of the sofa, had thrilled at the touch of an old velvet brocade, a wondrous texture that she could recognize, would have recognized among a thousand, without dropping her eyes on it. They stuck to the cabinet with a kind of dissimulated dread, while she painfully asked herself whether she should notice it, notice everything, or just pretend not to be affected. How could she pretend not to be affected, with the very pendants of the lustres tinkling at her and with Mrs Gereth, beside her and staring at her even as she herself stared at the cabinet, hunching up a back like Atlas under his globe? She was appalled at this image of what Mrs Gereth had on her shoulders. That lady was waiting and watching her, bracing herself, and preparing the same face of confession and defiance she had shown the day, at Poynton, she had been surprised in the corridor. It was farcical not to speak; and yet to exclaim, to participate, would give one a bad sense of being mixed up with a theft. This ugly word sounded, for herself, in Fleda's silence, and the very violence of it jarred her into a scared glance, as of a creature detected, to right and left. But what again the full picture most showed her was the far-away empty sockets, a scandal of nakedness in high, bare walls. She at last uttered something formal and incoherent – she didn't know what: it had no relation to either house. Then she felt Mrs Gereth's hand once more on her arm. 'I've arranged a charming room for you – it's really lovely. You'll be very happy there.' This was spoken with extraordinary sweetness and with a smile that meant, 'Oh, I know what you're thinking; but what does it matter when you're so loyally on my side?' It had come indeed to a question of 'sides', Fleda thought, for the whole place was in battle array. In the soft lamplight, with one fine feature after another looming up into sombre richness, it defied her not to pro-nounce it a triumph of taste. Her passion for beauty leaped back into life; and was not what now most appealed to it a certain gorgeous audacity? Mrs Gereth's high hand was, as mere great effect, the climax of the impression.

'It's too wonderful, what you've done with the house!' – the visitor met her friend's eyes. They lighted up with joy – that friend herself so pleased with what she had done. This was not at all, in its accidental air of enthusiasm, what Fleda wanted to have said: it offered her as stupidly announcing from the first minute on whose side she was. Such was clearly the way Mrs Gereth took it: she threw herself upon the delightful girl and tenderly embraced her again; so that Fleda soon went on, with a studied difference and a cooler inspec-tion: 'Why, you brought away absolutely everything!'

'Oh no, not everything; I saw how little I could get into this scrap of a house. I only brought away what I required.'

Fleda had got up; she took a turn round the room. 'You "required" the very best pieces – the *morceaux de musée,* the individual gems!'

'I certainly didn't want the rubbish, if that's what you mean.' Mrs Gereth, on the sofa, followed the direction of her companion's eyes; with the light of her satisfaction still in her face, she slowly rubbed her large, handsome hands.

53

Wherever she was, she was herself the great piece in the gallery. It was the first Fleda had heard of there being 'rubbish' at Poynton, but she didn't for the moment take up this insincerity; she only, from where she stood in the room, called out, one after the other, as if she had had a list in her hand, the pieces that in the great house had been scattered and that now, if they had a fault, were too much like a minuet danced on a hearth-rug. She knew them each, in every chink and charm – knew them by the personal name their distinctive sign or story had given them; and a second time she felt how, against her intention, this uttered knowledge struck her hostess as so much free approval. Mrs Gereth was never indifferent to approval, and there was nothing she could so love you for as for doing justice to her deep morality. There was a particular gleam in her eyes when Fleda exclaimed at last, dazzled by the display: 'And even the Maltese cross!' That description, though technically incorrect, had always been applied, at Poynton, to a small but marvellous crucifix of ivory, a masterpiece of delicacy, of expression, and of the great Spanish period, the existence and precarious accessibility of which she had heard of at Malta, years before, by an odd and romantic chance – a clue followed through mazes of secrecy till the treasure was at last unearthed.

'"Even" the Maltese cross?' Mrs Gereth rose as she sharply echoed the words. 'My dear child, you don't suppose I'd have sacrificed *that*! For what in the world would you have taken me?'

'A *bibelot* the more or the less,' Fleda said, 'could have made little difference in this grand general view of you. I take you simply for the greatest of all conjurers. You've operated with a quickness – and with a quietness!' Her voice trembled a little as she spoke, for the plain meaning of her words was that what her friend had achieved belonged to the class of operation essentially involving the protection of darkness. Fleda felt she really could say nothing at all if she couldn't say that she knew what the danger had been. She completed her thought by a resolute and perfectly candid question: 'How in the world did you get off with them?'

Mrs Gereth confessed to the fact of danger with a cynicism

that surprised the girl. 'By calculating, by choosing my time. I *was* quiet, and I *was* quick. I manoeuvred; then at the last rushed!' Fleda drew a long breath: she saw in the poor woman something much better than sophistical ease, a crude elation that was a comparatively simple state to deal with. Her elation, it was true, was not so much from what she had done as from the way she had done it – by as brilliant a stroke as any commemorated in the annals of crime. 'I succeeded because I had thought it all out and left nothing to chance: the whole process was organized in advance, so that the mere carrying it into effect took but a few hours. It was largely a matter of money: oh, I was horribly extravagant – I had to turn on so many people. But they were all to be had – a little army of workers, the packers, the porters, the helpers of every sort, the men with the mighty vans. It was a question of arranging in Tottenham Court Road and of paying the price. I haven't paid it yet; there'll be a horrid bill; but at least the thing's done! Expedition pure and simple was the essence of the bargain. "I can give you two days," I said; "I can't give you another second." They undertook the job, and the two days saw them through. The people came down on a Tuesday morning; they were off on the Thursday. I admit that some of them worked all Wednesday night. I had thought it all out; I stood over them; I showed them how. Yes, I coaxed them, I made love to them. Oh, I was inspired – they found me wonderful. I neither ate nor slept, but I was as calm as I am now. I didn't know what was in me; it was worth finding out. I'm very remarkable, my dear: I lifted tons with my own arms. I'm tired, very, very tired; but there's neither a scratch nor a nick, there isn't a teacup missing.' Magnificent both in her exhaustion and in her triumph, Mrs Gereth sank on the sofa again, the sweep of her eyes a rich synthesis and the restless friction of her hands a clear betrayal. 'Upon my word,' she laughed, 'they really look better here!'

Fleda had listened in awe. 'And no one at Poynton said anything? There was no alarm?'

'What alarm should there have been? Owen left me almost defiantly alone: I had taken a time that I had reason to believe was safe from a descent.' Fleda had another wonder, which she hesitated to express: it would scarcely do to ask Mrs Gereth if she hadn't stood in fear of her servants. She knew, moreover, some of the secrets of her humorous household rule, all made up of shocks to shyness and provocations to curiosity – a diplomacy so artful that several of the maids quite yearned to accompany her to Ricks. Mrs Gereth, reading sharply the whole of her visitor's thought, caught it up with fine frankness. 'You mean that I was watched – that he had his myrmidons, pledged to wire him if they should see what I was "up to"? Precisely. I know the three persons you have in mind: I had them in mind myself. Well, I took a line with them – I settled them.'

Fleda had had no one in particular in mind; she had never believed in the myrmidons; but the tone in which Mrs Gereth spoke added to her suspense. 'What did you do to them?'

'I took hold of them hard – I put them in the forefront. I made them work.'

'To move the furniture?'

'To help, and to help so as to please me. That was the way to take them; it was what they had least expected. I marched up to them and looked each straight in the eye, giving him the chance to choose if he'd gratify me or gratify my son. He gratified *me*. They were too stupid!'

Mrs Gereth massed herself there more and more as an immoral woman, but Fleda had to recognize that she too would have been stupid and she too would have gratified her. 'And when did all this take place?'

'Only last week; it seems a hundred years. We've worked here as fast as we worked there, but I'm not settled yet: you'll see in the rest of the house. However, the worst is over.'

'Do you really think so?' Fleda presently inquired. 'I mean, does he, after the fact, as it were, accept it?'

'Owen – what I've done? I haven't the least idea,' said Mrs Gereth.

'Does Mona?'

'You mean that she'll be the soul of the row?'

'I hardly see Mona as the "soul" of anything,' the girl replied. 'But have they made no sound? Have you heard nothing at all?'

'Not a whisper, not a step, in all the eight days. Perhaps they don't know. Perhaps they're crouching for a leap.'

'But wouldn't they have gone down as soon as you left?'

'They may not have known of my leaving.' Fleda wondered afresh; it struck her as scarcely supposable that some sign shouldn't have flashed from Poynton to London. If the storm was taking this term of silence to gather, even in Mona's breast, it would probably discharge itself in some startling form. The great hush of everyone concerned was strange; but when she pressed Mrs Gereth for some explanation of it, that lady only replied, with her brave irony: 'Oh, I took their breath away!' She had no illusions, however; she was still prepared to fight. What indeed was her spoliation of Poynton but the first engagement of a campaign?

All this was exciting, but Fleda's spirit dropped, at bedtime, in the chamber embellished for her pleasure, where she found several of the objects that in her earlier room she had most admired. These had been reinforced by other pieces from other rooms, so that the quiet air of it was a harmony without a break, the finished picture of a maiden's bower. It was the sweetest Louis Seize, all assorted and combined – old chastened, figured, faded France. Fleda was impressed anew with her friend's genius for composition. She could say to herself that no girl in England, that night, went to rest with so picked a guard; but there was no joy for her in her privilege, no sleep even for the tired hours that made the place, in the embers of the fire and the winter dawn, look grey somehow, and loveless. She couldn't care for such things when they came to her in such ways; there was a wrong about them all that turned them to ugliness. In the watches of the night she saw Poynton dishonoured; she had cared for it as a happy whole, she reasoned, and the parts of it now around her seemed to suffer like chopped limbs. Before going to bed she had walked about with Mrs Gereth and seen at whose expense the whole house had been furnished. At poor Owen's from top to bottom – there wasn't a chair he hadn't sat upon. The maiden aunt had been exterminated – no trace of her to tell her tale. Fleda tried to think of some of the things at Poynton still unappropriated, but her memory was a blank about them, and in trying to focus

57

the old combinations she saw again nothing but gaps and scars, a vacancy that gathered at moments into something worse. This concrete image was her greatest trouble, for it was Owen Gereth's face, his sad, strange eyes, fixed upon her now as they had never been. They stared at her out of the darkness, and their expression was more than she could bear: it seemed to say that he was in pain and that it was somehow her fault. He had looked to her to help him, and this was what her help had been. He had done her the honour to ask her to exert herself in his interest, confiding to her a task of difficulty, but of the highest delicacy. Hadn't that been exactly the sort of service she longed to render him? Well, her way of rendering it had been simply to betray him and hand him over to his enemy. Shame, pity, resentment oppressed her in turn ; in the last of these feelings the others were quickly submerged. Mrs Gereth had imprisoned her in that torment of taste ; but it was clear to her for an hour at least that she might hate Mrs Gereth.

Something else, however, when morning came, was even more intensely definite: the most odious thing in the world for her would be ever again to meet Owen. She took on the spot a resolve to neglect no precaution that could lead to her going through life without that accident. After this, while she dressed, she took still another. Her position had become, in a few hours, intolerably false ; in as few more hours as possible she would therefore put an end to it. The way to put an end to it would be to inform Mrs Gereth that, to her great regret, she couldn't be with her now, couldn't cleave to her to the point that everything about her so plainly urged. She dressed with a sort of violence, a symbol of the manner in which this purpose was precipitated. The more they parted company the less likely she was to come across Owen ; for Owen would be drawn closer to his mother now by the very necessity of bringing her down. Fleda, in the inconsequence of distress, wished to have nothing to do with her fall ; she had had too much to do with everything. She was well aware of the importance, before breakfast and in view of any light they might shed on the question of motive, of not suffering her invidious expression of a difference to be accompanied by the traces of tears ; but it none the less came to pass, downstairs, that after she had subtly put her back to the window, to make a mystery of the state of her eyes, she stupidly let a rich sob escape her before she could properly meet the consequences of being asked if she wasn't delighted with her room. This accident struck her on the spot as so grave that she felt the only refuge to be instant hypocrisy, some graceful impulse that would charge her emotion to the quickened sense of her friend's generosity – a demonstration entailing a flutter round the table and a renewed embrace, and not so successfully improvised but that Fleda fancied Mrs Gereth to have been only half reassured. She had been startled, at any rate, and she might remain suspicious: this reflection interposed by the time, after breakfast, the girl had recovered sufficiently to say what was in her heart. She accordingly didn't say it that morning at all: she had absurdly veered about; she had encountered the shock of the fear that Mrs Gereth, with sharpened eyes, might wonder why the deuce (she often wondered in that phrase) she had grown so warm about Owen's rights. She would doubtless, at a pinch, be able to defend them on abstract grounds, but that would involve a discussion, and the idea of a discussion made her nervous for her secret. Until in some way Poynton should return the blow and give her a cue, she must keep nervousness down ; and she called herself a fool for having forgotten, however briefly, that her one safety was in silence.

Directly after luncheon Mrs Gereth took her into the garden for a glimpse of the revolution – or at least, said the mistress of Ricks, of the great row – that had been decreed there ; but the ladies had scarcely placed themselves for this view before the younger one found herself embracing a prospect that opened in quite another quarter. Her attention was called to it, oddly, by the streamers of the parlourmaid's cap, which, flying straight behind the neat young woman who unexpectedly burst from the house and showed a long red face as she ambled over the grass, seemed to articulate in their flutter the name that Fleda lived at present only to catch. 'Poynton – Poynton!' said the morsels of muslin ; so that the parlour-maid became on the instant an actress in the drama, and Fleda, assuming pusillanimously that she herself was only a spectator, looked across the footlights at the exponent of the principal part. The manner in which this artist returned her look showed that she was equally preoccupied. Both were haunted alike by possibilities, but the apprehension of neither, before the announcement was made, took the form of the arrival at Ricks, in the flesh, of Mrs Gereth's victim. When the messenger informed them that Mr Gereth was in the drawing-room, the blank 'Oh!' emitted by Fleda was quite as precipitate as the sound of her hostess's lips, besides being, as she felt, much less pertinent. 'I thought it would be somebody,' that lady afterwards said ; 'but I expected on the whole a solicitor's clerk.' Fleda didn't mention that she herself had expected on the whole a pair of constables. She was surprised by Mrs Gereth's question to the parlourmaid.

'For whom did he ask?'

'Why, for *you,* of course, dearest friend!' Fleda interjected, falling instinctively into the address that embodied the intensest pressure. She wanted to put Mrs Gereth between her and her danger.

'He asked for Miss Vetch, mum,' the girl replied, with a face that brought startlingly to Fleda's ear the muffled chorus of the kitchen.

'Quite proper,' said Mrs Gereth austerely. Then to Fleda: 'Please go to him.'

'But what to do?'

'What you always do – to see what he wants.' Mrs Gereth dismissed the maid. 'Tell him Miss Vetch will come.' Fleda saw that nothing was in the mother's imagination at this moment but the desire not to meet her son. She had completely broken with him, and there was little in what had just happened to repair the rupture. It would now take more to do so than his presenting himself uninvited at her door. 'He's right in asking for you – he's aware that you're still our communicator ; nothing has occurred to alter that. To what he wishes to transmit through you I'm ready, as I've been ready before, to listen. As far as *I'*m concerned, if I couldn't meet him a month ago, how am I to meet him today? If he has come to say, "My dear mother, you're here, in the hovel into which I've flung you, with consolations that give me pleasure," I'll listen to him ; but on no other footing. That's what you're to ascertain,

please. You'll oblige me as you've obliged me before. There!'
Mrs Gereth turned her back and, with a fine imitation of
superiority, began to redress the miseries immediately before
her. Fleda meanwhile hesitated, lingered for some minutes
where she had been left, feeling secretly that her fate still had
her in hand. It had put her face to face with Owen Gereth, and
it evidently meant to keep her so. She was reminded afresh of
two things: one of which was that, though she judged her
friend's rigour, she had never really had the story of the scene
enacted in the great awestricken house between the mother and
the son weeks before – the day the former took to her bed in
her overthrow; the other was, that at Ricks as at Poynton, it
was before all things her place to accept thankfully a usefulness
not, she must remember, universally asknowledged. What
determined her at the last, while Mrs Gereth disappeared in
the shrubbery, was that, though she was at a distance from
the house and the drawing-room was turned the other way, she
could absolutely see the young man alone there with the
sources of his pain. She saw his simple stare at his tapestries,
heard his heavy tread on his carpets and the hard breath of
his sense of unfairness. At this she went to him fast.

CHAPTER 8

'I ASKED for you,' he said when she stood there, 'because I heard from the flyman who drove me from the station to the inn that he had brought you here yesterday. We had some talk, and he mentioned it.'

'You didn't know I was here?'

'No. I knew only that you had had, in London, all that you told me, that day, to do; and it was Mona's idea that after your sister's marriage you were staying on with your father. So I thought you were with him still.'

'I am,' Fleda replied, idealizing a little the fact. 'I'm here only for a moment. But do you mean,' she went on, 'that if you had known I was with your mother you wouldn't have come down?'

The way Owen hung fire at this question made it sound more playful than she had intended. She had, in fact, no consciousness of any intention but that of confining herself rigidly to her function. She could already see that, in whatever he had now braced himself for, she was an element he had not reckoned with. His preparation had been of a different sort – the sort congruous with his having been careful to go first and lunch solidly at the inn. He had not been forced to ask for her, but she became aware, in his presence, of a particular desire to make him feel that no harm could really come to him. She might upset him, as people called it, but she would take no advantage of having done so. She had never seen a person with whom she wished more to be light and easy, to be exceptionally human. The account he presently gave of the matter was that he indeed wouldn't have come if he had known she was on the spot; because then, didn't she see? he could have written to her. He would have had her there to let fly at his mother.

'That would have saved me – well, it would have saved me a lot. Of course I would rather see you than her,' he somewhat awkwardly added. 'When the fellow spoke of you, I assure you I quite jumped at you. In fact I've no real desire to see Mummy at all. If she thinks I *like* it – ! ' he sighed disgustedly. 'I only came down because it seemed better than any other way. I didn't want her to be able to say I hadn't been all right. I dare say you know she has taken everything; or if not quite everything, why, a lot more than one ever dreamed. You can see for yourself – she has got half the place down. She has got them crammed – you can see for yourself!' He had his old trick of artless repetition, his helpless iteration of the obvious; but he was sensibly different, for Fleda, if only by the difference of his clear face, mottled over and almost disfigured by little points of pain. He might have been a fine young man with a bad toothache; with the first even of his life. What ailed him above all, she felt was that trouble was new to him: he had never known a difficulty; he had taken all his fences, his world wholly the world of the personally possible, rounded indeed by a grey suburb into which he had never had occasion to stray. In this vulgar and ill-lighted region he had evidently now lost himself. 'We left it quite to her honour, you know,' he said ruefully.

'Perhaps you've a right to say that you left it a little to mine.' Mixed up with the spoils there, rising before him as if she were in a manner their keeper, she felt that she must absolutely dissociate herself. Mrs Gereth had made it impossible to do anything but give her away. 'I can only tell you that, on my side, I left it to her. I never dreamed either that she would pick out so many things.'

'And you don't really think it's fair, do you? You *don't*! ' He spoke very quickly; he really seemed to plead.

Fleda faltered a moment. 'I think she has gone too far.' Then she added: 'I shall immediately tell her that I've said that to you.'

He appeared puzzled by this statement, but he presently rejoined: 'You haven't then said to mamma what you think?'

'Not yet; remember that I only got here last night.' She appeared to herself ignobly weak. 'I had had no idea what she was doing; I was taken completely by surprise. She managed it wonderfully.'

'It's the sharpest thing I ever saw in *my* life!' They looked at each other with intelligence, in appreciation of the sharpness, and Owen quickly broke into a loud laugh. The laugh was in itself natural, but the occasion of it strange; and stranger still, to Fleda, so that she too almost laughed, the inconsequent charity with which he added: 'Poor dear old Mummy! That's one of the reasons I asked for you,' he went on – 'to see if you'd back her up.'

Whatever he said or did, she somehow liked him the better for it. 'How can I back her up, Mr Gereth, when I think, as I tell you, that she has made a great mistake?'

'A great mistake! That's all right.' He spoke – it wasn't clear to her why – as if this declaration were a great point gained.

'Of course there are many things she hasn't taken,' Fleda continued.

'Oh yes, a lot of things. But you wouldn't know the place, all the same.' He looked about the room with his discoloured, swindled face, which deepened Fleda's compassion for him, conjuring away any smile at so candid an image of the dupe. 'You'd know this one soon enough, wouldn't you? These are just the things she ought to have left. Is the whole house full of them?'

'The whole house,' said Fleda uncompromisingly. She thought of her lovely room.

'I never knew how much I cared for them. They're awfully valuable, aren't they?' Owen's manner mystified her; she was conscious of a return of the agitation he had produced in her on that last bewildering day, and she reminded herself that, now she was warned, it would be inexcusable of her to allow him to justify the fear that had dropped on her. 'Mother thinks I never took any notice, but I assure you I was awfully proud of everything. Upon my honour, I *was* proud, Miss Vetch.'

There was an oddity in his helplessness; he appeared to wish to persuade her and to satisfy himself that she sincerely felt how worthy he really was to treat what had happened as an injury. She could only exclaim, almost as helplessly as himself: 'Of course you did justice! It's all most painful. I shall instantly let your mother know,' she again declared, 'the way I've

64

spoken of her to you.' She clung to that idea as to the sign of her straightness.

'You'll tell her what you think she ought to do?' he asked with some eagerness.

'What she ought to do?'

'*Don't* you think it – I mean that she ought to give them up?'

'To give them up?' Fleda hesitated again.

'To send them back – to keep it quiet.' The girl had not felt the impulse to ask him to sit down among the monuments of his wrong, so that, nervously, awkwardly, he fidgeted about the room with his hands in his pockets and an effect of returning a little into possession through the formulation of his view. 'To have them packed and dispatched again, since she knows so well how. She does it beautifully' – he looked close at two or three precious pieces. 'What's sauce for the goose is sauce for the gander!'

He had laughed at his way of putting it, but Fleda remained grave. 'Is that what you came to say to her?'

'Not exactly those words. But I did come to say' – he stammered, then brought it out – 'I did come to say we must have them right back.'

'And did you think your mother would see you?'

'I wasn't sure, but I thought it right to try – to put it to her kindly, don't you see? If she won't see me, then she has herself to thank. The only other way would have been to set the lawyers at her.'

'I'm glad you didn't do that.'

'I'm dashed if I want to!' Owen honestly declared. 'But what's a fellow to do if she won't meet a fellow?'

'What do you call meeting a fellow?' Fleda asked, with a smile.

'Why, letting *me* tell her a dozen things she can have.'

This was a transaction that Fleda, after a moment, had to give up trying to represent to herself. 'If she won't do that – ?' she went on.

'I'll leave it all to my solicitor. *He* won't let her off: by Jove, I know the fellow!'

'That's horrible!' said Fleda, looking at him in woe.

'It's utterly beastly!'

His want of logic as well as his vehemence startled her; and with her eyes still on his she considered before asking him the question these things suggested. At last she asked it. 'Is Mona very angry?'

'Oh dear, yes!' said Owen.

She had perceived that he wouldn't speak of Mona without her beginning. After waiting fruitlessly now for him to say more, she continued: 'She has been there again? She has seen the state of the house?'

'Oh dear, yes!' Owen repeated.

Fleda disliked to appear not to take account of his brevity, but it was just because she was struck by it that she felt the pressure of the desire to know more. What it suggested was simply what her intelligence supplied, for he was incapable of any art of insinuation. Wasn't it at all events the rule of communication with him to say for him what he couldn't say? This truth was present to the girl as she inquired if Mona greatly resented what Mrs Gereth had done. He satisfied her promptly; he was standing before the fire, his back to it, his long legs apart, his hands, behind him, rather violently jiggling his gloves. 'She hates it awfully. In fact, she refuses to put up with it at all. Don't you see? – she saw the place with all the things.'

'So that of course she misses them.'

'Misses them – rather! She was awfully sweet on them.' Fleda remembered how sweet Mona had been, and reflected that if that was the sort of plea he had prepared it was indeed as well he shouldn't see his mother. This was not all she wanted to know, but it came over her that it was all she needed. 'You see it puts me in the position of not carrying out what I promised,' Owen said. 'As she says herself' – he hesitated an instant – 'it's just as if I had obtained her under false pretences.' Just before, when he spoke with more drollery than he knew, it had left Fleda serious; but now his own clear gravity had the effect of exciting her mirth. She laughed out, and he looked surprised, but went on: 'She regards it as a regular sell.'

Fleda was silent; but finally, as he added nothing, she exclaimed: 'Of course it makes a great difference!' She knew all she needed, but none the less she risked, after another pause, an interrogative remark. 'I forgot when it is that your marriage takes place?'

Owen came away from the fire and, apparently at a loss where to turn, ended by directing himself to one of the windows. 'It's a little uncertain ; the date isn't quite fixed.'

'Oh, I thought I remembered that at Poynton you had told me a day, and that it was near at hand.'

'I dare say I did ; it was for the 19th. But we've altered that – she wants to shift it.' He looked out of the window ; then he said: 'In fact, it won't come off till Mummy has come round.'

'Come round?'

'Put the place as it was.' In his offhand way he added: 'You know what I mean!'

He spoke not impatiently, but with a kind of intimate familiarity, the sweetness of which made her feel a pang for having forced him to tell her what was embarrassing to him, what was even humiliating. Yes, indeed, she knew all she needed: all she needed was that Mona had proved apt at putting down that wonderful patent-leather foot. Her type was misleading only to the superficial, and no one in the world was less superficial than Fleda. She had guessed the truth at Waterbath and she had suffered from it at Poynton ; at Ricks the only thing she could do was to accept it with the dumb exaltation that she felt rising. Mona had been prompt with her exercise of the member in question, for it might be called prompt to do that sort of thing before marriage. That she had indeed been premature who should say save those who should have read the matter in the full light of results? Neither at Waterbath nor at Poynton had even Fleda's thoroughness discovered all that there was – or rather, all that there was not – in Owen Gereth. 'Of course it makes all the difference!' she said in answer to his last words. She pursued, after considering: 'What you wish me to say from you then to your mother is that you demand immediate and practically complete restitution?'

'Yes, please. It's tremendously good of you.'

'Very well, then. Will you wait?'

'For Mummy's answer?' Owen stared and looked perplexed ; he was more and more fevered with so much vivid expression of his case. 'Don't you think that if I'm here she may hate it worse – think I may want to make her reply bang off?'

Fleda thought. 'You don't then?'

'I want to take her in the right way, don't you know? – treat her as if I gave her more than just an hour or two.'

'I see,' said Fleda. 'Then, if you don't wait – good-bye.'

This again seemed not what he wanted. 'Must *you* do it bang off?'

'I'm only thinking she'll be impatient – I mean, you know, to learn what will have passed between us.'

'I see,' said Owen, looking at his gloves. 'I can give her a day or two, you know. Of course I didn't come down to sleep,' he went on. 'The inn seems a horrid hole. I know all about the trains – having no idea you were here.' Almost as soon as his interlocutress he was struck with the absence of the visible, in this, as between effect and cause. 'I mean because in that case I should have felt I could stop over. I should have felt I could talk with you a blessed sight longer than with Mummy.'

'We've already talked a long time,' smiled Fleda.

'Awfully, haven't we?' He spoke with the stupidity she didn't object to. Inarticulate as he was, he had more to say; he lingered perhaps because he was vaguely aware of the want of sincerity in her encouragement to him to go. 'There's one thing, please,' he mentioned, as if there might be a great many others too. 'Please don't say anything about Mona.'

She didn't understand. 'About Mona?'

'About its being *her* that thinks she has gone too far.' This was still slightly obscure, but now Fleda understood. 'It mustn't seem to come from *her* at all, don't you know? That would only make Mummy worse.'

Fleda knew exactly how much worse, but she felt a delicacy about explicitly assenting. She was already immersed moreover in the deep consideration of what might make 'Mummy' better. She couldn't see as yet at all; she could only clutch at the hope of some inspiration after he should go. Oh, there was a remedy, to be sure, but it was out of the question; in spite of which, in the strong light of Owen's troubled presence, of his anxious face and restless step, it hung there before her for some minutes. She felt that, remarkably, beneath the decent rigour of his errand, the poor young man, for reasons, for weariness, for disgust, would have been ready not to insist. His fitness to fight his mother had left him – he wasn't in fighting trim. He had no natural avidity and even no special wrath ; he had none that had not been taught him, and it was doing his best to learn the lesson that had made him so sick. He had his delicacies, but he hid them away like presents before Christmas. He was hollow, perfunctory, pathetic ; he had been guided by another hand. That hand had naturally been Mona's, and it was heavy even now on his strong, broad back. Why then had he originally rejoiced so in its touch? Fleda dashed aside this question, for it had nothing to do with her problem. Her problem was to help him to live as a gentleman and carry through what he had undertaken ; her problem was to reinstate him in his rights. It was quite irrelevant that Mona had no intelligence of what she had lost – quite irrelevant that she was moved not by the privation, but by the insult : she had every reason to be moved, though she was so much more movable, in the vindictive way, at any rate, than one might have supposed – assuredly more than Owen himself had imagined.

'Certainly I shall not mention Mona,' Fleda said, 'and there won't be the slightest necessity for it. The wrong's quite sufficiently yours, and the demand you make is perfectly justified by it.'

'I can't tell you what it is to me to feel you on my side! ' Owen exclaimed.

'Up to this time,' said Fleda, after a pause, 'your mother has had no doubt of my being on hers.'

'Then of course she won't like your changing.'

'I dare say she won't like it at all.'

'Do you mean to say you'll have a regular kick-up with her? '

'I don't exactly know what you mean by a regular kick-up. We shall naturally have a great deal of discussion – if she consents to discuss the matter at all. That's why you must decidedly give her two or three days.'

'I see you think she *may* refuse to discuss it at all,' said Owen.

'I'm only trying to be prepared for the worst. You must remember that to have to withdraw from the ground she has taken, to make a public surrender of what she has publicly appropriated, will go uncommonly hard with her pride.'

Owen considered; his face seemed to broaden, but not into a smile. 'I suppose she's tremendously proud, isn't she?' This might have been the first time it had occurred to him.

'You know better than I,' said Fleda, speaking with high extravagance.

'I don't know anything in the world half so well as you. If I were as clever as you I might hope to get round her.' Owen hesitated; then he went on: 'In fact I don't quite see what even you can say or do that will really fetch her.'

'Neither do I, as yet. I must think – I must pray!' the girl pursued, smiling. 'I can only say to you that I'll try. I *want* to try, you know – I want to help you.' He stood looking at her so long on this that she added with much distinctness: 'So you must leave me, please, quite alone with her. You must go straight back.'

'Back to the inn?'

'Oh no, back to town. I'll write to you tomorrow.'

He turned about vaguely for his hat.

'There's a chance, of course, that she may be afraid.'

'Afraid, you mean, of the legal steps you may take?'

'I've got a perfect case – I could have her up. The Brigstocks say it's simple stealing.'

'I can easily fancy what the Brigstocks say!' Fleda permitted herself to remark without solemnity.

'It's none of their business, is it?' was Owen's unexpected rejoinder. Fleda had already noted that no one so slow could ever have had such rapid transitions.

She showed her amusement. 'They've a much better right to say it's none of mine.'

'Well, at any rate, you don't call her names.'

Fleda wondered whether Mona did; and this made it all the finer of her to exclaim in a moment: 'You don't know what I shall call her if she holds out!'

Owen gave her a gloomy glance; then he blew a speck off the crown of his hat. 'But if you do have a set-to with her?'

He paused so long for a reply that Fleda said: 'I don't think I know what you mean by a set-to.'

'Well, if she calls *you* names.'

'I don't think she'll do that.'

'What I mean to say is, if she's angry at your backing me up – what will you do then? She can't possibly like it, you know.'

'She may very well not like it; but everything depends. I must see what I shall do. You mustn't worry about me.'

She spoke with decision, but Owen seemed still unsatisfied. 'You won't go away, I hope?'

'Go away?'

'If she does take it ill of you.'

Fleda moved to the door and opened it. 'I'm not prepared to say. You must have patience and see.'

'Of course I must,' said Owen – 'of course, of course.' But he took no more advantage of the open door than to say: 'You want me to be off, and I'm off in a minute. Only, before I go, please answer me a question. If you *should* leave my mother, where would you go?'

Fleda smiled again. 'I haven't the least idea.'

'I suppose you'd go back to London.'

'I haven't the least idea,' Fleda repeated.

'You don't – a – live anywhere in particular, do you?' the young man went on. He looked conscious as soon as he had spoken; she could see that he felt himself to have alluded more grossly than he meant to the circumstances of her having, if one were plain about it, no home of her own. He had meant it as an illusion of a tender sort to all that she would sacrifice in the case of a quarrel with his mother; but there was indeed no graceful way of touching on that. One just couldn't be plain about it.

Fleda, wound up as she was, shrank from any treatment at all of the matter, and she made no answer to his question. 'I *won't* leave your mother,' she said. 'I'll produce an effect on her; I'll convince her absolutely.'

'I believe you will, if you look at her like that!'

She was wound up to such a height that there might well be a light in her pale, fine little face – a light that, while, for all return, at first, she simply shone back at him, was intensely

71

reflected in his own. 'I'll make her see it – I'll make her see it!'
She rang out like a silver bell. She had at that moment a perfect faith that she should succeed; but it passed into something
else when, the next instant, she became aware that Owen,
quickly getting between her and the door she had opened, was
sharply closing it, as might be said, in her face. He had done
this before she could stop him, and he stood there with his
hand on the knob and smiled at her strangely. Clearer than he
could have spoken it was the sense of those seconds of silence.

'When I got into this I didn't know you, and now that I
know you how can I tell you the difference? And *she's* so
different, so ugly and vulgar, in the light of this squabble. No,
like *you* I've never known one. It's another thing, it's a new
thing altogether. Listen to me a little: can't something be
done?' It was what had been in the air in those moments at
Kensington, and it only wanted words to be a committed act.
The more reason, to the girl's excited mind, why it shouldn't
have words; her one thought was not to hear, to keep the act
uncommitted. She would do this if she had to be horrid.

'Please let me out, Mr Gereth,' she said; on which he opened
the door with an hesitation so very brief that in thinking of
these things afterwards – for she was to think of them for ever
– she wondered in what tone she could have spoken. They went
into the hall, where she encountered the parlour-maid of
whom she inquired whether Mrs Gereth had come in.

'No miss; and I think she has left the garden. She has gone
up the back road.' In other words, they had the whole place to
themselves. It would haveb een a pleasure, in a different mood
to converse with that parlour-maid.

'Please open the house-door,' said Fleda.

Owen, as if in quest of his umbrella, looked vaguely about
the hall – looked even wistfully up the staircase – while the
neat young woman complied with Fleda's request. Owen's
eyes then wandered out of the open door. 'I think it's awfully
nice here,' he observed; 'I assure you I could do with it myself.'

'I should think you might, with half your things here! It's
Poynton itself – almost. Good-bye, Mr Gereth,' Fleda added.
Her intention had naturally been that the neat young woman,
opening the front door, should remain to close it on the

departing guest. That functionary, however, had acutely vanished behind a stiff flap of green baize which Mrs Gereth had not yet had time to abolish. Fleda put out her hand, but Owen turned away – he couldn't find his umbrella. She passed into the open air – she was determined to get him out ; and in a moment he joined her in the little plastered portico which had small resemblance to any feature of Poynton. It was, as Mrs Gereth had said, like the portico of a house in Brompton.

'Oh, I don't mean with all the things here,' he explained in regard to the opinion he had just expressed. 'I mean I could put up with it just as it was ; it had a lot of good things, don't you think? I mean if everything was back at Poynton, if everything was all right.' He brought out these last words with a sort of smothered sigh. Fleda didn't understand his explanation unless it had reference to another and more wonderful exchange – the restoration to the great house not only of its tables and chairs, but of its alienated mistress. This would imply the installation of his own life at Ricks, and obviously that of another person. Such another person could scarcely be Mona Brigstock. He put out his hand now ; and once more she heard his unsounded words: 'With everything patched up at the other place, I could live here with *you*. Don't you see what I mean?'

Fleda saw perfectly, and, with a face in which she flattered herself that nothing of this vision appeared, gave him her hand and said: 'Good-bye, good-bye.'

Owen held her hand very firmly and kept it even after an effort made by her to recover it – an effort not repeated, as she felt it best not to show she was flurried. That solution – of her living with him at Ricks – disposed of him beautifully, and disposed not less so of herself ; it disposed admirably too of Mrs Gereth. Fleda could only vainly wonder how it provided for poor Mona. While he looked at her, grasping her hand, she felt that now indeed she was paying for his mother's extravagance at Poynton – the vividness of that lady's public plea that little Fleda Vetch was the person to insure the general peace. It was to that vividness poor Owen had come back, and if Mrs Gereth had had more discretion little Fleda Vetch wouldn't have been in a predicament. She saw that Owen had at this moment his sharpest necessity of speech, and so long as he didn't release her hand she could only submit to him. Her defence would be perhaps to look blank and hard; so she looked as blank and as hard as she could, with the reward of an immediate sense that this was not a bit what he wanted. It even made him hang fire, as if he were suddenly ashamed of himself, were recalled to some idea of duty and of honour. Yet he none the less brought it out. 'There's one thing I dare say I ought to tell you, if you're going so kindly to act for me; though of course you'll see for yourself it's a thing it won't do to tell *her*.' What was it? He made her wait for it again, and while she waited, under firm coercion, she had the extraordinary impression that Owen's simplicity was in eclipse. His natural honesty was like the scent of a flower, and she felt at this moment as if her nose had been brushed by the bloom without the odour. The allusion was undoubtedly to his mother; and was not what he meant about the matter in question the opposite of what he said – that it just *would* do to tell her? It would have been the first time he had said the opposite of what he meant, and there was certainly a fascination in the phenomenon, as well as a challenge to suspense in the ambiguity. 'It's just that I understand from Mona, you know,' he stammered; 'it's just that she has made no bones about bringing home to me – ' He tried to laugh, and in the effort he faltered again.

'About bringing home to you?' – Fleda encouraged him.

He was sensible of it, he achieved his performance. 'Why, that if I don't get the things back – every blessed one of them except a few *she'll* pick out – she won't have anything more to say to me.'

Fleda, after an instant, encouraged him again. 'To say to you?'

'Why, she simply won't marry me, don't you see?'

Owen's legs, not to mention his voice, had wavered while he spoke, and she felt his possession of her hand loosen so that she was free again. Her stare of perception broke into a lively laugh. 'Oh, you're all right, for you *will* get them. You will; you're quite safe; don't worry!' She fell back into the house with her hand on the door. 'Good-bye, good-bye.' She repeated it several times, laughing bravely, quite waving him away and, as he didn't move and save that he was on the other side of it, closing the door in his face quite as he had closed that of the drawing-room in hers. Never had a face, never at least had such a handsome one, been so presented to that offence. She even held the door a minute, lest he should try to come in again. At last, as she heard nothing, she made a dash for the stairs and ran up.

CHAPTER 9

IN knowing a while before all she needed, Fleda had been far
from knowing as much as that; so that once upstairs, where, in
her room, with her sense of danger and trouble, the age of
Louis-Seize suddenly struck her as wanting in taste and point,
she felt that she now for the first time knew her temptation. Owen had put it before her with an art beyond his own
dream. Mona would cast him off if he didn't proceed to extremities; if his negotiation with his mother should fail he
would be completely free. That negotiation depended on a
young lady to whom he had pressingly suggested the condition
of his freedom; and as if to aggravate the young lady's predicament designing fate had sent Mrs Gereth, as the parlour-
maid said, 'up the back roads'. This would give the young lady
more time to make up her mind that nothing should come of
the negotiation. There would be different ways of putting the
question to Mrs Gereth, and Fleda might profitably devote the
moments before her return to a selection of the way that would
most surely be tantamount to failure. This selection indeed
required no great adroitness; it was so conspicuous that failure
would be the reward of an effective introduction of Mona.
If that abhorred name should be properly invoked Mrs Gereth
would resist to the death, and before envenomed resistance
Owen would certainly retire. His retirement would be into
single life, and Fleda reflected that he had now gone away
conscious of having practically told her so. She could only
say, as she waited for the back road to disgorge, that she hoped
it was a consciousness he enjoyed. There was something *she*
enjoyed; but that was a very different matter. To know that
she had become to him an object of desire gave her wings that
she felt herself flutter in the air: it was like the rush of a flood
into her own accumulations. These stored depths had been
fathomless and still, but now, for half an hour, in the empty
house, they spread till they overflowed. He seemed to have
made it right for her to confess to herself her secret. Strange

76

then there should be for him in return nothing that such a confession could make right! How could it make right that he should give up Mona for another woman? His attitude was a sorry appeal to Fleda to legitimate that. But he didn't believe it himself, and he had none of the courage of his suggestion. She could easily see how wrong everything must be when a man so made to be manly was wanting in courage. She had upset him, as people called it, and he had spoken out from the force of the jar of finding her there. He had upset her too, heaven knew, but she was one of those who could pick themselves up. She had the real advantage, she considered, of having kept him from seeing that she had been overthrown.

She had moreover at present completely recovered her feet, though there was in the intensity of the effort required to do so a vibration which throbbed away into an immense allowance for the young man. How could she after all know what, in the disturbance wrought by his mother, Mona's relations with him might have become? If he had been able to keep his wits, such as they were, more about him he would probably have felt – as sharply as she felt on his behalf – that so long as those relations were not ended he had no right to say even the little he had said. He had no right to appear to wish to draw in another girl to help him to an escape. If he was in a plight he must get out of the plight himself, he must get out of it first, and anything he should have to say to anyone else must be deferred and detached. She herself, at any rate – it was her own case that was in question – couldn't dream of assisting him save in the sense of their common honour. She could never be the girl to be drawn in, she could never lift her finger against Mona. There was something in her that would make it a shame to her for ever to have owed her happiness to an interference. It would seem intolerably vulgar to her to have 'ousted' the daughter of the Brigstocks; and merely to have abstained even wouldn't assure her that she had been straight. Nothing was really straight but to justify her little pensioned presence by her use; and now, won over as she was to heroism, she could see her use only as some high and delicate deed. She couldn't do anything at all, in short, unless she could do it with a kind of pride, and there would be nothing to be proud of in having arranged for poor Owen to get off easily. Nobody had a right to get off easily from pledges so deep, so sacred. How could Fleda doubt they had been tremendous when she knew so well what any pledge of her own would be? If Mona was so formed that she could hold such vows light, that was Mona's peculiar business. To have loved Owen apparently, and yet to have loved him only so much, only to the extent of a few tables and chairs, was not a thing she could so much as try to grasp. Of a different way of loving him she was herself ready to give an instance, an instance of which the beauty indeed would not be generally known. It would not perhaps if revealed be generally understood, inasmuch as the effect of the particular pressure she proposed to exercise would be, should success attend it, to keep him tied to an affection that had died a sudden and violent death. Even in the ardour of her meditation Fleda remained in sight of the truth that it would be an odd result of her magnanimity to prevent her friend's shaking off a woman he disliked. If he didn't dislike Mona, what was the matter with him? And if he did, Fleda asked, what was the matter with her own silly self?

Our young lady met this branch of the temptation it pleased her frankly to recognize by declaring that to encourage any such cruelty would be tortuous and base. She had nothing to do with his dislikes; she had only to do with his good nature and his good name. She had joy of him just as he was, but it was of these things she had the greatest. The worst aversion and the liveliest reaction moreover wouldn't alter the fact – since one was facing facts – that but the other day his strong arms must have clasped a remarkably handsome girl as close as she had permitted. Fleda's emotion at this time was a wonderous mixture, in which Mona's permissions and Mona's beauty figured powerfully as aids to reflection. She herself had no beauty, and *her* permissions were the stony stares she had just practised in the drawing-room – a consciousness of a kind appreciably to add to the particular sense of triumph that made her generous. I may not perhaps too much diminish the merit of that generosity if I mention that it could take the flight we are considering just because really, with the telescope of her long thought, Fleda saw what might bring her out of the wood. Mona herself would bring her out; at the least Mona possibly might. Deep down plunged the idea that even should she achieve what she had promised Owen, there was still the contingency of Mona's independent action. She might by that time, under stress of temper or of whatever it was that was now moving her, have said or done the things there is no patching up. If the rupture should come from Waterbath they might all be happy yet. This was a calculation that Fleda wouldn't have committed to paper, but it affected the total of her sentiments. She was meanwhile so remarkably constituted that while she refused to profit by Owen's mistake, even while she judged it and hastened to cover it up, she could drink a sweetness from it that consorted little with her wishing it mightn't have been made. There was no harm done, because he had instinctively known, poor dear, with whom to make it, and it was a compensation for seeing him worried that he hadn't made it with some horrid mean girl who would immediately have dished him by making a still bigger one. Their protected error (for she indulged a fancy that it was hers too) was like some dangerous, lovely living thing that she had caught and could keep – keep vivid and helpless in the cage of her own passion and look at and talk to all day long. She had got it well locked up there by the time that, from an upper window, she saw Mrs Gereth again in the garden. At this she went down to meet her.

CHAPTER 10

FLEDA'S line had been taken, her word was quite ready; on the terrace of the painted pots she broke out before her interlocutress could put a question. 'His errand was perfectly simple: he came to demand that you shall pack everything straight up again and send it back as fast as the railway will carry it.'

The back road had apparently been fatiguing to Mrs Gereth; she rose there rather white and wan with her walk. A certain sharp thinness was in her ejaculation of 'Oh!' – after which she glanced about her for a place to sit down. The movement was a criticism of the order of events that offered such a piece of news to a lady coming in tired; but Fleda could see that in turning over the possibilities this particular peril was the one that during the last hour her friend had turned up oftenest. At the end of the short, grey day, which had been moist and mild, the sun was out; the terrace looked to the south, and a bench, formed as to legs and arms of iron representing knotted boughs, stood against the warmest wall of the house. The mistress of Ricks sank upon it and presented to her companion the handsome face she had composed to hear everything. Strangely enough, it was just this fine vessel of her attention that made the girl most nervous about what she must drop in. 'Quite a "demand", dear, is it?' asked Mrs Gereth, drawing in her cloak.

'Oh, that's what I should call it!' Fleda laughed, to her own surprise.

'I mean with the threat of enforcement and that sort of thing.'

'Distinctly with the threat of enforcement – what would be called, I suppose, coercion.'

'What sort of coercion?' said Mrs Gereth.

'Why, legal, don't you know? – what he calls setting the lawyers at you.'

'Is that what he calls it?' She seemed to speak with disinterested curiosity.

'That's what he calls it,' said Fleda.

Mrs Gereth considered an instant. 'Oh, the lawyers!' she exclaimed lightly. Seated there almost cosily in the reddening winter sunset, only with her shoulders raised a little and her mantle tightened as if from a slight chill, she had never yet looked to Fleda so much in possession nor so far from meeting unsuspectedness half-way. 'Is he going to send them down here?'

'I dare say he thinks it may come to that.'

'The lawyers can scarcely do the packing,' Mrs Gereth humorously remarked.

'I suppose he means them – in the first place, at least – to try to talk you over.'

'In the first place, eh? And what does he mean in the second?'

Fleda hesitated; she had not foreseen that so simple an inquiry could disconcert her. 'I'm afraid I don't know.'

'Didn't you ask?' Mrs Gereth spoke as if she might have said, 'What then were you doing all the while?'

'I didn't ask very much,' said her companion. 'He has been gone some time. The great thing seemed to be to understand clearly that he wouldn't be content with anything less than what he mentioned.'

'My just giving everything back?'

'Your just giving everything back.'

'Well, darling, what did you tell him?' Mrs Gereth blandly inquired.

Fleda faltered again, wincing at the term of endearment, at what the words took for granted, charged with the confidence she had now committed herself to betray. 'I told him I would tell you!' She smiled, but she felt that her smile was rather hollow and even that Mrs Gereth had begun to look at her with some fixedness.

'Did he seem very angry?'

'He seemed very sad. He takes it very hard,' Fleda added.

'And how does *she* take it?'

81

'Ah, that – that I felt a delicacy about asking.'

'So you didn't ask?' The words had the note of surprise.

Fleda was embarrassed; she had not made up her mind definitely to lie. 'I didn't think you'd care.' That small untruth she would risk.

'Well – I don't!' Mrs Gereth declared; and Fleda felt less guilty to hear her, for the statement was as inexact as her own. 'Didn't you say anything in return?' Mrs Gereth presently continued.

'Do you mean in the way of justifying you?'

'I didn't mean to trouble you to do that. My justification,' said Mrs Gereth, sitting there warmly and, in the lucidity of her thought, which nevertheless hung back a little, dropping her eyes on the gravel – 'my justification was all the past. My justification was the cruelty – ' But at this, with a short, sharp gesture, she checked herself. 'It's too good of me to talk – now.' She produced these sentences with a cold patience, as if addressing Fleda in the girl's virtual and actual character of Owen's representative. Our young lady crept to and fro before the bench, combating the sense that it was occupied by a judge, looking at her boot-toes, reminding herself in doing so of Mona, and lightly crunching the pebbles as she walked. She moved about because she was afraid, putting off from moment to moment the exercise of the courage she had been sure she possessed. That courage would all come to her if she could only be equally sure that what she should be called upon to do for Owen would be to suffer. She had wondered, while Mrs Gereth spoke, how that lady would describe her justification. She had described it as if to be irreproachably fair, give her adversary the benefit of every doubt, and then dismiss the question for ever. 'Of course,' Mrs Gereth went on, 'if we didn't succeed in showing him at Poynton the ground we took, it's simply that he shuts his eyes. What I supposed was that you would have given him your opinion that if I was the woman so signally to assert myself, I'm also the woman to rest upon it imperturbably enough.'

Fleda stopped in front of her hostess. 'I gave him my opinion that you're very logical, very obstinate, and very proud.'

'Quite right, my dear: I'm a rank bigot – about that sort of thing!' and Mrs Gereth jerked her head at the contents of the house. 'I've never denied it. I'd kidnap – to save them, to convert them – the children of heretics. When I know I'm right I go to the stake. Oh, he may burn me alive!' she cried with a happy face. 'Did he abuse me?' she then demanded.

Fleda had remained there, gathering in her purpose. 'How little you know him!'

Mrs Gereth stared, then broke into a laugh that her companion had not expected. 'Ah, my dear, certainly not so well as you!' The girl, at this, turned away again – she felt she looked too conscious; and she was aware that, during a pause, Mrs Gereth's eyes watched her as she went. She faced about afresh to meet them, but what she met was a question that reinforced them. 'Why had you a "delicacy" as to speaking of Mona?'

She stopped again before the bench, and an inspiration came to her. 'I should think *you* would know,' she said with proper dignity.

Blankness was for a moment on Mrs Gereth's brow; then light broke – she visibly remembered the scene in the breakfast-room after Mona's night at Poynton. 'Because I contrasted you – told him *you* were the one?' Her eyes looked deep. 'You were – you are still!'

Fleda gave a bold dramatic laugh. 'Thank you, my love – with all the best things at Ricks!'

Mrs Gereth considered, trying to penetrate, as it seemed; but at last she brought out roundly: 'For you, you know, I'd send them back!'

The girl's heart gave a tremendous bound; the right way dawned upon her in a flash. Obscurity indeed the next moment engulfed this course, but for a few thrilled seconds she had understood. To send the things back 'for her' meant of course to send them back if there were even a dim chance that she might become mistress of them. Fleda's palpitation was not allayed as she asked herself what portent Mrs Gereth had suddenly perceived of such a chance: that perception could only from a sudden suspicion of her secret. This suspicion, in turn, was a tolerably straight consequence of that implied view of the propriety of surrender from which, she was well aware, she could say nothing to dissociate herself. What she first felt was that if she wished to rescue the spoils she wished also to rescue her secret. So she looked as innocent as she could and said as quickly as possible: 'For me? Why in the world for me?'

'Because you're so awfully keen.'

'Am I? Do I strike you so? You know I hate him,' Fleda went on.

She had the sense for a while of Mrs Gereth's regarding her with the detachment of some stern, clever stranger. 'Then what's the matter with you? Why do you want me to give in?'

Fleda hesitated; she felt herself reddening. 'I've only said your son wants it. I haven't said *I* do.'

'Then say it and have done with it!'

This was more peremptory than any word her friend, though often speaking in her presence with much point, had ever yet directly addressed to her. It affected her like the crack of a whip, but she confined herself, with an effort, to taking it as a reminder that she must keep her head. 'I know he has his engagement to carry out.'

'His engagement to marry? Why, it's just that engagement we loathe!'

'Why should *I* loathe it?' Fleda asked with a strained smile. Then, before Mrs Gereth could reply, she pursued: 'I'm thinking of his general undertaking – to give her the house as she originally saw it.'

'To give her the house!' Mrs Gereth brought up the words from the depth of the unspeakable. The effort was like the moan of an autumn wind; it was in the power of such an image to make her turn pale.

'I'm thinking,' Fleda continued, 'of the simple question of his keeping faith on an important clause of his contract: it doesn't matter whether it's with a stupid girl or with a monster of cleverness. I'm thinking of his honour and his good name.'

'The honour and good name of a man you hate?'

'Certainly,' the girl resolutely answered. 'I don't see why you should talk as if one had a petty mind. You don't think so.

84

It's not on that assumption you've ever dealt with me. I can do your son justice, as he put his case to me.'

'Ah, then he did put his case to you!' Mrs Gereth exclaimed, with an accent of triumph. 'You seemed to speak just now as if really nothing of any consequence had passed between you.'

'Something always passes when one has a little imagination,' our young lady declared.

'I take it you don't mean that Owen has any!' Mrs Gereth cried with her large laugh.

Fleda was silent a moment. 'No, I don't mean that Owen has any,' she returned at last.

'Why is it you hate him so?' her hostess abruptly inquired.

'Should I love him for all he has made you suffer?'

Mrs Gereth slowly rose at this and, coming across the walk, took her young friend in her arms and kissed her. She then passed into one of Fleda's an arm perversely and imperiously sociable. 'Let us move a little,' she said, holding her close and giving a slight shiver. They strolled along the terrace, and she brought out another question. 'He *was* eloquent, then, poor dear – he poured forth the story of his wrongs?'

Fleda smiled down at her companion, who, cloaked and perceptibly bowed, leaned on her heavily and gave her an odd, unwonted sense of age and cunning. She took refuge in an evasion. 'He couldn't tell me anything that I didn't know pretty well already.'

'It's very true that you know everything. No, dear, you haven't a petty mind; you've a lovely imagination and you're the nicest creature in the world. If you were inane, like most girls – like everyone, in fact – I would have insulted you, I would have outraged you, and then you would have fled from me in terror. No, now that I think of it,' Mrs Gereth went on, 'you wouldn't have fled from me; nothing, on the contrary, would have made you budge. You would have cuddled into your warm corner, but you would have been wounded and weeping and martyrized, and you would have taken every opportunity to tell people I'm a brute – as indeed I should have been!' They went to and fro, and she would not allow Fleda, who laughed and protested, to attenuate with any light civility this spirited picture. She praised her cleverness and her patience; then she said it was getting cold and dark and they must go in to tea. She delayed quitting the place, however, and reverted instead to Owen's ultimatum, about which she asked another question or two; in particular whether it had struck Fleda that he really believed she would comply with such a summons.

'I think he really believes that if I try hard enough I can make you': after uttering which words our young lady stopped short and emulated the embrace she had received a few moments before.

'And you've promised to try: I see. You didn't tell me that, either,' Mrs Gereth added as they went on. 'But you're rascal enough for anything!' While Fleda was occupied in thinking in what terms she could explain why she had indeed been rascal enough for the reticence thus denounced, her companion broke out with an inquiry somewhat irrelevant and even in form somewhat profane. 'Why the devil, at any rate, doesn't it come off?'

Fleda hesitated. 'You mean their marriage?'

'Of course I mean their marriage!'

Fleda hesitated again. 'I haven't the least idea.'

'You didn't ask him?'

'Oh, how in the world can you fancy?' She spoke in a shocked tone.

'Fancy your putting a question so indelicate? *I* should have put it – I mean in your place; but I'm quite coarse, thank God!' Fleda felt privately that she herself was coarse, or at any rate would presently have to be; and Mrs Gereth, with a purpose that struck the girl as increasing, continued: 'What, then, *was* the day to be? Wasn't it just one of these?'

'I'm sure I don't remember.'

It was part of the great rupture and an effect of Mrs Gereth's character that up to this moment she had been completely and haughtily indifferent to that detail. Now, however, she had a visible reason for being clear about it. She bethought herself and she broke out – 'Isn't the day past?' Then, stopping short, she added: 'Upon my word, they must have put it off!' As Fleda made no answer to this she sharply went on: '*Have* they put it off?'

'I haven't the least idea,' said the girl.

Her hostess was looking at her hard again. 'Didn't he tell you – didn't he say anything about it?'

Fleda, meanwhile, had had time to make her reflections, which were moreover the continued throb of those that had occupied the interval between Owen's departure and his mother's return. If she should now repeat his words, this wouldn't at all play the game of her definite vow; it would only play the game of her little gagged and blinded desire. She could calculate well enough the effect of telling Mrs Gereth how she had had it from Owen's troubled lips that Mona was only waiting for the restitution and would do nothing without it. The thing was to obtain the restitution without imparting that knowledge. The only way, also, not to impart it was not to tell any truth at all about it; and the only way to meet this last condition was to reply to her companion, as she presently did: 'He told me nothing whatever: he didn't touch on the subject.'

'Not in any way?'

'Not in any way.'

Mrs Gereth watched Fleda and considered. 'You haven't any idea if they are waiting for the things?'

'How should I have? I'm not in their counsels.'

'I dare say they are – or that Mona is.' Mrs Gereth reflected again; she had a bright idea. 'If I don't give in, I'll be hanged if she'll not break off.'

'She'll never, never break off!' said Fleda.

'Are you sure?'

'I can't be sure, but it's my belief.'

'Derived from him?'

The girl hung fire a few seconds. 'Derived from him.'

Mrs Gereth gave her a long last look, then turned abruptly away. 'It's an awful bore you didn't really get it out of him! Well, come to tea,' she added rather dryly, passing straight into the house.

CHAPTER 11

THE sense of her adversary's dryness, which was ominous of something she couldn't read, made Fleda, before complying, linger a little on the terrace; she felt the need moreover of taking breath after such a flight into the cold air of denial. When at last she rejoined Mrs Gereth she found her erect before the drawing-room fire. Their tea had been set out in the same quarter, and the mistress of the house, for whom the preparation of it was in general a high and undelegated function, was in an attitude to which the hissing urn made no appeal. This omission, for Fleda, was such a further sign of something to come that, to disguise her apprehension, she immediately and without an apology took the duty in hand; only, however, to be promptly reminded that she was performing it confusedly and not counting the journeys of the little silver shovel she emptied into the pot. 'Not *five,* my dear – the usual three,' said her hostess, with the same dryness; watching her then in silence while she clumsily corrected her mistake. The tea took some minutes to draw, and Mrs Gereth availed herself of them suddenly to exclaim: 'You haven't yet told me, you know, how it is you propose to "make" me!'

'Give everything back?' Felda looked into the pot again and uttered her question with a briskness that she felt to be a little overdone. 'Why, by putting the question well before you; by being so eloquent that I shall persuade you, shall act upon you; by making you sorry for having gone so far,' she said boldly; 'by simply and earnestly asking it of you, in short; and by reminding you at the same time that it's the first thing I ever have so asked. Oh, you've done things for me – endless and beautiful things,' she exclaimed; 'but you've done them all from your own generous impulse. I've never so much as hinted to you to lend me a postage stamp.'

'Give me a cup of tea,' said Mrs Gereth. A moment later, taking the cup, she replied: 'No, you've never asked me for a postage stamp.'

'That gives me a pull!' Fleda returned, smiling.

'Puts you in the situation of expecting that I shall do this thing just simply to oblige you?'

The girl hesitated. 'You said a while ago that for me you *would* do it.'

'For you, but not for your eloquence. Do you understand what I mean by the difference?' Mrs Gereth asked as she stood stirring her tea.

Fleda, to postpone answering, looked round, while she drank it, at the beautiful room. 'I don't in the least like, you know, your having taken so much. It was a great shock to me, on my arrival here, to find you had done so.'

'Give me some more tea,' said Mrs Gereth ; and there was a moment's silence as Fleda poured out another cup. 'If you were shocked, my dear, I'm bound to say you concealed your shock.'

'I know I did. I was afraid to show it.'

Mrs Gereth drank off her second cup. 'And you're not afraid now?'

'No, I'm not afraid now.'

'What has made the difference?'

'I've pulled myself together' Fleda paused ; then she added : 'and I've seen Mr Owen.'

'You've seen Mr Owen' – Mrs Gereth concurred. She put down her cup and sank into a chair, in which she leaned back, resting her head and gazing at her young friend. 'Yes, I did tell you a while ago that for you I'd do it. But you haven't told me yet what you'll do in return.'

Fleda thought an instant. 'Anything in the wide world you may require.'

'Oh, "anything" is nothing at all! That's too easily said.' Mrs Gereth, reclining more completely, closed her eyes with an air of disgust, an air indeed of inviting slumber.

Fleda looked at her quiet face, which the appearance of slumber always made particularly handsome ; she noted how much the ordeal of the last few weeks had added to its indications of age. 'Well then, try me with something. What is it you demand?'

At this, opening her eyes, Mrs Gereth sprang straight up. 'Get him away from her!'

Fleda marvelled: her companion had in an instant become young again. 'Away from Mona? How in the world – ?'

'By not looking like a fool!' cried Mrs Gereth very sharply. She kissed her, however, on the spot, to make up for this roughness, and summarily took off her hat, which, on coming into the house, our young lady had not removed. She applied a friendly touch to the girl's hair and gave a businesslike pull to her jacket. 'I say don't look like an idiot, because you happen not to be one, not the least bit. *I*'m idiotic; I've been so, I've just discovered, ever since our first days together. I've been a precious donkey; but that's another affair.'

Fleda, as if she humbly assented, went through no form of controverting this; she simply stood passive to her companion's sudden refreshment of her appearance. 'How *can* I get him away from her?' she presently demanded.

'By letting yourself go.'

'By letting myself go?' She spoke mechanically, still more like an idiot, and felt as if her face flamed out the insincerity of her question. It was vividly back again, the vision of the real way to act upon Mrs Gereth. This lady's movements were now rapid; she turned off from her as quickly as she had seized her, and Fleda sat down to steady herself for full responsibility.

Her hostess, without taking up her ejaculation, gave a violent poke at the fire and then faced her again. 'You've done two things, then, today – haven't you? – that you've never done before. One has been asking me the service, or favour, or concession – whatever you call it – that you just mentioned; the other has been telling me – certainly too for the first time – an immense little fib.'

'An immense little fib?' Fleda felt weak; she was glad of the support of her seat.

'An immense big one, then!' said Mrs Gereth irritatedly. 'You don't in the least "hate" Owen, my darling. You care for him very much. In fact, my own, you're in love with him – there! Don't tell me any more lies!' cried Mrs Gereth with a voice and a face in the presence of which Fleda recognized that there was nothing for her but to hold herself and take them. When once the truth was out, it was out, and she could see more and more every instant that it would be the only way. She accepted therefore what had to come; she leaned back her head and closed her eyes as her companion had done just before. She would have covered her face with her hands but for the still greater shame. 'Oh, you're a wonder, a wonder,' said Mrs Gereth ; 'you're magnificent, and I was right, as soon as I saw you, to pick you out and trust you!' Fleda closed her eyes tighter at this last word, but her friend kept it up. 'I never dreamed of it till a while ago, when, after he had come and gone, we were face to face. Then something stuck out of you ; it strongly impressed me, and I didn't know at first quite what to make of it. It was that you had just been with him and that you were not natural. Not natural to *me*,' she added with a smile. 'I pricked up my ears, and all that this might mean dawned upon me when you said you had asked nothing about Mona. It put me on the scent, but I didn't show you, did I? I felt it was *in* you, deep down, and that I must draw it out. Well, I *have* drawn it, and it's a blessing. Yesterday, when you shed tears at breakfast, I was awfully puzzled. What has been the matter with you all the while? Why, Fleda, it isn't a crime, don't you know that?' cried the delighted woman. 'When I was a girl I was always in love, and not always with such nice people as Owen. I didn't behave as well as you ; compared with you I think I must have been horrid. But if you're proud and reserved, it's your own affair ; I'm proud too, though I'm not reserved – that's what spoils it. I'm stupid, above all – that's what I am ; so dense that I really blush for it. However, no one but you could have deceived me. If I trusted you, moreover, it was exactly to be cleverer than myself. You must be so now more than ever!' Suddenly Fleda felt her hands grasped: Mrs Gereth had plumped down at her feet and was leaning on her knees. 'Save him – save him: you *can*!' she passionately pleaded. 'How could you *not* like him, when he's such a dear? He *is* a dear, darling; there's no harm in my own boy! You can do what you will with him – you know you can! What else does he give us all this time for? Get him away from her; it's as if he besought you to, poor wretch! Don't abandon him to such a fate, and I'll never abandon *you*. Think of him with that creature, that future! If you'll take him I'll give up everything. There, it's a solemn promise, the most sacred of my life! Get the better of her, and he shall have every stick I removed. Give me your word, and I'll accept it. I'll write for the packers tonight!'

Fleda, before this, had fallen forward on her companion's neck, and the two women, clinging together, had got up while the younger wailed on the other's bosom. 'You smooth it down because you see more in it than there can ever be ; but after my hideous double game how will you be able to believe in me again?'

'I see in it simply what *must* be, if you've a single spark of pity. Where on earth was the double game, when you've behaved like such a saint? You've been beautiful, you've been exquisite, and all our trouble is over.'

Fleda, drying her eyes, shook her head ever so sadly. 'No, Mrs Gereth, it isn't over. I can't do what you ask – I can't meet your condition.'

Mrs Gereth stared ; the cloud gathered in her face again. 'Why, in the name of goodness, when you adore him? I know what you see in him,' she declared in another tone. 'You're right!'

Fleda gave a faint, stubborn smile. 'He cares for her too much.'

'Then why doesn't he marry her? He's giving you an extra-ordinary chance.'

'He doesn't dream I've ever thought of him,' said Fleda. 'Why should he, if you didn't?'

'It wasn't with me you were in love, my duck.' Then Mrs Gereth added : 'I'll go and tell him.'

'If you do any such thing, you shall never see me again, – absolutely, literally never!'

Mrs Gereth looked hard at her young friend, showing she saw she must believe her. 'Then you're perverse, you're wicked. Will you swear he doesn't know?'

'Of course he doesn't know!' cried Fleda indignantly.

Her interlocutress was silent a little. 'And that he has no feeling on *his* side?'

'For me?' Fleda stared. 'Before he has even married her?'

Mrs Gereth gave a sharp laugh at this. 'He ought at least to appreciate your wit. Oh, my dear, you *are* a treasure! Doesn't he appreciate anything? Has he given you absolutely no symptom – not looked a look, not breathed a sigh?'

'The case,' said Fleda coldly, 'is as I've had the honour to state it.'

'Then he's as big a donkey as his mother! But you know you must account for their delay,' Mrs Gereth remarked.

'Why must I?' Fleda asked after a moment.

'Because you were closeted with him here so long. You can't pretend at present, you know, not to have any art.'

The girl hesitated an instant; she was conscious that she must choose between two risks. She had had a secret and the secret was gone. Owen had one, which was still unbruised, and the greater risk now was that his mother should lay her formidable hand upon it. All Fleda's tenderness for him moved her to protect it; so she faced the smaller peril. 'Their delay,' she brought herself to reply, 'may perhaps be Mona's doing. I mean because he has lost her the things.'

Mrs Gereth jumped at this. 'So that she'll break altogether if I keep them?'

Fleda winced. 'I've told you what I believe about that. She'll make scenes and conditions; she'll worry him. But she'll hold him fast; she'll never give him up.'

Mrs Gereth turned it over. 'Well, I'll keep them, to try her,' she finally pronounced; at which Fleda felt quite sick, as if she had given everything and got nothing.

CHAPTER 12

'I MUST in common decency let him know that I've talked of the matter with you,' she said to her hostess that evening. 'What answer do you wish me to write to him?'

'Write to him that you must see him again,' said Mrs Gereth.

Fleda looked very blank. 'What on earth am I to see him for?'

'For anything you like.'

The girl would have been struck with the levity of this had she not already, in an hour, felt the extent of the change suddenly wrought in her commerce with her friend – wrought above all, to that friend's view, in her relation to the great issue. The effect of what had followed Owen's visit was to make that relation the very key of the crisis. Pressed upon her, goodness knew, the crisis had been, but it now seemed to put forth big, encircling arms – arms that squeezed till they hurt and she must cry out. It was as if everything at Ricks had been poured into a common receptacle, a public ferment of emotion and zeal, out of which it was ladled up to be tasted and talked about ; everything at least but the one little treasure of knowledge that she kept back. She ought to have liked this, she reflected, because it meant sympathy, meant a closer union with the source of so much in her life that had been beautiful and renovating ; but there were fine instincts in her that stood off. She had had – and it was not merely at this time – to recognize that there were things for which Mrs Gereth's *flair* was not so happy as for bargains and 'marks'. It wouldn't be happy now as to the best action on the knowledge she had just gained ; yet as from this moment they were still more intimately together, so a person deeply in her debt would simply have to stand and meet what was to come. There were ways in which she could sharply incommode such a person, and not only with the best conscience in the world, but with a sort of brutality of good intentions. One of the straightest of these

strokes, Fleda saw, would be the dance of delight over the
mystery Mrs Gereth had laid bare – the loud, lawful, tactless
joy of the explorer leaping upon the strand. Like any other
lucky discoverer, she would take possession of the fortunate
island. She was nothing if not practical: almost the only thing
she took account of in her young friend's soft secret was the
excellent use she could make of it – a use so much to her taste
that she refused to feel a hindrance in the quality of the
material. Fleda put into Mrs Gereth's answer to her question a
good deal more meaning than it would have occurred to her
a few hours before that she was prepared to put, but she had
on the spot a foreboding that even so broad a hint would live
to be bettered.

'Do you suggest that I shall propose to him to come down
here again?' she presently inquired.

'Dear, no; say that you'll go up to town and meet him.' It
was bettered, the broad hint; and Fleda felt this to be still
more the case when, returning to the subject before they went
to bed, her companion said: 'I make him over to you wholly,
you know – to do what you please with. Deal with him in your
own clever way – I ask no questions. All I ask is that you
succeed.'

'That's charming,' Fleda replied, 'but it doesn't tell me a bit,
you'll be so good as to consider, in what terms to write to him.
It's not an answer from you to the message I was to give you.'

'The answer to his message is perfectly distinct: he shall
have everything in the place the minute he'll say he'll marry
you.'

'You really pretend,' Fleda asked, 'to think me capable of
transmitting him that news?'

'What else can I really pretend when you threaten so to
cast me off if I speak the word myself?'

'Oh, if *you* speak the word!' the girl murmured very gravely,
but happy at least to know that in this direction Mrs Gereth
confessed herself warned and helpless. Then she added: 'How
can I go on living with you on a footing of which I so deeply
disapprove? Thinking as I do that you've despoiled him far
more than is just or merciful – for if I expected you to take
something, I didn't in the least expect you to take everything

– how can I stay here without a sense that I'm backing you up in your cruelty and participating in your ill-gotten gains?' Fleda was determined that if she had the chill of her exposed and investigated state she would also have the convenience of it, and that if Mrs Gereth popped in and out of the chamber of her soul she would at least return the freedom. 'I shall quite hate, you know, in a day or two, every object that surrounds you – become blind to all the beauty and rarity that I formerly delighted in. Don't think me harsh; there's no use in my not being frank now. If I leave you, everything's at an end.'

Mrs Gereth, however, was imperturbable: Fleda had to recognize that her advantage had become too real. 'It's too beautiful, the way you care for him; it's music in my ears. Nothing else but such a passion could make you say such things ; that's the way I should have been too, my dear. Why didn't you tell me sooner? I'd have gone right in for you ; I never would have moved a candlestick. Don't stay with me if it torments you ; don't, if you suffer, be where you see the old rubbish. Go up to town – go back for a little to your father's. It need be only for a little: two or three weeks will see us through. Your father will take you and be glad, if you only will make him understand what it's a question of – of your getting yourself off his hands for ever. *I'*ll make him understand, you know, if you feel shy. I'd take you up myself, I'd go with you, to spare your being bored; we'd put up at an hotel and we might amuse ourselves a bit. We haven't had much pleasure since we met, have we? But of course that wouldn't suit our book. I should be a bugaboo to Owen – I should be fatally in the way. Your chance is there – your chance is to be alone ; for God's sake, use it to the right end. If you're in want of money I've a little I can give you. But I ask no questions – not a question as small as your shoe! '

She asked no questions, but she took the most extraordinary things for granted. Fleda felt this still more at the end of a couple of days. On the second of these our young lady wrote to Owen ; her emotion had to a certain degree cleared itself – there was something she could say briefly. If she had given everything to Mrs Gereth and as yet got nothing, so she had on the other hand quickly reacted – it took but a night – against the discouragement of her first check. Her desire to serve him was too passionate, the sense that he counted upon her too sweet: these things caught her up again and gave her a new patience and a new subtlety. It shouldn't really be for nothing that she had given so much ; deep within her burned again the resolve to get something back. So what she wrote to Owen was simply that she had had a great scene with his mother, but that he must be patient and give her time. It was difficult, as they both had expected, but she was working her hardest for him. She had made an impression – she would do everything to follow it up. Meanwhile he must keep intensely quiet and take no other steps ; he must only trust her and pray for her and believe in her perfect loyalty. She made no allusion whatever to Mona's attitude, nor to his not being, as regarded that young lady, master of the situation ; but she said in a postcript, in reference to his mother, 'Of course she wonders a good deal why your marriage doesn't take place.' After the letter had gone she regretted having used the word 'loyalty', there were two or three milder terms which she might as well have employed. The answer she immediately received from Owen was a little note of which she met all the deficiencies by describing it to herself as pathetically simple, but which, to prove that Mrs Gereth might ask as many questions as she liked, she at once made his mother read. He had no art with his pen, he had not even a good hand, and his letter, a short profession of friendly confidence, consisted of but a few familiar and colourless words of acknowledgement and assent. The gist of it was that he would certainly, since Miss Vetch recommended it, not hurry mamma too much. He would not for the present cause her to be approached by anyone else, but he would nevertheless continue to hope that she would see she *must* come round. 'Of course, you know,' he added, 'she can't keep me waiting indefinitely. Please give her my love and tell her that. If it can be done peaceably I know you're just the one to do it.'

Fleda had awaited his rejoinder in deep suspense ; such was her imagination of the possibility of his having, as she tacitly phrased it, let himself go on paper that when it arrived she was at first almost afraid to open it. There was indeed a distinct danger, for if he should take it into his head to write her love-letters the whole chance of aiding him would drop: she would have to return them, she would have to decline all further communication with him: it would be quite the end of the business. This imagination of Fleda's was a faculty that easily embraced all the heights and depths and extremities of things; that made a single mouthful, in particular, of any tragic or desperate necessity. She was perhaps at first just a trifle disappointed not to find in the note in question a syllable that strayed from the text; but the next moment she had risen to a point of view from which its presented itself as a production almost inspired in its simplicity. It was simple even for Owen, and she wondered what had given him the cue to be more so than usual. Then she saw how natures that are right just do the things that are right. He wasn't clever – his manner of writing showed it; but the cleverest man in England couldn't have had more the instinct that, under the circumstances, was the supremely happy one, the instinct of giving her something that would do beautifully to be shown to Mrs Gereth. This was a kind of divination, for naturally he couldn't know the line Mrs Gereth was taking. It was furthermore explained – and that was the most touching part of all – by his wish that she herself should notice how awfully well he was behaving. His very bareness called her attention to his virtue; and these were the exact fruits of her beautiful and terrible admonition. He was cleaving to Mona; he was doing his duty; he was making tremendously sure he should be without reproach.

If Fleda handed this communication to her friend as a triumphant gage of the innocence of the young man's heart, her elation lived but a moment after Mrs Gereth had pounced upon the tell-tale spot in it. 'Why in the world, then,' that lady cried, 'does he still not breathe a breath about the day, the *day*, the DAY?' She repeated the word with a crescendo of superior acuteness; she proclaimed that nothing could be more marked than its absence – and absence that simply spoke volumes. What did it prove in fine but that she was producing the effect she had toiled for – that she had settled or was rapidly settling Mona?

Such a challenge Fleda was obliged in some manner to take up. 'You may be settling Mona,' she returned with a smile, 'but I can hardly regard it as sufficient evidence that you're settling Mona's lover.'

'Why not, with such a studied omission on his part to gloss over in any manner the painful tension existing between them – the painful tension that, under providence, I've been the means of bringing about? He gives you by his silence clear notice that his marriage is practically off.'

'He speaks to me of the only thing that concerns me. He gives me clear notice that he abates not one jot of his demand.'

'Well, then, let him take the only way to get it satisfied.'

Fleda had no need to ask again what such a way might be, nor was her support removed by the fine assurance with which Mrs Gereth could make her argument wait upon her wish. These days, which dragged their length into a strange, uncomfortable fortnight, had already borne more testimony to that element than all the other time the two women had passed together. Our young lady had been at first far from measuring the whole of a feature that Owen himself would probably have described as her companion's 'cheek'. She lived now in a kind of bath of boldness, felt as if a fierce light poured in upon her from windows open wide; and the singular part of the ordeal was that she couldn't protest against it fully without incurring, even to her own mind, some reproach of ingratitude, some charge of smallness. If Mrs Gereth's apparent determination to hustle her into Owen's arms was accompanied with an air of holding her dignity rather cheap, this was after all only as a consequence of her being held in respect to some other attributes rather dear. It was a new version of the old story of being kicked upstairs. The wonderful woman was the same woman who, in the summer, at Poynton, had been so puzzled to conceive why a good-natured girl shouldn't have contributed more to the personal rout of the Brigstocks – shouldn't have been grateful even for the handsome puff of Fleda Vetch. Only her passion was keener now and her scruple more absent; the fight made a demand upon her, and her pugnacity had become one with her constant habit of using such weapons as she could pick up. She had no imagination about anybody's life save on the side she bumped against. Fleda was quite aware that she would have otherwise been a rare creature; but a rare creature was originally just what she had struck her as being. Mrs Gereth had really no perception of anybody's nature – had only one question about persons: were they clever or stupid? To be clever meant to know the marks. Fleda knew them by direct inspiration, and a warm recognition of this had been her friend's tribute to her character. The girl had hours, now, of sombre wishing that she might never see anything good again: that kind of experience was evidently not an infallible source of peace. She would be more at peace in some vulgar little place that should owe its *cachet* to Tottenham Court Road. There were nice strong horrors in West Kensington; it was as if they beckoned her and wooed her back to them. She had a relaxed recollection of Waterbath; and of her reasons for staying on at Ricks the force was rapidly ebbing. One of these was her pledge to Owen – her vow to press his mother close; the other was the fact that of the two discomforts, that of being prodded by Mrs Gereth and that of appearing to run after somebody else, the former remained for a while the more endurable.

As the days passed, however, it became plainer to Fleda that her only chance of success would be in lending herself to this low appearance. Then, moreover, at last, her nerves settling the question, the choice was simply imposed by the violence done to her taste – to whatever was left of that high principle, at least, after the free and reckless meeting, for months, of great drafts and appeals. It was all very well to try to evade discussion: Owen Gereth was looking to her for a struggle, and it wasn't a bit of a struggle to be disgusted and dumb. She was on too strange a footing – that of having presented an ultimatum and having had it torn up in her face. In such a case as that the envoy always departed; he never sat gaping and dawdling before the city. Mrs Gereth, every morning, looked publicly into the *Morning Post,* the only newspaper she received; and every morning she treated the blankness of that journal as fresh evidence that everything was 'off'. What did the *Post* exist for but to tell you your children were wretchedly married? – so that if such a source of misery was dry, what could you do but infer that for once you had miraculously escaped? She almost taunted Fleda with supineness in not getting something out of somebody – in the same breath indeed in which she drenched her with a kind of appreciation more onerous to the girl than blame. Mrs Gereth herself had of course washed her hands of the matter ; but Fleda knew people who knew Mona and would be sure to be in her confidence – inconceivable people who admired her and had the privilege of Waterbath. What was the use therefore of being the most natural and the easiest of letter-writers, if no sort of side-light – in some pretext for correspondence – was, by a brilliant creature, to be got out of such barbarians? Fleda was not only a brilliant creature, but she heard herself commended in these days for new and strange attractions ; she figured suddenly, in the queer conversations of Ricks, as a distinguished, almost as a dangerous beauty. That retouching of her hair and dress in which her friend had impulsively indulged on a first glimpse of her secret was by implication very frequently repeated. She had the sense not only of being advertised and offered, but of being counselled and enlightened in ways that she scarcely understood – arts obscure even to a poor girl who had had, in good society and motherless poverty, to look straight at realities and fill out blanks.

These arts, when Mrs Gereth's spirits were high, were handled with a brave and cynical humour with which Fleda's fancy could keep no step: they left our young lady wondering what on earth her companion wanted her to do. 'I want you to cut in ! ' – that was Mrs Gereth's familiar and comprehensive phrase for the course she prescribed. She challenged again and again Fleda's picture, as she called it (though the sketch was too slight to deserve the name), of the indifference to which a prior attachment had committed the proprietor of Poynton. 'Do you mean to say that, Mona or no Mona, he could see you that way, day after day, and not have the ordinary feelings of a man?' This was the sort of interrogation to which Fleda was fitfully and irrelevantly treated. She had grown almost used to the refrain. 'Do you mean to say that when, the other day, one had quite made you over to him, the great gawk, and he was, on this very spot, utterly alone with you – ' The poor girl at this point never left any doubt of what she meant to say, but Mrs Gereth could be trusted to break out in another place and at another time. At last Fleda wrote to her father that he must take her in for a while; and when, to her companion's delight, she returned to London, that lady went with her to the station and wafted her on her way. The *Morning Post* had been delivered as they left the house, and Mrs Gereth had brought it with her for the traveller, who never spent a penny on a newspaper. On the platform, however, when this young person was ticketed, labelled, and seated, she opened it at the window of the carriage, exclaiming as usual, after looking into it a moment: 'Nothing – nothing – nothing: don't tell *me*!' Every day that there was nothing was a nail in the coffin of the marriage. An instant later the train was off, but, moving quickly beside it, while Fleda leaned inscrutably forth, Mrs Gereth grasped her friend's hand and looked up with wonderful eyes. 'Only let yourself go, darling – only let yourself go!'

CHAPTER 13

THAT she desired to ask no questions Mrs Gereth conscientiously proved by closing her lips tight after Fleda had gone to London. No letter from Ricks arrived at West Kensington, and Fleda, with nothing to communicate that could be to the taste of either party, forbore to open a correspondence. If her heart had been less heavy she might have been amused to perceive how much rope this reticence of Ricks seemed to signify to her that she could take. She had at all events no good news for her friend save in the sense that her silence was not bad news. She was not yet in a position to write that she had 'cut in'; but neither, on the other hand, had she gathered material for announcing that Mona was undisseverable from her prey. She had made no use of the pen so glorified by Mrs Gereth to wake up the echoes of Waterbath; she had sedulously abstained from inquiring what in any quarter, far or near, was said or suggested or supposed. She only spent a matutinal penny on the *Morning Post*; she only saw, on each occasion, that that inspired sheet had as little to say about the imminence as about the abandonment of certain nuptials. It was at the same time obvious that Mrs Gereth triumphed on these occasions much more than she trembled, and that with a few such triumphs repeated she would cease to tremble at all. What was most manifest, however, was that she had had a rare preconception of the circumstances that would have ministered, had Fleda been disposed, to the girl's cutting in. It was brought home to Fleda that these circumstances would have particularly favoured intervention; she was quickly forced to do them a secret justice. One of the effects of her intimacy with Mrs Gereth was that she had quite lost all sense of intimacy with anyone else. The lady of Ricks had made a desert around her, possessing and absorbing her so utterly that other partakers had fallen away. Hadn't she been admonished, months before, that people considered they had lost her and were reconciled on the whole to the privation? Her present position in the great

103

unconscious town defined itself as obscure: she regarded it at any rate with eyes suspicious of that lesson. She neither wrote notes nor received them; she indulged in no reminders nor knocked at any doors; she wandered vaguely in the western wilderness or cultivated shy forms of that 'household art' for which she had had a respect before tasting the bitter tree of knowledge. Her only plan was to be as quiet as a mouse, and when she failed in the attempt to lose herself in the flat suburb she felt like a lonely fly crawling over a dusty chart.

How had Mrs Gereth known in advance that if she had chosen to be 'vile' (that was what Fleda called it) everything would happen to help her? – especially the way her poor father, after breakfast, doddered off to his club, showing seventy when he was really fifty-seven, and leaving her richly alone for the day. He came back about midnight, looking at her very hard and not risking long words – only making her feel by inimitable touches that the presence of his family compelled him to alter all his hours. She had in their common sitting-room the company of the objects he was fond of saying that he had collected – objects, shabby and battered, of a sort that appealed little to his daughter: old brandy-flasks and matchboxes, old calendars and hand-books, intermixed with an assortment of pen-wipers and ashtrays, a harvest he had gathered in from penny bazaars. He was blandly unconscious of that side of Fleda's nature which had endeared her to Mrs Gereth, and she had often heard him wish to goodness there was something striking she cared for. Why didn't she try collecting something? – it didn't matter what. She would find it gave an interest to life, and there was no end of little curiosities one could easily pick up. He was conscious of having a taste for fine things which his children had unfortunately not inherited. This indicated the limits of their acquaintance with him – limits which, as Fleda was now sharply aware, could only leave him to wonder what the mischief she was there for. As she herself echoed this question to the letter she was not in a position to clear up the mystery. She couldn't have given a name to her errand in town or explained it save by saying that she had had to get away from Ricks. It was intensely provisional, but what was to come next? Nothing could come next but a deeper anxiety. She had neither a home nor an outlook – nothing in all the wide world but a feeling of suspense.

Of course she had her duty – her duty to Owen – a definite undertaking, reaffirmed, after his visit to Ricks, under her hand and seal ; but there was no sense of possession attached to that ; there was only a horrible sense of privation. She had quite moved from under Mrs Gereth's wide wing ; and now that she was really among the penwipers and ashtrays she was swept, at the thought of all the beauty she had forsworn, by short wild gusts of despair. If her friend should really keep the spoils she would never return to her. If that friend should on the other hand part with them, what on earth would there be to return to? The chill struck deep as Fleda thought of the mistress of Ricks reduced, in vulgar parlance, to what she had on her back : There was nothing to which she could compare such an image but her idea of Marie Antoinette in the Conciergerie, or perhaps the vision of some tropical birds, the creature of hot, dense forests, dropped on a frozen moor to pick up a living. The mind's eye could see Mrs Gereth, indeed, only in her thick, coloured air ; it took all the light of her treasures to make her concrete and distinct. She loomed for a moment, in any mere house, gaunt and unnatural ; then she vanished as if she had suddenly sunk into a quicksand. Fleda lost herself in the rich fancy of how, if *she* were mistress of Poynton, a whole province, as an abode, should be assigned there to the august queenmother. She would have returned from her campaign with her baggage-train and her loot, and the palace would unbar its shutters and the morning flash back from its halls. In the event of a surrender the poor woman would never again be able to begin to collect : She was now too old and too moneyless, and times were altered and good things impossibly dear. A surrender, furthermore, to any daughter-in-law save an oddity like Mona needn't at all be an abdication in fact ; any other fairly nice girl whom Owen should have taken it into his head to marry would have been positively glad to have, for the museum, a custodian who was a walking catalogue and who understood beyond anyone in England the hygiene and temperament of rare pieces. A fairly nice girl would somehow be away a good deal and would at such times count it a blessing to feel Mrs Gereth at her post.

Fleda had fully recognized, the first days, that, quite apart from any question of letting Owen know where she was, it would be a charity to give him some sign: it would be weak, it would be ugly, to be diverted from that kindness by the fact that Mrs Gereth had attached a tinkling bell to it. A frank relation with him was only superficially discredited: she ought for his own sake to send him a word of cheer. So she repeatedly reasoned, but she as repeatedly delayed performance: if her general plan had been to be as still as a mouse, an interview like the interview at Ricks would be an odd contribution to that ideal. Therefore with a confused preference of practice to theory she let the days go by; she felt that nothing was so imperative as the gain of precious time. She shouldn't be able to stay with her father forever, but she might now reap the benefit of having married her sister. Maggie's union had been built up round a small spare room. Concealed in this apartment she might try to paint again, and abetted by the grateful Maggie – for Maggie at least was grateful – she might try to dispose of her work. She had not indeed struggled with a brush since her visit to Waterbath, where the sight of the family splotches had put her immensely on her guard. Poynton moreover had been an impossible place for producing; no active art could flourish there but a Buddhistic contemplation. It had stripped its mistress clean of all feeble accomplishments; her hands were imbrued neither with ink nor with water-colour. Close to Fleda's present abode was the little shop of a man who mounted and framed pictures and desolately dealt in artists' materials. She sometimes paused before it to look at a couple of shy experiments for which its dull window constituted publicity, small studies placed there for sale and full of warning to a young lady without fortune and without talent. Some such young lady had brought them forth in sorrow; some such young lady, to see if they had been snapped up, had passed and repassed as helplessly as she herself was doing. They never had been, they never would be, snapped up; yet they were quite above the actual attainment of some other young ladies. It was a matter of discipline with Fleda to take an occasional

106

lesson from them ; besides which, when she now quitted the house, she had to look for reasons after she was out. The only place to find them was in the shop-windows. They made her feel like a servant girl taking her 'afternoon', but that didn't signify: perhaps some day she would resemble such a person still more closely. This continued a fortnight, at the end of which the feeling was suddenly dissipated. She had stopped as usual in the presence of the little pictures ; then, as she turned away, she had found herself face to face with Owen Gereth.

At the sight of him two fresh waves passed quickly across her heart, one at the heels of the other. The first was an instant perception that this encounter was not an accident ; the second a consciousness as prompt that the best place for it was the street. She knew before he told her that he had been to see her, and the next thing she knew was that he had had information from his mother. Her mind grasped these things while he said with a smile: 'I saw only your back, but I was sure. I was over the way. I've been at your house.'

'How came you to know my house?' Fleda asked.

'I like that!' he laughed. 'How came you not to let me know that you were there?'

Fleda, at this, thought it best also to laugh. 'Since I didn't let you know, why did you come?'

'Oh, I say!' cried Owen. 'Don't add insult to injury. Why in the world didn't you let me know? I came because I want awfully to see you.' He hesitated, then he added: 'I got the tip from mother: she has written to me – fancy!'

They still stood where they had met. Fleda's instinct was to keep him there ; the more so that she could already see him take for granted that they would immediately proceed together to her door. He rose before her with a different air: he looked less ruffled and bruised than he had done at Ricks, he showed a recovered freshness. Perhaps, however, this was only because she had scarcely seen him at all as yet in London form, as he would have called it – 'turned out' as he was turned out in town. In the country, heated with the chase and splashed with the mire, he had always reminded her of a picturesque peasant in national costume. This costume, as Owen wore it, varied from day to day; it was as copious as the wardrobe of an actor ; but it never failed of suggestions of the earth and the weather, the hedges and the ditches, the beasts and the birds. There had been days when it struck her as all nature in one pair of boots. It didn't make him now another person that he was delicately dressed, shining and splendid – that he had a higher hat and light gloves with black seams, and a spear-like umbrella ; but it made him, she soon decided, really handsomer, and that in turn gave him – for she never could think of him, or indeed of some other things, without the aid of his vocabulary – a tremendous pull. Yes, this was for the moment, as he looked at her, the great fact of their situation – his pull was tremendous. She tried to keep the acknowledgement of it from trembling in her voice as she said to him with more surprise than she really felt: 'You've then reopened relations with her?'

'It's she who has reopened them with me. I got her letter this morning. She told me you were here and that she wished me to know it. She didn't say much ; she just gave me your address. I wrote her back, you know, "Thanks no end. Shall go today." So we *are* in correspondence again, aren't we? She means of course that you've something to tell me from her, eh? But if you have, why haven't you let a fellow know?' He waited for no answer to this, he had so much to say. 'At your house, just now, they told me how long you've been here. Haven't you known all the while that I'm counting the hours ; I left a word for you – that I would be back at six ; but I'm awfully glad to have caught you so much sooner. You don't mean to say you're not going home!' he exclaimed in dismay. 'The young woman there told me you went out early.'

'I've been out a very short time,' said Fleda, who had hung back with the general purpose of making things difficult for him. The street would make them difficult ; she could trust the street. She reflected in time, however, that to betray to him she was afraid to admit him would give him more a feeling of facility than of anything else. She moved on with him after a moment, letting him direct their course to her door, which was only round a corner: she considered as they went that it might not prove such a stroke to have been in London so long and yet not to have called him. She desired he should feel she was perfectly simple with him, and there was no simplicity in that.

None the less, on the steps of the house, though she had a key, she rang the bell; and while they waited together and she averted her face she looked straight into the depths of what Mrs Gereth had meant by giving him the 'tip'. This had been perfidious, had been monstrous of Mrs Gereth, and Fleda wondered if her letter had contained only what Owen repeated.

CHAPTER 14

WHEN Owen and Fleda were in her father's little place and,
among the brandy-flasks and pen-wipers, still more disconcerted and divided, the girl – to do something, though it would
make him stay – had ordered tea, he put the letter before her
quite as if he had guessed her thought. 'She's still a bit nasty –
fancy!' He handed her the scrap of a note which he had pulled
out of his pocket and from its envelope. 'Fleda Vetch,' it ran,
'is at 10 Raphael Road, West Kensington. Go to see her, and
try, for God's sake, to cultivate a glimmer of intelligence.'
When in handing it back to him she took in his face she saw
that its heightened colour was the effect of his watching her
read such an allusion to his want of wit. Fleda knew what it
was an allusion to, and his pathetic air of having received this
buffet, tall and fine and kind as he stood there, made her
conscious of not quite concealing her knowledge. For a minute
she was kept silent by an angered sense of the trick that had
been played her. It was a trick because Fleda considered there
had been a covenant; and the trick consisted of Mrs Gereth's
having broken the spirit of their agreement while conforming
in a fashion to the letter. Under the girl's menace of a complete
rupture she had been afraid to make of her secret the use she
itched to make ; but in the course of these days of separation
she had gathered pluck to hazard an indirect betrayal. Fleda
measured her hesitations and the impulse which she had finally
obeyed and which the continued procrastination of Waterbath
had encouraged, had at last made irresistible. If in her high-
handed manner of playing their game she had not named the
thing hidden, she had named the hiding-place. It was over the
sense of this wrong that Fleda's lips closed tight: she was
afraid of aggravating her case by some ejaculation that would
make Owen prick up his ears. A great, quick effort, however,
helped her to avoid the danger ; with her constant idea of keeping cool and repressing a visible flutter, she found herself able
to choose her words. Meanwhile he had exclaimed with his

uncomfortable laugh: 'That's a good one for me, Miss Vetch, isn't it?'

'Of course you know by this time that your mother's very sharp,' said Fleda.

'I think I can understand well enough when I know what's to be understood,' the young man asserted. 'But I hope you won't mind my saying that you've kept me pretty well in the dark about that. I've been waiting, waiting, waiting; so much has depended on your news. If you've been working for me I'm afraid it has been a thankless job. Can't she say what she'll do, one way or the other? I can't tell in the least where I am, you know. I haven't really learnt from you, since I saw you there, where *she* is. You wrote me to be patient, and upon my soul I have been. But I'm afraid you don't quite realize what I'm to be patient with. At Waterbath, don't you know? I've simply to account and answer for the damned things. Mona looks at me and waits, and I, hang it, I look at you and do the same.' Fleda had gathered fuller confidence as he continued; so plain was it that she had succeeded in not dropping into his mind the spark that might produce the glimmer invoked by his mother. But even this fine assurance gave a start when, after an appealing pause, he went on: 'I hope, you know, that after all you're not keeping anything back from me.'

In the full face of what she was keeping back such a hope could only make her wince; but she was prompt with her explanations in proportion as she felt they failed to meet him. The smutty maid came in with tea-things, and Fleda, moving several objects, eagerly accepted the diversion of arranging a place for them on one of the tables. 'I've been trying to break your mother down because it has seemed there may be some chance of it. That's why I've let you go on expecting it. She's too proud to veer round all at once, but I think I speak correctly in saying that I've made an impression.'

In spite of ordering tea she had not invited him to sit down; she herself made a point of standing. He hovered by the window that looked into Raphael Road; she kept at the other side of the room; the stunted slavey, gazing wide-eyed at the beautiful gentleman and either stupidly or cunningly bringing

111

but one thing at a time, came and went between the tea-tray and the open door.

'You pegged at her so hard?' Owen asked.

'I explained to her fully your position and put before her much more strongly than she liked what seemed to me her absolute duty.'

Owen waited a little. 'And having done that, you departed?'

Fleda felt the full need of giving a reason for her departure; but at first she only said with cheerful frankness: 'I departed.'

Her companion again looked at her in silence. 'I thought you had gone to her for several months.'

'Well,' Fleda replied, 'I couldn't stay. I didn't like it. I didn't like it at all – I couldn't bear it,' she went on. 'In the midst of those trophies of Poynton, living with them, touching them, using them, I felt as if I were backing her up. As I was not a bit of an accomplice, as I hate what she has done, I didn't want to be, even to the extent of the mere look of it – what is it you call such people? – an accessory after the fact.' There was something she kept back so rigidly that the joy of uttering the rest was double. She felt the sharpest need of giving him all the other truth. There was a matter as to which she had deceived him, and there was a matter as to which she had deceived Mrs Gereth, but her lack of pleasure in deception as such came home to her now. She busied herself with the tea and, to extend the occupation, cleared the table still more, spreading out the coarse cups and saucers and the vulgar little plates. She was aware that she produced more confusion than symmetry, but she was also aware that she was violently nervous. Owen tried to help her with something: this made rather for disorder. 'My reason for not writing to you,' she pursued, 'was simply that I was hoping to hear more from Ricks. I've waited from day to day for that.'

'But you've heard nothing?'

'Not a word.'

'Then what I understand,' said Owen, 'is that, practically, you and Mummy have quarrelled. And you've done it – I mean you personally – for *me*.'

'Oh no, we haven't quarrelled a bit!' Then with a smile: 'We've only diverged.'

'You've diverged uncommonly far!' – Owen laughed back. Fleda, with her hideous crockery and her father's collections, could conceive that these objects, to her visitor's perception even more strongly than to her own, measured the length of the swing from Poynton and Ricks; she was aware too that her high standards figured vividly enough even to Owen's simplicity to make him reflect that West Kensington was a tremendous fall. If she had fallen it was because she had acted for him. She was all the more content he should thus see she *had* acted, as the cost of it, in his eyes, was none of her own showing. 'What seems to have happened,' he exclaimed, 'is that you've had a row with her and yet not moved her!'

Fleda considered a moment; she was full of the impression that, notwithstanding her scant help, he saw his way clearer than he had seen it at Ricks. He might mean many things; and what if the many should mean in their turn only one? 'The difficulty is, you understand, that she doesn't really see into your situation.' She hesitated. 'She doesn't comprehend why your marriage hasn't yet taken place.'

Owen stared. 'Why, for the reason I told you: that Mona won't take another step till mother has given full satisfaction. Everything must be there. You see, everything *was* there the day of that fatal visit.'

'Yes, that's what I understood from you at Ricks,' said Fleda; 'but I haven't repeated it to your mother.' She had hated, at Ricks, to talk with him about Mona, but now that scruple was swept away. If he could speak of Mona's visit as fatal, she need at least not pretend not to notice it. It made all the difference that she had tried to assist him and had failed: to give him any faith in her service she must give him all her reasons but one. She must give him, in other words, with a corresponding omission, all Mrs Gereth's. 'You can easily see that, as she dislikes your marriage, anything that may seem to make it less certain works in her favour. Without my telling her, she has suspicions and views that are simply suggested by your delay. Therefore it didn't seem to me right to make them worse. By holding off long enough, she thinks she may put an end to your engagement. If Mona's waiting, she believes she may at last tire Mona out.' That, in all conscience, Fleda felt was lucid enough.

So the young man, following her attentively, appeared equally to feel. 'So far as that goes,' he promptly declared, 'she *has* at last tired Mona out.' He uttered the words with a strange approach to hilarity.

Fleda's surprise at this aberration left her a moment looking at him. 'Do you mean your marriage is off?'

Owen answered with a kind of gay despair. 'God knows, Miss Vetch, where or when or what my marriage is! If it isn't "off", it certainly, at the point things have reached, isn't *on*. I haven't seen Mona for ten days, and for a week I haven't heard from her. She used to write me every week, don't you know? She won't budge from Waterbath, and I haven't budged from town.' Then he suddenly broke out: 'If she *does* chuck me, will mother come round?'

Fleda, at this, felt that her heroism had come to its real test – felt that in telling him the truth she should effectively raise a hand to push his impediment out of the way. Was the knowledge that such a motion would probably dispose forever of Mona capable of yielding to the conception of still giving her every chance she was entitled to? That conception was heroic, but at the same moment it reminded Fleda of the place it had held in her plan, she was also reminded of the not less urgent claim of the truth. Ah, the truth – there was a limit to the impunity with which one could juggle with it! Wasn't what she had most to remember the fact that Owen had a right to his property and that he had also her vow to stand by him in the effort to recover it? How did she stand by him if she hid from him the single way to recover it of which she was quite sure? For an instant that seemed to her the fullest of her life she debated. 'Yes,' she said at last, 'if your marriage is really abandoned, she will give up everything she has taken.'

'That's just what makes Mona hesitate!' Owen honestly exclaimed. 'I mean the idea that I shall get back the things only if she gives me up.'

Fleda thought an instant. 'You mean makes her hesitate to keep you – not hesitate to renounce you?'

Owen looked a trifle bewildered. 'She doesn't see the use of hanging on, as I haven't even yet put the matter into legal hands. She's awfully keen about that, and awfully disgusted that I don't. She says it's the only real way, and she thinks I'm afraid to take it. She has given me time and then has given me again more. She says I give Mummy too much. She says I'm a muff to go pottering on. That's why she's drawing off so hard, don't you see?'

'I don't see very clearly. Of course you must give her what you offered her ; of course you must keep your word. There must be no mistake about *that*! ' the girl declared.

Owen's bewilderment visibly increased. 'You think, then, as she does, that I *must* send down the police?'

The mixture of reluctance and dependence in this made her feel how much she was failing him. She had the sense of 'chucking' him too. 'No, no, not yet! ' she said, though she had really no other and no better course to prescribe. 'Doesn't it occur to you,' she asked in a moment, 'that if Mona is, as you say, drawing away, she may have, in doing so, a very high motive? She knows the immense value of all the objects detained by your mother, and to restore the spoils of Poynton, she is ready – is that it! – to make a sacrifice. The sacrifice is that of an engagement she had entered upon with joy.'

Owen had been blank a moment before, but he followed this argument with success – a success so immediate that it enabled him to produce with decision: 'Ah, she's not that sort! She wants them herself,' he added ; 'she wants to feel they're hers ; she doesn't care whether I have them or not! And if she can't get them she doesn't want *me*. If she can't get them she doesn't want anything at all.'

This was categoric ; Fleda drank it in. 'She takes such an interest in them?'

'So it appears.'

'So much that they're *all*, and that she can let everything else absolutely depend upon them?'

Owen weighed her question as if he felt the responsibility of his answer. But that answer came in a moment, and, as Fleda could see, out of a wealth of memory. 'She never wanted them particularly till they seemed to be in danger. Now she has an idea about them ; and when she gets hold of an idea – Oh dear me!' He broke off, pausing and looking away as with a sense of the futility of expression: it was the first time Fleda had ever heard him explain a matter so pointedly or embark at all on a generalization. It was striking, it was touching to her, as he faltered, that he appeared but half capable of floating his generalization to the end. The girl, however, was so far competent to fill up his blank as that she had divined, on the occasion of Mona's visit to Poynton, what would happen in the event of the accident at which he glanced. She had there with her own eyes seen Owen's betrothed get hold of an idea. 'I say, you know, *do* give me some tea!' he went on irrelevantly and familiarly.

Her profuse preparations had all this time had no sequel, and, with a laugh that she felt to be awkward, she hastily complied with his request. 'It's sure to be horrid,' she said ; 'we don't have at all good things.' She offered him also bread and butter, of which he partook, holding his cup and saucer in his other hand and moving slowly about the room. She poured herself a cup, but not to take it ; after which, without wanting it, she began to eat a small stale biscuit. She was struck with the extinction of the unwillingness she had felt at Ricks to contribute to the bandying between them of poor Mona's name ; and under this influence she presently resumed: 'Am I to understand that she engaged herself to marry you without caring for you?'

Owen looked out into Raphael Road. 'She *did* care for me awfully. But she can't stand the strain.'

'The strain of what?'

'Why of the whole wretched thing.'

'The whole thing has indeed been wretched, and I can easily conceive its effect upon her,' Fleda said.

Her visitor turned sharp round. 'You *can*?' There was a light in his strong stare. 'You can understand it's spoiling her temper and making her come down on *me*? She behaves as if I were of no use to her at all!'

Fleda hesitated. 'She's rankling under the sense of her wrong.'

'Well, was it *I*, pray, who perpetrated the wrong? Ain't I doing what I can to get the thing arranged?'

116

The ring of his question made his anger at Mona almost resemble for a minute an anger at Fleda ; and this resemblance in turn caused our young lady to observe how handsome he looked when he spoke, for the first time in her hearing, with that degree of heat, and used, also for the first time, such a term as 'perpetrated'. In addition, his challenge rendered still more vivid to her the mere flimsiness of her own aid. 'Yes, you've been perfect,' she said. 'You've had a most difficult part. You've *had* to show tact and patience, as well as firmness, with your mother, and you've strikingly shown them. It's I who, quite unintentionally, have deceived you. I haven't helped you at all to your remedy.'

'Well, you wouldn't at all events have ceased to like me, would you? ' Owen demanded. It evidently mattered to him to know if she really justified Mona. 'I mean of course if you *had* liked me – like me as *she* liked me,' he explained.

Fleda looked this inquiry in the face only long enough to recognize that, in her embarrassment, she must take instant refuge in a superior one. 'I can answer that better if I know how kind to her you've been. *Have* you been kind to her? ' she asked as simply as she could.

'Why, rather, Miss Vetch! ' Owen declared. 'I've done every blessed thing she wished. I rushed down to Ricks, as you saw, with fire and sword, and the day after that I went to see her at Waterbath.' At this point he checked himself, though it was just the point at which her interest deepened. A different look had come into his face as he put down his empty teacup. 'But why should I tell you such things, for any good it does me? I gather that you've no suggestion to make me now except that I shall request my solicitor to act. *Shall* I request him to act? '

Fleda scarcely heard his words ; something new had suddenly come into her mind. 'When you went to Waterbath after seeing me,' she asked, 'did you tell her all about that? '

Owen looked conscious. 'All about it? '

'That you had had a long talk with me, without seeing your mother at all? '

'Oh yes, I told her exactly, and that you had been most awfully kind, and that I had placed the whole thing in your hands.'

'Fleda was silent a moment. 'Perhaps that displeased her,' she at last suggested.

'It displeased her fearfully,' said Owen, looking very queer.

'Fearfully?' broke from the girl. Somehow, at the word, she was startled.

'She wanted to know what right you had to meddle. She said you were not honest.'

'Oh!' Fleda cried, with a long wail. Then she controlled herself. 'I see.'

'She abused you, and I defended you. She denounced you –'

She checked him with a gesture. 'Don't tell me what she did!' She had coloured up to her eyes, where, as with the effect of a blow in the face, she quickly felt the tears gathering. It was a sudden drop in her great flight, a shock to her attempt to watch over what Mona was entitled to. While she had been straining her very soul in this attempt, the object of her magnanimity had been pronouncing her 'not honest'. She took it all in, however, and after an instant was able to smile. She would not have been surprised to learn, indeed, that her smile was strange. 'You said a while ago that your mother and I quarrelled about you. It's much more true that you and Mona have quarrelled about *me*.'

Owen hesitated, but at last he brought it out. 'What I mean to say is, don't you know, that Mona, if you don't mind my saying so, has taken it into her head to be jealous.'

'I see,' said Fleda. 'Well, I dare say our conferences have looked very odd.'

'They've looked very beautiful, and they've been very beautiful. Oh, I've told her the sort you are!' the young man pursued.

'That of course hasn't made her love me better.'

'No, nor love me,' said Owen. 'Of course, you know, she says she loves me.'

'And do you say you love her?'

'I say nothing else – I say it all the while. I said it the other day a dozen times.' Fleda made no immediate rejoinder to this, and before she could choose one he repeated his question of a moment before. '*Am* I to tell my solicitor to act?'

She had at that moment turned away from this solution,

118

precisely because she saw in it the great chance of her secret. If she should determine him to adopt it she might put out her hand and take him. It would shut in Mrs Gereth's face the open door of surrender: she would flare up and fight, flying the flag of a passionate, an heroic defence. The case would obviously go against her, but the proceedings would last longer than Mona's patience or Owen's propriety. With a formal rupture he would be at large; and she had only to tighten her fingers round the string that would raise the curtain on that scene. 'You tell me you "say" you love her, but is there nothing more in it than your saying so? You wouldn't say so, would you, if it's not true? What in the world has become, in so short a time, of the affection that led to your engagement?'

'The deuce knows what has become of it, Miss Vetch!' Owen cried. 'It seemed all to go to pot as this horrid struggle came on.' He was close to her now, and, with his face lighted again by the relief of it, he looked all his helpless history into her eyes. 'As I saw you and noticed you more, as I knew you better and better, I felt less and less – I couldn't help it – about anything or anyone else. I wished I had known you sooner – I knew I should have liked you better than anyone in the world. But it wasn't you who made the difference,' he eagerly continued, 'and I was awfully determined to stick to Mona to the death. It was she herself who made it, upon my soul, by the state she got into, the way she sulked, the way she took things, and the way she let me have it! She destroyed our prospects and our happiness, upon my honour. She made just the same smash of them as if she had kicked over that tea-table. She wanted to know all the while what was passing between us, between you and me; and she wouldn't take my solemn assurance that nothing was passing but what might have directly passed between me and old Mummy. She said a pretty girl like you was a nice old Mummy for me, and, if you'll believe it, she never called you anything else but that. I'll be hanged if I haven't been good, haven't I? I haven't breathed a breath of any sort to you, have I? You'd have been down on me hard if I had, wouldn't you? You're down on me pretty hard as it is, I think, aren't you? But I don't care what you say now, or what Mona says, either, or a single rap what anyone says: she has

119

given me at last, by her confounded behaviour, a right to speak out, to utter the way I feel about it. The way I feel about it, don't you know, is that it had all better come to an end. You ask me if I don't love her, and I suppose it's natural enough you should. But you ask it at the very moment I'm half mad to say to you that there's only one person on the whole earth I *really* love, and that that person – ' Here Owen pulled up short, and Fleda wondered if it was from the effect of his perceiving, through the closed door, the sound of steps and voices on the landing of the stairs. She had caught this sound herself with surprise and a vague uneasiness: it was not an hour at which her father ever came in, and there was no present reason why she should have a visitor. She had a fear, which after a few seconds deepened: a visitor was at hand ; the visitor would be simply Mrs Gereth. That lady wished for a near view of the consequence of her note to Owen. Fleda straightened herself with the instant thought that if this was what Mrs Gereth desired Mrs Gereth should have it in a form not to be mistaken. Owen's pause was the matter of a moment, but during that moment our young couple stood with their eyes holding each other's eyes and their ears catching the suggestion, still through the door, of a murmured conference in the hall. Fleda had begun to make the movement to cut it short when Owen stopped her with a grasp of her arm. 'You're surely able to guess,' he said, with his voice dropped and her arm pressed as she had never known such a drop or such a pressure – 'you're surely able to guess the one person on earth I love?'

The handle of the door turned, and Fleda had only time to jerk at him: 'Your mother!'

The door opened, and the smutty maid, edging in, announced 'Mrs Brigstock!'

CHAPTER 15

MRS BRIGSTOCK, in the doorway, stood looking from one of
the occupants of the room to the other ; then they saw her
eyes attach themselves to a small object that had lain hitherto
unnoticed on the carpet. This was the biscuit of which, on
giving Owen his tea, Fleda had taken a perfunctory nibble:
she had immediately laid it on the table, and that subsequently, in some precipitate movement, she should have
brushed it off was doubtless a sign of the agitation that
possessed her. For Mrs Brigstock there was apparently more
in it than met the eye. Owen at any rate picked it up, and
Fleda felt as if he were removing the traces of some scene that
the newspapers would have characterized as lively. Mrs Brigstock clearly took in also the sprawling tea-things and the
mark as of high water in the full faces of her young friends.
These elements made the little place a vivid picture of
intimacy. A minute was filled by Fleda's relief at finding her
visitor not to be Mrs Gereth, and a longer space by the
ensuing sense of what was really more compromising in the
actual apparition. It dimly occurred to her that the lady of
Ricks had also written to Waterbath. Not only had Mrs Brigstock never paid her a call, but Fleda would have been unable
to figure her so employed. A year before the girl had spent
a day under her roof, but never feeling that Mrs Brigstock
regarded this as constituting a bond. She had never stayed in
any house but Poynton where the imagination of a bond, one
way or the other, prevailed. After the first astonishment she
dashed gayly at her guest, emphasizing her welcome and wondering how her whereabouts had become known at Waterbath.
Had not Mrs Brigstock quitted that residence for the very
purpose of laying her hand on the associate of Mrs Gereth's
misconduct? The spirit in which this hand was to be laid our
young lady was yet to ascertain ; but she was a person who
could think ten thoughts at once – a circumstance which, even
putting her present plight at its worst, gave her a great

121

advantage over a person who required easy conditions for dealing even with one. The very vibration of the air, however, told her that whatever Mrs Brigstock's spirit might originally have been, it had been sharply affected by the sight of Owen. He was essentially a surprise: she had reckoned with everything that concerned him but his presence. With that, in awkward silence, she was reckoning now, as Fleda could see, while she effected with friendly aid an embarrassed transit to the sofa. Owen would be useless, would be deplorable: that aspect of the case Fleda had taken in as well. Another aspect was that he would admire her, adore her, exactly in proportion as she herself should rise gracefully superior. Fleda felt for the first time free to let herself 'go', as Mrs Gereth had said, and she was full of the sense that to 'go' meant now to aim straight at the effect of moving Owen to rapture at her simplicity and tact. It was her impression that he had no positive dislike of Mona's mother; but she couldn't entertain that notion without a glimpse of the implication that he had a positive dislike of Mrs Brigstock's daughter. Mona's mother declined tea, declined a better seat, declined a cushion, declined to remove her boa: Fleda guessed that she had not come on purpose to be dry, but that the voice of the invaded room had itself given her the hint.

'I just came on the mere chance,' she said. 'Mona found yesterday, somewhere, the card of invitation to your sister's marriage that you sent us, or your father sent us, some time ago. We couldn't be present – it was impossible; but as it had this address on it I said to myself that I might find you here.'

'I'm very glad to be at home,' Fleda responded.

'Yes, that doesn't happen very often, does it?' Mrs Brigstock looked round afresh at Fleda's home.

'Oh, I came back from Ricks last week. I shall be here now till I don't know when.'

'We thought it very likely you would have come back. We knew of course of your having been at Ricks. If I didn't find you I thought I might perhaps find Mr Vetch,' Mrs Brigstock went on.

'I'm sorry he's out. He's always out – all day long.'

Mrs Brigstock's round eyes grew rounder. 'All day long?'

'All day long,' Fleda smiled.

'Leaving you quite to yourself?'

'A good deal to myself, but a little, today, as you see, to Mr Gereth – ' and the girl looked at Owen to draw him into their sociability. For Mrs Brigstock he had immediately sat down; but the movement had not corrected the sombre stiffness taking possession of him at the sight of her. Before he found a response to the appeal addressed to him Fleda turned again to her other visitor. 'Is there any purpose for which you would like my father to call on you?'

Mrs Brigstock received this question as if it were not to be unguardedly answered; upon which Owen intervened with pale irrelevance: 'I wrote to Mona this morning of Miss Vetch's being in town; but of course the letter hadn't arrived when you left home.'

'No, it hadn't arrived. I came up for the night – I've several matters to attend to.' Then looking with an intention of fixedness from one of her companions to the other, 'I'm afraid I've interrupted your conversation,' Mrs Brigstock said. She spoke without effectual point, had the air of merely announcing the fact. Fleda had not yet been confronted with the question of the sort of person Mrs Brigstock was; she had only been confronted with the question of the sort of person Mrs Gereth scorned her for being. She was really, somehow, no sort of person at all, and it came home to Fleda that if Mrs Gereth could see her at this moment she would scorn her more than ever. She had a face of which it was impossible to say anything but that it was pink, and a mind that it would be possible to describe only if one had been able to mark it in a similar fashion. As nature had made this organ neither green nor blue nor yellow, there was nothing to know it by: it strayed and bleated like an unbranded sheep. Fleda felt for it at this moment much of the kindness of compassion, since Mrs Brigstock had brought it with her to do something for her that she regarded as delicate. Fleda was quite prepared to help it to perform, if she should be able to gather what it wanted to do. What she gathered, however, more and more, was that it wanted to do something different from what it had wanted to do in leaving Waterbath. There was still

nothing to enlighten her more specifically in the way her
visitor continued: 'You must be very much taken up. I believe
you quite espouse his dreadful quarrel.'

Fleda vaguely demurred. 'His dreadful quarrel?'

'About the contents of the house. Aren't you looking after
them for him?'

'She knows how awfully kind you've been to me,' Owen
said. He showed such discomfiture that he really gave away
their situation; and Fleda found herself divided between the
hope that he would take leave and the wish that he should
see the whole of what the occasion might enable her to bring
to pass for him.

She explained to Mrs Brigstock. 'Mrs Gereth, at Ricks, the
other day, asked me particularly to see him for her.'

'And did she ask you also particularly to see him here in
town?' Mrs Brigstock's hideous bonnet seemed to argue for
the unsophisticated truth; and it was on Fleda's lips to reply
that such had indeed been Mrs Gereth's request. But she
checked herself, and before she could say anything else Owen
had addressed their companion.

'I made a point of letting Mona know that I should be
here, don't you see? That's exactly what I wrote her this
morning.'

'She would have had no doubt you would be here, if you
had a chance,' Mrs Brigstock returned. 'If your letter had
arrived it might have prepared me for finding you here at tea.
In that case I certainly wouldn't have come.'

'I'm glad, then, it didn't arrive. Shouldn't you like him to
go?' Fleda asked.

Mrs Brigstock looked at Owen and considered: nothing
showed in her face but that it turned a deeper pink. 'I should
like him to go with *me*.' There was no menace in her tone,
but she evidently knew what she wanted. As Owen made no
response to this Fleda glanced at him to invite him to assent;
then, for fear that he wouldn't, and would thereby make his
case worse, she took upon herself to declare that she was sure
he would be very glad to meet such a wish. She had no sooner
spoken than she felt that the words had a bad effect of
intimacy: she had answered for him as if she had been his

124

wife. Mrs Brigstock continued to regard him as if she had observed nothing, and she continued to address Fleda: 'I've not seen him for a long time – I've particular things to say to him.'

'So have I things to say to you, Mrs Brigstock!' Owen interjected. With this he took up his hat as if for an immediate departure.

The other visitor meanwhile turned to Fleda. 'What is Mrs Gereth going to do?'

'Is that what you came to ask me?' Fleda demanded.

'That and several other things.'

'Then you had much better let Mr Gereth go, and stay by yourself and make me a pleasant visit. You can talk with him when you like, but it is the first time you've been to see me.'

This appeal had evidently a certain effect; Mrs Brigstock visibly wavered. 'I can't talk with him whenever I like,' she returned; 'he hasn't been near us since I don't know when. But there are things that have brought me here.'

'They are not things of any importance,' Owen, to Fleda's surprise, suddenly asserted. He had not at first taken up Mrs Brigstock's expression of a wish to carry him off: Fleda could see that the instinct at the bottom of this was that of standing by her, of seeming not to abandon her. But abruptly, all his soreness working within him, it had struck him that he should abandon her still more if he should leave her to be dealt with by her other visitor. 'You must allow me to say, you know, Mrs Brigstock, that I don't think you should come down on Miss Vetch about anything. It's very good of her to take the smallest interest in us and our horrid little squabble. If you want to talk about it, talk about it with *me*.' He was flushed with the idea of protecting Fleda, of exhibiting his consideration for her. 'I don't like your cross-questioning her, don't you see? She's as straight as a die: *I*'ll tell you all about her!' he declared with an excited laugh. 'Please come off with me and let her alone.'

Mrs Brigstock, at this, became vivid at once; Fleda thought she looked most peculiar. She stood straight up, with a queer distention of her whole person and of everything in her face but her mouth, which she gathered into a small, tight orifice.

125

Fleda was painfully divided ; her joy was deep within, but it was more relevant to the situation that she should not appear to associate herself with the tone of familiarity in which Owen addressed a lady who had been, and was perhaps still, about to become his mother-in-law. She laid on Mrs Brigstock's arm a repressive hand. Mrs Brigstock, however, had already exclaimed on her having so wonderful a defender. 'He speaks, upon my word, as if I had come here to be rude to you !'

At this, grasping her hard, Fleda laughed ; then she achieved the exploit of delicately kissing her. 'I'm not in the least afraid to be alone with you, or of your tearing me to pieces. I'll answer any question that you can possibly dream of putting to me.'

'I'm the proper person to answer Mrs Brigstock's questions,' Owen broke in again, 'and I'm not a bit less ready to meet them than you are.' He was firmer than she had ever seen him : it was as if she had not known he could be so firm.

'But she'll only have been here a few minutes. What sort of a visit is that? ' Fleda cried.

'It has lasted long enough for my purpose. There was something I wanted to know, but I think I know it now.'

'Anything you don't know I dare say I can tell you ! ' Owen observed as he impatiently smoothed his hat with the cuff of his coat.

Fleda by this time desired immensely to keep his companion, but she saw she could do so only at the cost of provoking on his part a further exhibition of the sheltering attitude, which he exaggerated precisely because it was the first thing, since he had begun to 'like' her, that he had been able frankly to do for her. It was not in her interest that Mrs Brigstock should be more struck than she already was with that benevolence. 'There may be things you know that I don't,' she presently said to her, with a smile. 'But I've a sort of sense that you're labouring under some great mistake.'

Mrs Brigstock, at this, looked into her eyes more deeply and yearningly than she had supposed Mrs Brigstock could look ; it was the flicker of a certain willingness to give her a chance. Owen, however, quickly spoiled everything. 'Nothing is more probable than that Mrs Brigstock is doing what you

126

say; but there's no one in the world to whom you owe an explanation. I may owe somebody one – I dare say I do; but not you, no!'

'But what if there's one that it's no difficulty at all for me to give?' Fleda inquired. 'I'm sure that's the only one Mrs Brigstock came to ask, if she came to ask any at all.'

Again the good lady looked hard at her young hostess. 'I came, I believe, Fleda, just, you know, to plead with you.'

Fleda, with a bright face, hesitated a moment. 'As if I were one of those bad women in a play?'

The remark was disastrous. Mrs Brigstock, on whom her brightness was lost, evidently thought it singularly free. She turned away, as from a presence that had really defined itself as objectionable, and Fleda had a vain sense that her good humour, in which there was an idea, was taken for impertinence, or at least for levity. Her allusion was improper, even if she herself wasn't; Mrs Brigstock's emotion simplified: it came to the same thing. 'I'm quite ready,' that lady said to Owen rather mildly and woundedly. 'I do want to speak to you very much.'

'I'm completely at your service.' Owen held out his hand to Fleda. 'Good-bye, Miss Vetch. I hope to see you again tomorrow.' He opened the door for Mrs Brigstock, who passed before the girl with an oblique, averted salutation. Owen and Fleda, while he stood at the door, then faced each other darkly and without speaking. Their eyes met once more for a long moment, and she was conscious there was something in hers that the darkness didn't quench, that he had never seen before and that he was perhaps never to see again. He stayed long enough to take it – to take it with a sombre stare that just showed the dawn of wonder; then he followed Mrs Brigstock out of the house.

CHAPTER 16

HE had uttered the hope that he should see her the next day,
but Fleda could easily reflect that he wouldn't see her if she
were not there to be seen. If there was a thing in the world
she desired at that moment, it was that the next day should
have no point of resemblance with the day that had just
elapsed. She accordingly aspired to an absence: she would go
immediately down to Maggie. She ran out that evening and
telegraphed to her sister, and in the morning she quitted
London by an early train. She required for this step no reason
but the sense of necessity. It was a strong personal need ; she
wished to interpose something, and there was nothing she
could interpose but distance, but time. If Mrs Brigstock had
to deal with Owen she would allow Mrs Brigstock the chance.
To be there, to be in the midst of it, was the reverse of what
she craved: she had already been more in the midst of it than
had ever entered into her plan. At any rate she had renounced
her plan ; she had no plan now but the plan of separation.
This was to abandon Owen, to give up the fine office of helping him back to his own ; but when she had undertaken that
office she had not foreseen that Mrs Gereth would defeat it
by a manoeuvre so simple. The scene at her father's rooms had
extinguished all offices, and the scene at her father's rooms
was of Mrs Gereth's producing. Owen, at all events, must now
act for himself: he had obligations to meet, he had satisfac-
tions to give, and Fleda fairly ached with the wish that he
might be equal to them. She never knew the extent of her
tenderness for him till she became conscious of the present
force of her desire that he should be superior, be perhaps even
sublime. She obscurely made out that superiority, that sub-
limity, mightn't after all be fatal. She closed her eyes and lived
for a day or two in the mere beauty of confidence. It was with
her on the short journey ; it was with her at Maggie's ; it
glorified the mean little house in the stupid little town. Owen
had grown larger to her: he would do, like a man, whatever

he should have to do. He wouldn't be weak – not as she was: she herself was weak exceedingly.

Arranging her few possessions in Maggie's fewer receptacles, she caught a glimpse of the bright side of the fact that her old things were not such a problem as Mrs Gereth's. Picking her way with Maggie through the local puddles, diving with her into smelly cottages and supporting her, at smellier shops, in firmness over the weight of joints and the taste of cheese, it was still her own secret that was universally interwoven. In the puddles, the cottages, the shops she was comfortably alone with it ; that comfort prevailed even while, at the evening meal, her brother-in-law invited her attention to a diagram, drawn with a fork on too soiled a tablecloth, of the scandalous drains of the Convalescent Home. To be alone with it she had come away from Ricks ; and now she knew that to be alone with it she had come away from London. This advantage was of course menaced, but not immediately destroyed, by the arrival, on the second day, of the note she had been sure she should receive from Owen. He had gone to West Kensington and found her flown, but he had got her address from the little maid and then hurried to a club and written to her. 'Why have you left me just when I want you most?' he demanded. The next words, it was true, were more reassuring on the question of his steadiness.

I don't know what your reason may be [they went on] nor why you've not left a line for me; but I don't think you can feel that I did anything yesterday that it wasn't right for me to do. As regards Mrs Brigstock, certainly I just felt what was right and I did it. She had no business whatever to attack you that way, and I should have been ashamed if I had left her there to worry you. I won't have you worried by anyone; no one shall be disagreeable to you but me. I didn't mean to be so yesterday, and I don't today; but I'm perfectly free now to want you, and I want you much more than you've allowed me to explain. You'll see if I'm not all right, if you'll let me come to you. Don't be afraid – I'll not hurt you nor trouble you. I give you my honour I'll not hurt anyone. Only I *must* see you, on what I had to say to Mrs B. She was nastier than I thought she could be, but I'm behaving like an angel. I assure you I'm all right – that's exactly what I want you to see. You owe me something, you know, for what you said you would do and haven't done; what your departure without a word gives me to understand – doesn't it? – that you definitely can't do. Don't simply forsake me. See me, if you only see me once. I sha'n't wait for any leave – I shall come down tomorrow. I've been looking into trains and find there's something that will bring me down just after lunch and something very good for getting me back. I won't stop long. For God's sake, be there.

This communication arrived in the morning, but Fleda would still have had time to wire a protest. She debated on that alternative ; then she read the note over and found in one phrase an exact statement of her duty. Owen's simplicity had expressed it, and her subtlety had nothing to answer. She owed him something for her obvious failure, and what she owed him was to receive him. If indeed she had known he would make this attempt she might have been held to have gained nothing by her flight. Well, she had gained what she had gained – she had gained the interval. She had no compunction for the greater trouble she should give the young man ; it was now doubtless right that he should have as much trouble as possible. Maggie, who thought she was in her confidence, but was immensely not, had reproached her for having left Mrs Gereth, and Maggie was just in this proportion gratified to hear of the visitor with whom, early in the afternoon, she would have to ask to be left alone. Maggie liked to see far, and now she could sit upstairs and rake the whole future. She had known that, as she familiarly said, there was something the matter with Fleda, and the value of that knowledge was augmented by the fact that there was apparently also something the matter with Mr Gereth.

Fleda, downstairs, learned soon enough what this was. It was simply that, as he announced the moment he stood before her, he was now all right. When she asked him what he meant by that state he replied that he meant he could practically regard himself henceforth as a free man: he had had at West Kensington, as soon as they got into the street, such a horrid scene with Mrs Brigstock.

'I knew what she wanted to say to me: that's why I was determined to get her off. I knew I shouldn't like it, but I was perfectly prepared,' said Owen. 'She brought it out as soon as

130

we got round the corner; she asked me point-blank if I was in love with you.'

'And what did you say to that?'

'That it was none of her business.'

'Ah,' said Fleda, 'I'm not so sure!'

'Well, *I* am, and I'm the person most concerned. Of course I didn't use just those words: I was perfectly civil, quite as civil as she. But I told her I didn't consider she had a right to put me any such question. I said I wasn't sure that even Mona had, with the extraordinary line, you know, that Mona has taken. At any rate the whole thing, the way *I* put it, was between Mona and me; and between Mona and me, if she didn't mind, it would just have to remain.'

Fleda was silent a little. 'All that didn't answer her question.'

'Then you think I ought to have told her?'

Again our young lady reflected. 'I think I'm rather glad you didn't.'

'I knew what I was about,' said Owen. 'It didn't strike me that she had the least right to come down on us that way and ask for explanations.'

Fleda looked very grave, weighing the whole matter. 'I dare say that when she started, when she arrived, she didn't mean to "come down".'

'What then did she mean to do?'

'What she said to me just before she went: she meant to plead with me.'

'Oh, I heard her!' said Owen. 'But plead with you for what?'

'For you, of course – to entreat me to give you up. She thinks me awfully designing – that I've taken some sort of possession of you.'

Owen stared. 'You haven't lifted a finger! It's I who have taken possession.'

'Very true, you've done it all yourself.' Fleda spoke gravely and gently, without a breath of coquetry. 'But those are shades between which she's probably not obliged to distinguish. It's enough for her that we're singularly intimate.'

'I am, but you're not!' Owen exclaimed.

Fleda gave a dim smile. 'You make me at least feel that

I'm learning to know you very well when I hear you say such a thing as that. Mrs Brigstock came to get round me, to supplicate me,' she went on ; 'but to find you there, looking so much at home, paying me a friendly call and shoving the tea-things about – that was too much for her patience. She doesn't know, you see, that I'm after all a decent girl. She simply made up her mind on the spot that I'm a very bad case.'

'I couldn't stand the way she treated you, and that was what I had to say to her,' Owen returned.

'She's simple and slow, but she's not a fool: I think she treated me, on the whole, very well.' Fleda remembered how Mrs Gereth had treated Mona when the Brigstocks came down to Poynton.

Owen evidently thought her painfully perverse. 'It was you who carried it off ; you behaved like a brick. And so did I, I consider. If you only knew the difficulty I had! I told her you were the noblest and straightest of women.'

'That can hardly have removed her impression that there are things I put you up to.'

'It didn't,' Owen replied with candour. 'She said our relation, yours and mine, isn't innocent.'

'What did she mean by that?'

'As you may suppose, I particularly inquired. Do you know what she had the cheek to tell me?' Owen asked. 'She didn't better it much: she said she meant that it's excessively unnatural.'

Fleda considered afresh. 'Well, it is!' she brought out at last.

'Then, upon my honour, it's only you who make it so!' Her perversity was distinctly too much for him. 'I mean you make it so by the way you keep me off.'

'Have I kept you off today?' Fleda sadly shook her head, raising her arms a little and dropping them.

Her gesture of resignation gave him a pretext for catching at her hand, but before he could take it she had put it behind her. They had been seated together on Maggie's single sofa, and her movement brought her to her feet, while Owen, looking at her reproachfully, leaned back in discouragement.

'What good does it do me to be here when I find you only a stone?'

She met his eyes with all the tenderness she had not yet uttered, and she had not known till this moment how great was the accumulation. 'Perhaps, after all,' she risked, 'there may be even in a stone still some little help for you.'

Owen sat there a minute staring at her. 'Ah, you're beautiful, more beautiful than anyone,' he broke out, 'but I'll be hanged if I can ever understand you! On Tuesday, at your father's, you were beautiful – as beautiful, just before I left, as you are at this instant. But the next day, when I went back, I found it had apparently meant nothing ; and now, again, that you let me come here and you shine at me like an angel, it doesn't bring you an inch nearer to saying what I want you to say.' He remained a moment longer in the same position ; then he jerked himself up. 'What I want you to say is that you like me – what I want you to say is that you pity me.' He sprang up and came to her. 'What I want you to say is that you'll *save* me!'

Fleda hesitated. 'Why do you need saving, when you announced to me just now that you're a free man?'

He too hesitated, but he was not checked. 'It's just for the reason that I'm free. Don't you know what I mean, Miss Vetch? I want you to marry me.'

Fleda, at this, put out her hand in charity ; she held his own, which quickly grasped it a moment, and if he had described her as shining at him it may be assumed that she shone all the more in her deep, still smile. 'Let me hear a little more about your freedom first,' she said. 'I gather that Mrs Brigstock was not wholly satisfied with the way you disposed of her question.'

'I dare say she wasn't. But the less she's satisfied the more I'm free.'

'What bearing have *her* feelings, pray?' Fleda asked.

'Why, Mona's much worse than her mother. She wants much more to give me up.'

'Then why doesn't she do it?'

'She will, as soon as her mother gets home and tells her.'

'Tells her what?' Fleda inquired.

133

'Why, that I'm in love with *you*!'

Fleda debated. 'Are you so very sure she will?'

'Certainly I'm sure, with all the evidence I already have. That will finish her!' Owen declared.

This made his companion thoughtful again. 'Can you take such pleasure in her being "finished" – a poor girl you've once loved?'

Owen waited long enough to take in the question; then with a serenity startling even to her knowledge of his nature, 'I don't think I can have *really* loved her, you know,' he replied.

Fleda broke into a laugh which gave him a surprise as visible as the emotion it testified to. 'Then how am I to know that you "really" love – anybody else?'

'Oh, I'll show you that!' said Owen.

'I must take it on trust,' the girl pursued. 'And what if Mona doesn't give you up?' she added.

Owen was baffled but a few seconds; he had thought of everything. 'Why, that's just where you come in.'

'To save you? I see. You mean I must get rid of her for you.' His blankness showed for a little that he felt the chill of her cold logic; but as she waited for his rejoinder she knew to which of them it cost most. He gasped a minute, and that gave her time to say: 'You see, Mr Owen, how impossible it is to talk of such things yet!'

Like lightning he had grasped her arm. 'You mean you *will* talk of them?' Then as he began to take the flood of assent from her eyes: 'You *will* listen to me? Oh, you dear, you dear – when, when?'

'Ah, when it isn't mere misery!' The words had broken from her in a sudden loud cry, and what next happened was that the very sound of her pain upset her. She heard her own true note; she turned short away from him; in a moment she had burst into sobs; in another his arms were round her; the next she had let herself go so far that even Mrs Gereth might have seen it. He clasped her, and she gave herself – she poured out her tears on his breast; something prisoned and pent throbbed and gushed; something deep and sweet surged up – something that came from far within and far off, that had begun with the sight of him in his indifference and had

134

never had rest since then. The surrender was short, but the relief was long: she felt his lips upon her face and his arms tightened with his full divination. What she did, what she *had* done, she scarcely knew: she only was aware, as she broke from him again, of what had taken place in his own quick breast. What had taken place was that, with the click of a spring, he saw. He had cleared the high wall at a bound ; they were together without a veil. She had not a shred of a secret left ; it was as if a whirlwind had come and gone, laying low the great false front that she had built up stone by stone. The strangest thing of all was the momentary sense of desolation.

'Ah, all the while you *cared*?' Owen read the truth with a wonder so great that it was visibly almost a sadness, a terror caused by his sudden perception of where the impossibility was not. That made it all perhaps elsewhere.

'I cared, I cared, I cared!' Fleda moaned it as defiantly as if she were confessing a misdeed. 'How couldn't I care? But you mustn't, you must never, never ask! It isn't for us to talk about! ' she insisted. 'Don't speak of it, don't speak! '

It was easy indeed not to speak when the difficulty was to find words. He clasped his hands before her as he might have clasped them at an altar ; his pressed palms shook together while he held his breath and while she stilled herself in the effort to come round again to the real and the right. He helped this effort, soothing her into a seat with a touch as light as if she had really been something sacred. She sank into a chair and he dropped before her on his knees ; she fell back with closed eyes and he buried his face in her lap. There was no way to thank her but this act of prostration, which lasted, in silence, till she laid consenting hands on him, touched his head and stroked it, held it in her tenderness till he acknowledged his long density. He made the avowal seem only his – made her, when she rose again, raise him at last, softly, as if from the abasement of shame. If in each other's eyes now, however, they saw the truth, this truth, to Fleda, looked harder even than before – all the harder that when, at the very moment she recognized it, he murmured to her ecstatically, in fresh possession of her hands, which he drew up to his breast, holding them tight there with both his own: 'I'm saved, I'm

135

saved – I *am*! I'm ready for anything. I have your word. Come!' he cried, as if from the sight of a response slower than he needed, and in the tone he so often had of a great boy at a great game.

She had once more disengaged herself, with the private vow that he shouldn't yet touch her again. It was all too horribly soon – her sense of this was rapidly surging back. 'We mustn't talk, we mustn't talk; we must *wait*!' she intensely insisted. 'I don't know what you mean by your freedom; I don't see it. I don't feel it. Where is it yet, where, your freedom? If it's real there's plenty of time, and if it isn't there's more than enough. I hate myself,' she protested, 'for having anything to say about her: it's like waiting for dead men's shoes! What business is it of mine what she does? She has her own trouble and her own plan. It's too hideous to watch her and count on her!'

Owen's face, at this, showed a reviving dread, the fear of some darksome process of her mind. 'If you speak for yourself I can understand, but why is it hideous for *me*?'

'Oh, I mean for myself!' Fleda said impatiently.

'*I* watch her, *I* count on her: how can I do anything else? If I count on her to let me definitely know how we stand, I do nothing in life but what she herself has led straight up to. I never thought of asking you to "get rid of her" for me, and I never would have spoken to you if I hadn't held that I *am* rid of her, that she has backed out of the whole thing. Didn't she do so from the moment she began to put it off? I had already applied for the licence; the very invitations were half addressed. Who but she, all of a sudden, demanded an unnatural wait? It was none of *my* doing; I had never dreamed of anything but coming up to the scratch.' Owen grew more and more lucid, and more confident of the effect of his lucidity. 'She called it "taking a stand", to see what mother would do. I told her mother would do what I would make her do; and to that she replied that she would like to see me make her first. I said I would arrange that everything should be all right, and she said she really preferred to arrange it herself. It was a flat refusal to trust me in the smallest degree. Why then had she pretended so tremendously to care for me? And of course, at present,' said Owen, 'she trusts me, if possible, still less.'

Fleda paid this statement the homage of a minute's muteness. 'As to that, naturally, she has reason.'

'Why on earth has she reason?' Then, as his companion, moving away, simply threw up her hands, 'I never looked at you – not to call looking – till she had regularly driven me to it,' he went on. 'I know what I'm about. I do assure you I'm all right!'

'You're not all right – you're all wrong!' Fleda cried in despair. 'You mustn't stay here, you mustn't!' she repeated with clear decision. 'You make me say dreadful things, and I feel as if I made *you* say them.' But before he could reply she took it up in another tone. 'Why in the world, if everything had changed, didn't you break off?'

'I? – ' The inquiry seemed to have moved him to stupefaction. 'Can you ask me that question when I only wanted to please you? Didn't you seem to show me, in your wonderful way, that that was exactly how? I didn't break off just on purpose to leave it to *her*. I didn't break off so that there shouldn't be a thing to be said against me.'

The instant after her challenge Fleda had faced him again in self-reproof. 'There *isn't* a thing to be said against you, and I don't know what nonsense you make me talk! You *have* pleased me, and you've been right and good, and it's the only comfort, and you must go. Everything must come from Mona, and if it doesn't come we've said entirely too much. You must leave me alone – for ever.'

'For ever?' Owen gasped.

'I mean unless everything is different.'

'Everything *is* different – when I *know*!'

Fleda winced at what he knew; she made a wild gesture which seemed to whirl it out of the room. The mere allusion was like another embrace. 'You know nothing – and you must go and wait! You mustn't break down at this point.'

He looked about him and took up his hat: it was as if, in spite of frustration, he had got the essence of what he wanted and could afford to agree with her to the extent of keeping up the forms. He covered her with his fine, simple smile, but

137

made no other approach. 'Oh, I'm so awfully happy!' he exclaimed.

She hesitated: she would only be impeccable even though she should have to be sententious. 'You'll be happy if you're perfect!' she risked.

He laughed out at this, and she wondered if, with a newborn acuteness, he saw the absurdity of her speech, and that no one was happy just because no one could be what she so lightly prescribed. 'I don't pretend to be perfect, but I shall find a letter tonight!'

'So much the better, if it's the kind of one you desire.' That was the most she could say, and having made it sound as dry as possible she lapsed into a silence so pointed as to deprive him of all pretext for not leaving her. Still, nevertheless, he stood there, playing with his hat and filling the long pause with a strained and anxious smile. He wished to obey her thoroughly, to appear not to presume on any advantage he had won from her; but there was clearly something he longed for beside. While he showed this by hanging on she thought of two other things. One of these was that his countenance, after all, failed to bear out his description of his bliss. As for the other, it had no sooner come into her head than she found it seated, in spite of her resolution, on her lips. It took the form of an inconsequent question. 'When did you say Mrs Brigstock was to have gone back?'

Owen stared. 'To Waterbath? She was to have spent the night in town, don't you know? But when she left me, after our talk, I said to myself that she would take an evening train. I know I made her want to get home.'

'Where did you separate?' Fleda asked.

'At the West Kensington station – she was going to Victoria. I had walked with her there, and our talk was all on the way.'

Fleda pondered a moment. 'If she did go back that night you would have heard from Waterbath by this time.'

'I don't know,' said Owen. 'I thought I might hear this morning.'

'She can't have gone back,' Fleda declared. 'Mona would have written on the spot.'

'Oh yes, she *will* have written bang off!' Owen cheerfully conceded.

Fleda thought again. 'Then, even in the event of her mother's not having got home till the morning, you would have had your letter at the latest today. You see she has had plenty of time.'

Owen hesitated; then, 'Oh, she's all right!' he laughed. 'I go by Mrs Brigstock's certain effect on her – the effect of the temper the old lady showed when we parted. Do you know what she asked me?' he sociably continued. 'She asked me in a kind of nasty manner if I supposed you "really" cared anything about me. Of course I told her I supposed you didn't – not a solitary rap. How could I suppose you *do,* with your extraordinary ways? It doesn't matter; I could see she thought I lied.'

'You should have told her, you know, that I had seen you in town only that one time,' Fleda observed.

'By Jove, I did – for *you*! It was only for you.'

Something in this touched the girl so that for a moment she could not trust herself to speak. 'You're an honest man,' she said at last. She had gone to the door and opened it. 'Good-bye.'

Even yet, however, he hung back ; and she remembered how, at the end of his hour at Ricks, she had been put to it to get him out of the house. He had in general a sort of cheerful slowness which helped him at such times, though she could now see his strong fist crumple his big, stiff gloves as if they had been paper. 'But even if there's no letter – ' he began. He began, but there he left it.

'You mean, even if she doesn't let you off? Ah, you ask me too much!' Fleda spoke from the tiny hall, where she had taken refuge between the old barometer and the old mackintosh. 'There are things too utterly for yourselves alone. How can I tell? What do I know? Good-bye, good-bye! If she doesn't let you off, it will be because she *is* attached to you.'

'She's not, she's not: there's nothing in it! Doesn't a fellow know? – except with *you*!' Owen ruefully added. With this he came out of the room, lowering his voice to secret supplication, pleading with her really to meet him on the ground of the negation of Mona. It was this betrayal of his need of support and sanction that made her retreat – harden herself in the effort to save what might remain of all she had given, given probably for nothing. The very vision of him as he thus morally clung to her was the vision of a weakness somewhere in the core of his bloom, a blessed manly weakness of which, if she had only the valid right, it would be all a sweetness to take care. She faintly sickened, however, with the sense that there was as yet no valid right poor Owen could give. 'You can take it from my honour, you know,' he whispered, 'that she loathes me.'

Fleda had stood clutching the knob of Maggie's little painted stair-rail ; she took, on the stairs, a step backward. 'Why then doesn't she prove it in the only clear way?'

'She *has* proved it. Will you believe it if you see the letter?'

'I don't want to see any letter,' said Fleda. 'You'll miss your train.'

Facing him, waving him away, she had taken another upward step ; but he sprang to the side of the stairs and brought his hand, above the banister, down hard on her wrist. 'Do you mean to tell me that I must marry a woman I hate?'

From her step she looked down into his raised face. 'Ah, you see it's not true that you're free!' She seemed almost to exult. 'It's not true – it's not true!'

He only, at this, like a buffeting swimmer, gave a shake of his head and repeated his question. 'Do you mean to tell me I must marry such a woman?'

Fleda hesitated ; he held her fast. 'No. Anything is better than that.'

'Then, in God's name, what must I do?'

'You must settle that with her. You mustn't break faith. Anything is better than that. You must at any rate be utterly sure. She *must* love you – how can she help it? *I* wouldn't give you up!' said Fleda. She spoke in broken bits panting out her words. 'The great thing is to keep faith. Where *is* a man if he doesn't? If he doesn't he may be so cruel. So cruel, so cruel, so cruel!' Fleda repeated. 'I couldn't have a hand in *that,* you know: that's my position – that's mine. You offered her marriage: it's a tremendous thing for her.' Then looking at him another moment, '*I* wouldn't give you up!' she said again. He still had hold of her arm; she took in his blank alarm. With a quick dip of her face she reached his hand with her lips, pressing them to the back of it with a force of her words. 'Never, never, never!' she cried; and before he could succeed in seizing her she had turned and, scrambling up the stairs, got away from him even faster than she had got away from him at Ricks.

CHAPTER 17

TEN days after his visit she received a communication from
Mrs Gereth – a telegram of eight words, exclusive of signa-
ture and date. 'Come up immediately and stay with me here' –
it was characteristically sharp, as Maggie said; but, as Maggie
added, it was also characteristically kind. 'Here' was an hotel
in London, and Maggie had embraced a condition of life
which already began to produce in her some yearning for
hotels in London. She would have responded in an instant, and
she was surprised that her sister seemed to hesitate. Fleda's
hesitation, which lasted but an hour, was expressed in that
young lady's own mind by the reflection that in obeying her
friend's summons she shouldn't know what she should be 'in
for'. Her friend's summons, however, was but another name
for her friend's appeal ; and Mrs Gereth's bounty had laid her
under obligations more sensible than any reluctance. In the
event – that is at the end of her hour – she testified to her
gratitude by taking the train and to her mistrust by leaving
her luggage. She went as if she had gone up for the day. In
the train, however, she had another thoughtful hour, during
which it was her mistrust that mainly deepened. She felt as if
for ten days she had sat in darkness, looking to the east for a
dawn that had not yet glimmered. Her mind had lately been
less occupied with Mrs Gereth ; it had been so exceptionally
occupied with Mona. If the sequel was to justify Owen's
prevision of Mrs Brigstock's action upon her daughter, this
action was at the end of a week as much a mystery as ever.
The stillness, all round, had been exactly what Fleda desired,
but it gave her for the time a deep sense of failure, the sense
of a sudden drop from a height at which she had all things
beneath her. She had nothing beneath her now ; she herself
was at the bottom of the heap. No sign had reached her from
Owen – poor Owen, who had clearly no news to give about
his precious letter from Waterbath. If Mrs Brigstock had
hurried back to obtain that this letter should be written, Mrs

Brigstock might then have spared herself so great an inconvenience. Owen had been silent for the best of all reasons – the reason that he had had nothing in life to say. If the letter had not been written he would simply have had to introduce some large qualification into his account of his freedom. He had left his young friend under her refusal to listen to him until he should be able, on the contrary, to extend that picture ; and his present submission was all in keeping with the rigid honesty that his young friend had prescribed.

It was this that formed the element through which Mona loomed large ; Fleda had enough imagination, a fine enough feeling for life, to be impressed with such an image of successful immobility. The massive maiden at Waterbath *was* successful from the moment she could entertain her resentments as if they had been poor relations who needn't put her to expense. She was a magnificent dead weight ; there was something positive and portentous in her quietude. 'What game are they all playing?' poor Fleda could only ask ; for she had an intimate conviction that Owen was now under the roof of his betrothed. That was stupefying if he really hated Mona ; and if he didn't really hate her what had brought him to Raphael Road and to Maggie's? Fleda had no real light, but she felt that to account for the absence of any result of their last meeting would take a supposition of the full sacrifice to charity that she had held up before him. If he had gone to Waterbath it had been simply because he had to go. She had as good as told him that he would have to go ; that this was an inevitable incident of his keeping perfect faith – faith so literal that the smallest subterfuge would always be a reproach to him. When she tried to remember that it was for herself he was taking his risk, she felt how weak a way that was of expressing Mona's supremacy. There would be no need of keeping him up if there were nothing to keep him up to. Her eyes grew wan as she discerned in the impenetrable air that Mona's thick outline never wavered an inch. She wondered fitfully what Mrs Gereth had by this time made of it, and reflected with a strange elation that the sand on which the mistress of Ricks had built a momentary triumph was quaking beneath the surface. As the *Morning Post* still held its peace, she would be, of course, more confident ;

but the hour was at hand at which Owen would have absolutely to do either one thing or the other. To keep perfect faith was to inform against his mother, and to hear the police at her door would be Mrs Gereth's awakening. How much she was beguiled Fleda could see from her having been for a whole month quite as deep and dark as Mona. She had let her young friend alone because of the certitude, cultivated at Ricks, that Owen had done the opposite. He had done the opposite indeed, but much good had that brought forth! To have sent for her now, Fleda felt, was from this point of view wholly natural: she had sent for her to show at last how much she had scored. If, however, Owen was really at Waterbath the refutation of that boast was easy.

Fleda found Mrs Gereth in modest apartments and with an air of fatigue in her distinguished face – a sign, as she privately remarked, of the strain of that effort to be discreet of which she herself had been having the benefit. It was a constant feature of their relation that this lady could make Fleda blench a little, and that the effect proceeded from the intense pressure of her confidence. If the confidence had been heavy even when the girl, in the early flush of devotion, had been able to feel herself most responsive, it drew her heart into her mouth now that she had reserves and conditions, now that she couldn't simplify with the same bold hand as her protectress. In the very brightening of the tired look, and at the moment of their embrace, Fleda felt on her shoulders the return of the load, so that her spirit frankly quailed as she asked herself what she had brought up from her trusted seclusion to support it. Mrs Gereth's free manner always made a joke of weakness, and there was in such a welcome a richness, a kind of familiar nobleness, that suggested shame to a harried conscience. Something had happened, she could see, and she could also see, in the bravery that seemed to announce it had changed everything, a formidable assumption that what had happened was that a healthy young woman must like. The absence of luggage had made this young woman feel meagre even before her companion, taking in the bareness at a second glance, exclaimed upon it and roundly rebuked her. Of course she had expected her to stay.

Fleda thought best to show bravery too, and to show it from

the first. 'What you expected, dear Mrs Gereth, is exactly what I came up to ascertain. It struck me as right to do that first. I mean to ascertain, without making preparations.'

'Then you'll be so good as to make them on the spot!' Mrs Gereth was most emphatic. 'You're going abroad with me.'

Fleda wondered, but she also smiled. 'Tonight – tomorrow?'

'In as few days as possible. That's all that's left for me now.' Fleda's heart, at this, gave a bound; she wondered to what particular difference in Mrs Gereth's situation as last known to her it was an allusion. 'I've made my plan,' her friend continued: 'I go for at least a year. We shall go straight to Florence; we can manage there. I of course don't look to you, however,' she added, 'to stay with me all that time. That will require to be settled. Owen will have to join us as soon as possible; he may not be quite ready to get off with us. But I'm convinced it's quite the right thing to go. It will make a good change; it will put in a decent interval.'

Fleda listened; she was deeply mystified. 'How kind you are to me!' she presently said. The picture suggested so many questions that she scarcely knew which to ask first. She took one at a venture. 'You really have it from Mr Gereth that he'll give us his company?'

If Mr Gereth's mother smiled in response to this, Fleda knew that her smile was a tacit criticism of such a form of reference to her son. Fleda habitually spoke of him as Mr Owen, and it was a part of her present vigilance to appear to have relinquished that right. Mrs Gereth's manner confirmed a certain impression of her pretending to more than she felt; her very first words had conveyed it, and it reminded Fleda of the conscious courage with which, weeks before, the lady had met her visitor's first startled stare at the clustered spoils of Poynton. It was her practice to take immensely for granted whatever she wished. 'Oh, if you'll answer for him, it will do quite as well!' she said. Then she put her hands on the girl's shoulders and held them at arm's length, as if to shake them a little, while in the depths of her shining eyes Fleda discovered something obscure and unquiet. 'You bad, false thing, why didn't you tell me?' Her tone softened her harshness, and her visitor had never had such a sense of her indulgence. Mrs

Gereth could show patience; it was a part of the general bribe, but it was also like the handing in of a heavy bill before which Fleda could only fumble in a penniless pocket. 'You must perfectly have known at Ricks, and yet you practically denied it. That's why I call you bad and false!' It was apparently also why she again almost roughly kissed her.

'I think that before I answer you I had better know what you're talking about,' Fleda said.

Mrs Gereth looked at her with a slight increase of hardness. 'You've done everything you need for modesty, my dear! If he's sick with love of you, you haven't had to wait for me to inform you.'

Fleda hesitated. 'Has he informed *you*, dear Mrs Gereth?'

Dear Mrs Gereth smiled sweetly. 'How could he, when our situation is such that he communicates with me only through you, and that you are so tortuous you conceal everything?'

'Didn't he answer the note in which you let him know that I was in town?' Fleda asked.

'He answered it sufficiently by rushing off on the spot to see you.'

Mrs Gereth met that allusion with a prompt firmness that made almost insolently light of any ground of complaint, and Fleda's own sense of responsibility was now so vivid that all resentments turned comparatively pale. She had no heart to produce a grievance; she could only, left as she was with the little mystery on her hands, produce, after a moment, a question. 'How then do you come to know that your son has ever thought –'

'That he would give his ears to get you?' Mrs Gereth broke in. 'I had a visit from Mrs Brigstock.'

Fleda opened her eyes. 'She went down to Ricks?'

'The day after she had found Owen at your feet. She knows everything.'

Fleda shook her head sadly; she was more startled than she cared to show. This odd journey of Mrs Brigstock's, which, with a simplicity equal for once to Owen's, she had not divined, now struck her as having produced the hush of the last ten days. 'There are things she doesn't know!' she presently exclaimed.

'She knows he would do anything to marry you.'

'He hasn't told her so,' Fleda said.

'No, but he has told you. That's better still!' laughed Mrs Gereth. 'My dear child,' she went on with an air that affected the girl as a sort of blind profanity, 'don't try to make yourself out better than you are. *I* know what you are. I haven't lived with you so much for nothing. You're not quite a saint in heaven yet. Lord, what a creature you'd have thought me in my good time! But you do like it, fortunately, you idiot. You're pale with your passion, you sweet thing. That's exactly what I wanted to see. I can't for the life of me think where the shame comes in.' Then with a finer significance, a look that seemed to Fleda strange, she added: 'It's all right.'

'I've seen him but twice,' said Fleda.

'But twice?' Mrs Gereth still smiled.

'On the occasion, at papa's, that Mrs Brigstock told you of, and one day, since then, down at Maggie's.'

'Well, those things are between yourselves, and you seem to me both poor creatures at best.' Mrs Gereth spoke with a rich humour which tipped with light for an instant a real conviction. 'I don't know what you've got in your veins: you absurdly exaggerated the difficulties. But enough is as good as a feast, and when once I get you abroad together – !' She checked herself as if from excess of meaning; what might happen when she should get them abroad together was to be gathered only from the way she slowly rubbed her hands.

The gesture, however, made the promise so definite that for a moment her companion was almost beguiled. But there was nothing to account, as yet, for the wealth of Mrs Gereth's certitude: the visit of the lady of Waterbath appeared but half to explain it. 'Is it permitted to be surprised,' Fleda deferentially asked, 'at Mrs Brigstock's thinking it would help her to see you?'

'It's never permitted to be surprised at the aberrations of born fools,' said Mrs Gereth. 'If a cow should try to calculate, that's the kind of happy thought she'd have. Mrs Brigstock came down to plead with me.'

Fleda mused a moment. 'That's what she came to do with *me*,' she then honestly returned. 'But what did she expect to get of you, with your opposition so marked from the first?'

'She didn't know I want *you*, my dear. It's a wonder, with all my violence – the gross publicity I've given my desires. But she's as stupid as an owl – she doesn't feel your charm.'

Fleda felt herself flush slightly, but she tried to smile. 'Did you tell her all about it? Did you make her understand you want me?'

'For what do you take me? I wasn't such a donkey.'

'So as not to aggravate Mona?' Fleda suggested.

'So as not to aggravate Mona, naturally. We've had a narrow course to steer, but thank God we're at last in the open!'

'What do you call the open, Mrs Gereth?' Fleda demanded. Then as the other faltered: 'Do you know where Mr Owen is today?'

Mrs Gereth stared. 'Do you mean he's at Waterbath? Well, that's your own affair. I can bear it if *you* can.'

'Wherever he is, I can bear it,' Fleda said. 'But I haven't the least idea where he is.'

'Then you ought to be ashamed of yourself!' Mrs Gereth broke out with a change of note that showed how deep a passion underlay everything she had said. The poor woman, catching her companion's hand, however, the next moment, as if to retract something of this harshness, spoke more patiently. 'Don't you understand, Fleda, how immensely, how devotedly, I've trusted you?' Her tone was indeed a supplication.

Fleda was infinitely shaken; she was silent a little. 'Yes, I understand. Did she go to you to complain of me?'

'She came to see what she could do. She had been tremendously upset, the day before, by what had taken place at your father's, and she had posted down to Ricks on the inspiration of the moment. She hadn't meant it on leaving home; it was the sight of you closeted there with Owen that had suddenly determined her. The whole story, she said, was written in your two faces: she spoke as if she had never seen such an exhibition. Owen was on the brink, but there might still be time to save him, and it was with this idea she had bearded me in my den. "What won't a mother do, you know?" – that was one of the things she said. What wouldn't a mother do indeed? I thought I had sufficiently shown her what! She tried to break

148

me down by an appeal to my good nature, as she called it, and from the moment she opened on *you,* from the moment she denounced Owen's falsity, I was as good-natured as she could wish. I understood that it was a plea for mere mercy, that you and he between you were killing her child. Of course I was delighted that Mona should be killed, but I was studiously kind to Mrs Brigstock. At the same time I was honest. I didn't pretend to anything I couldn't feel. I asked her why the marriage hadn't taken place months ago, when Owen was perfectly ready ; and I showed her how completely that fatuous mistake on Mona's part cleared his responsibility. It was she who had killed *him* – it was she who had destroyed his affection, his illusions. Did she want him now when he was estranged, when he was disgusted, when he had a sore grievance? She reminded me that Mona had a sore grievance too, but she admitted that she hadn't come to me to speak of that. What she had come to me for was not to get the old things back, but simply to get Owen. What she wanted was that I would, in simple pity, see fair play. Owen had been awfully bedevilled – she didn't call it that, she called it "misled" – but it was simply you who had bedevilled him. He would be all right still if I would see that you were out of the way. She asked me point-blank if it was possible I could want him to marry you.'

Fleda had listened in unbearable pain and growing terror, as if her interlocutress, stone by stone, were piling some fatal mass upon her breast. She had the sense of being buried alive, smothered in the mere expansion of another will ; and now there was but one gap left to the air. A single word, she felt, might close it, and with the question that came to her lips as Mrs Gereth paused she seemed to herself to ask, in cold dread, for her doom. 'What did you say to that?' she inquired.

'I was embarrassed, for I saw my danger – the danger of her going home and saying to Mona that I was backing you up. It had been a bliss to learn that Owen had really turned to you, but my joy didn't put me off my guard. I reflected intensely for a few seconds ; then I saw my issue.'

'Your issue?' Fleda murmured.

'I remembered how you had tied my hands about saying a word to Owen.'

Fleda wondered. 'And did you remember the little letter that, with your hands tied, you still succeeded in writing to him?'

'Perfectly ; my little letter was a model of reticence. What I remembered was all that in those few words I forbade myself to say. I had been an angel of delicacy – I had effaced myself like a saint. It was not for me to have done all that and then figure to such a woman as having done the opposite. Besides, it was none of her business.'

'Is that what you said to her?' Fleda asked.

'I said to her that her question revealed a total misconception of the nature of my present relations with my son. I said to her that I had no relations with him at all, and that nothing had passed between us for months. I said to her that my hands were spotlessly clean of any attempt to make him make up to you. I said to her that I had taken from Poynton what I had a right to take, but had done nothing else in the world. I was determined that if I had bit my tongue off to oblige you I would at least have the righteousness that my sacrifice gave me.'

'And was Mrs Brigstock satisfied with your answer?'

'She was visibly relieved.'

'It was fortunate for you,' said Fleda, 'that she's apparently not aware of the manner in which, almost under her nose, you advertised me to him at Poynton.'

Mrs Gereth appeared to recall that scene ; she smiled with a serenity remarkably effective as showing how cheerfully used she had grown to invidious allusions to it. 'How should she be aware of it?'

'She would if Owen had described your outbreak to Mona.'

'Yes, but he didn't describe it. All his instinct was to conceal it from Mona. He wasn't conscious, but he was already in love with you!' Mrs Gereth declared.

Fleda shook her head wearily. 'No – I was only in love with him!'

Here was a faint illumination with which Mrs Gereth instantly mingled her fire. 'You dear old wretch!' she exclaimed ; and she again, with ferocity, embraced her young friend.

Fleda submitted like a sick animal: she would submit to everything now. 'Then what further passed?'

'Only that she left me thinking she had got something.'

'And what had she got?'

'Nothing but her luncheon. But *I* got everything!'

'Everything?' Fleda quavered.

Mrs Gereth, struck apparently by something in her tone, looked at her from a tremendous height. 'Don't fail me now!'

It sounded so like a menace that, with a full divination at last, the poor girl fell weakly into a chair. 'What on earth have you done?'

Mrs Gereth stood there in all the glory of a great stroke. 'I've settled you.' She filled the room, to Fleda's scared vision, with the glare of her magnificence. 'I've sent everything back.'

'Everything?' Fleda gasped.

'To the smallest snuff-box. The last load went yesterday. The same people did it. Poor little Ricks is empty.' Then as if, for a crowning splendour, to check all deprecation: 'They're yours, you goose!' Mrs Gereth concluded, holding up her handsome head and rubbing her white hands. Fleda saw that there were tears in her deep eyes.

CHAPTER 18

SHE was slow to take in the announcement, but when she had done so she felt it to be more than her cup of bitterness would hold. Her bitterness was her anxiety, the taste of which suddenly sickened her. What had she become, on the spot, but a traitress to her friend? The treachery increased with the view of the friend's motive, a motive magnificent as a tribute to her value. Mrs Gereth had wished to make sure of her and had reasoned that there would be no such way as by a large appeal to her honour. If it be true, as men have declared, that the sense of honour is weak in women, some of the bearings of this stroke might have thrown a light on the question. What was now, at all events, put before Fleda was that she had been made sure of, for the greatness of the surrender imposed an obligation as great. There was an expression she had heard used by young men with whom she danced: the only word to fit Mrs Gereth's intention was that Mrs Gereth had designed to 'fetch' her. It was a calculated, it was a crushing bribe ; it looked her in the eyes and said simply: 'That's what I do for you!' What Fleda was to do in return required no pointing out. The sense, at present, of how little she had done made her almost cry aloud with pain ; but her first endeavour, in the face of the fact, was to keep such a cry from reaching her companion. How little she had done Mrs Gereth didn't yet know, and possibly there would be still some way of turning round before the discovery. On her own side too Fleda had almost made one: she had known she was wanted, but she had not after all conceived how magnificently much. She had been treated by her friend's act as a conscious prize, but what made her a conscious prize was only the power the act itself imputed to her. As high, bold diplomacy it dazzled and carried her off her feet. She admired the noble risk of it, a risk Mrs Gereth had faced for the utterly poor creature that the girl now felt herself. The change it instantly wrought in her was, moreover, extraordinary: it transformed at a touch her emotion on the subject

152

of concessions. A few weeks earlier she had jumped at the duty of pleading for them, practically quarrelling with the lady of Ricks for her refusal to restore what she had taken. She had been sore with the wrong to Owen, she had bled with the wounds of Poynton; now however, as she heard of the replenishment of the void that had so haunted her, she came as near sounding an alarm as if from the deck of a ship she had seen a person she loved jump into the sea. Mrs Gereth had become in a flash the victim; poor little Ricks had been laid bare in a night. If Fleda's feeling about the old things had taken precipitate form the form would have been a frantic command. It was indeed for mere want of breath that she didn't shout: 'Oh, stop them – it's no use; bring them back – it's too late!' And what most kept her breathless was her companion's very grandeur. Fleda distinguished as never before the purity of such a passion; it made Mrs Gereth august and almost sublime. It was absolutely unselfish – she cared nothing for mere possession. She thought solely and incorruptibly of what was best for the things; she had surrendered them to the presumptive care of the one person of her acquaintance who felt about them as she felt herself, and whose long lease of the future would be the nearest approach that could be compassed to committing them to a museum. Now it was indeed that Fleda knew what rested on her; now it was also that she measured as if for the first time Mrs Gereth's view of the natural influence of a fine acquisition. She had adopted the idea of blowing away the last doubt of what her young friend would gain, of making good still more than she was obliged to make it the promise of weeks before. It was one thing for the girl to have heard that in a certain event restitution would be made; it was another for her to see the condition, with a noble trust, treated in advance as performed, and to be able to feel that she should have only to open a door to find every old piece in every old corner. To have played such a card was therefore, practically, for Mrs Gereth, to have won the game. Fleda had certainly to recognize that, so far as the theory of the matter went, the game had been won. Oh, she had been made sure of!

She couldn't, however, succeed for so many minutes in deferring her exposure. 'Why didn't you wait, dearest? Ah, why didn't you wait?' – if that inconsequent appeal kept rising to her lips to be cut short before it was spoken, this was only because at first the humility of gratitude helped her to gain time, enabled her to present herself very honestly as too overcome to be clear. She kissed her companion's hands, she did homage at her feet, she murmured soft snatches of praise, and yet in the midst of it all was conscious that what she really showed most was the wan despair at her heart. She saw Mrs Gereth's glimpse of this despair suddenly widen, heard the quick chill of her voice pierce through the false courage of endearments. 'Do you mean to tell me at such an hour as this that you've really lost him?'

The tone of the question made the idea a possibility for which Fleda had nothing from this moment but terror. 'I don't know, Mrs Gereth; how can I say?' she asked. 'I've not seen him for so long; as I told you just now, I don't even know where he is. That's by no fault of his,' she hurried on: 'he would have been with me every day if I had consented. But I made him understand, the last time, that I'll receive him again only when he's able to show me that his release has been complete and definite. Oh, he can't yet, don't you see, and that's why he hasn't been back. It's far better than his coming only that we should both be miserable. When he does come he'll be in a better position. He'll be tremendously moved by the splendid thing you've done. I know you wish me to feel that you've done it as much for me as for Owen, but your having done it for me is just what will delight him most! When he hears of it,' said Fleda, in desperate optimism, 'when he hears of it – ' There indeed, regretting her advance, she quite broke down. She was wholly powerless to say what Owen would do when he heard of it. 'I don't know what he won't make of you and how he won't hug you!' she had to content herself with lamely declaring. She had drawn Mrs Gereth to a sofa with a vague instinct of pacifying her and still, after all, gaining time ; but it was a position in which her great duped benefactress, portentously patient again during this demonstration, looked far from inviting a 'hug'. Fleda found herself tricking out the situation with artificial flowers, trying to talk even herself into the fancy that Owen, whose name she now made simple and sweet, might come in upon them at any moment. She felt an immense need to be understood and justified; she averted her face in dread from all that she might have to be forgiven. She pressed on her companion's arm as if to keep her quiet till she should really know, and then, after a minute, she poured out the clear essence of what in happier days had been her 'secret'. 'You mustn't think I don't adore him when I've told him so to his face. I love him so that I'd die for him – I love him so that it's horrible. Don't look at me therefore as if I had not been kind, as if I had not been as tender as if he were dying and my tenderness were what would save him. Look at me as if you believe me, as if you feel what I've been through. Darling Mrs Gereth, I could kiss the ground he walks on. I haven't a rag of pride ; I used to have, but it's gone. I used to have a secret, but everyone knows it now, and anyone who looks at me can say, I think, what's the matter with me. It's not so very fine, my secret, and the less one really says about it the better ; but I want you to have it from me because I was stiff before. I want you to see for yourself that I've been brought as low as a girl can very well be. It serves me right,' Fleda laughed, 'if I was ever proud and horrid to you! I don't know what you wanted me, in those days at Ricks, to do, but I don't think you can have wanted much more than what I've done. The other day at Maggie's I did things that made me, afterwards, think of you! I don't know what girls may do ; but if he doesn't know that there isn't an inch of me that isn't his – ! ' Fleda sighed as if she couldn't express it ; she piled it up, as she would have said ; holding Mrs Gereth with dilated eyes, she seemed to sound her for the effect of these words. 'It's idiotic,' she wearily smiled ; 'it's so strange that I'm almost angry for it, and the strangest part of all is that it isn't even happiness. It's anguish – it was from the first; from the first there was a bitterness and a kind of dread. But I owe you every word of the truth. You don't do him justice, either: he's a dear, I assure you he's a dear. I'd trust him to the last breath ; I don't think you really know him. He's ever so much cleverer than he makes a show of ; he's remarkable in his own shy way. You told me at Ricks that you wanted me to let myself go, and I've "gone" quite far enough to discover as much as that, as well as all sorts of other delightful things about him. You'll tell me I make myself out worse than I am,' said the girl, feeling more and more in her companion's attitude a quality that treated her speech as a desperate rigmarole and even perhaps as a piece of cold immodesty. She wanted to make herself out 'bad' – it was a part of her justification; but it suddenly occured to her that such a picture of her extravagance imputed a want of gallantry to the young man. 'I don't care for anything you think,' she declared, 'because Owen, don't you know, sees me as I am. He's so kind that it makes up for everything!'

This attempt at gaiety was futile; the silence with which, for a minute, her adversary greeted her troubled plea brought home to her afresh that she was on the bare defensive. 'Is it a part of his kindness never to come near you?' Mrs Gereth inquired at last. 'Is it a part of his kindness to leave you without an inkling of where he is?' She rose again from where Fleda had kept her down; she seemed to tower there in the majesty of her gathered wrong. 'Is it a part of his kindness that, after I've toiled as I've done for six days, and with my own weak hands, which I haven't spared, to denude myself, in your interest, to that point that I've nothing left, as I may say, but what I have on my back – it is a part of his kindness that you're not even able to produce him for me?'

There was a high contempt in this which was for Owen quite as much, and in the light of which Fleda felt that her effort at plausibility had been mere grovelling. She rose from the sofa with an humiliated sense of rising from ineffectual knees. That discomfort, however, lived but an instant: it was swept away in a rush of loyalty to the absent. She herself could bear his mother's scorn; but to avert it from his sweet innocence she broke out with a quickness that was like the raising of an arm. 'Don't blame him – don't blame him: he'd do anything on earth for me! It was I,' said Fleda, eagerly, 'who sent him back to her; I made him go; I pushed him out of the house; I declined to have anything to say to him except on another footing.'

Mrs Gereth stared as at some gross material ravage. 'Another footing? What other footing?'

'The one I've already made so clear to you: my having it in

black and white, as you may say, from her that she freely gives him up.'

'Then you think he lies when he tells you that he has recovered his liberty?'

Fleda hesitated a moment; after which she exclaimed with a certain hard pride: 'He's enough in love with me for anything!'

'For anything, apparently, except to act like a man and impose his reason and his will on your incredible folly. For anything except to put an end, as any man worthy of the name, would have put it, to your systematic, to your idiotic perversity. What are you, after all, my dear, I should like to know, that a gentleman who offers you what Owen offers should have to meet such wonderful exactions, to take such extraordinary precautions about your sweet little scruples?' Her resentment rose to a strange insolence which Fleda took full in the face and which, for the moment at least, had the horrible force to present to her vengefully a showy side of the truth. It gave her a blinding glimpse of lost alternatives. 'I don't know what to think of him,' Mrs Gereth went on; 'I don't know what to call him: I'm so ashamed of him that I can scarcely speak of him even to *you*. But indeed I'm so ashamed of you both together that I scarcely know in common decency where to look.' She paused to give Fleda the full benefit of this remarkable statement; then she exclaimed: 'Anyone but a jackass would have tucked you under his arm and marched you off to the Registrar!'

Fleda wondered; with her free imagination she could wonder even while her cheek stung from a slap. 'To the Registrar?'

'That would have been the sane, sound, immediate course to adopt. With a grain of gumption you'd both instantly have felt it. *I* should have found a way to take you, you know, if I'd been what Owen's supposed to be. *I* should have got the business over first; the rest could come when you liked! Good God, girl, your place was to stand before me as a woman honestly married. One doesn't know what one has hold of in touching you, and you must excuse my saying that you're literally unpleasant to me to meet as you are. Then at least we could have talked, and Owen, if he had the ghost of a sense

157

of humour, could have snapped his fingers at your refinements.'

This stirring speech affected our young lady as if it had been the shake of a tambourine borne towards her from a gypsy dance: her head seemed to go round and she felt a sudden passion in her feet. The emotion, however, was but meagrely expressed in the flatness with which she heard herself presently say: 'I'll go to the Registrar now.'

'Now?' Magnificent was the sound Mrs Gereth threw into this monosyllable. 'And pray who's to take you?' Fleda gave a colourless smile, and her companion continued: 'Do you literally mean that you can't put your hand upon him?' Fleda's wan grimace appeared to irritate her; she made a short, imperious gesture. 'Find him for me, you fool – *find* him for me!'

'What do you want of him,' Fleda sadly asked, 'feeling as you do to both of us?'

'Never mind how I feel, and never mind what I say when I'm furious!' Mrs Gereth still more incisively added. 'Of course I cling to you, you wretches, or I shouldn't suffer as I do. What I want of him is to see that he takes you; what I want of him is to go with you myself to the place.' She looked round the room as if, in feverish haste, for a mantle to catch up; she bustled to the window as if to spy out a cab: she would allow half an hour for the job. Already in her bonnet, she had snatched from the sofa a garment for the street: she jerked it on as she came back. 'Find him, find him,' she repeated; 'come straight out with me, to try, at least, to get at him!'

'How can I get at him? He'll come when he's ready,' Fleda replied.

Mrs Gereth turned on her sharply. 'Ready for what? Ready to see me ruined without a reason or a reward?'

Fleda was silent; the worst of it all was that there was something unspoken between them. Neither of them dared to utter it, but the influence of it was in the girl's tone when she returned at last, with great gentleness: 'Don't be harsh to me – I'm very unhappy.' The words produced a visible impression on Mrs Gereth, who held her face averted and sent off through the window a gaze that kept pace with the long caravan of her treasures. Fleda knew she was watching it wind up the avenue of Poynton – Fleda participated indeed fully in the vision; so that after a little the most consoling thing seemed to her to add: 'I don't see why in the world you take so for granted that he's, as you say, "lost".'

Mrs Gereth continued to stare out of the window, and her stillness denoted some success in controlling herself. 'If he's not lost, why are you unhappy?'

'I'm unhappy because I torment you, and you don't understand me.'

'No, Fleda, I don't understand you,' said Mrs Gereth, finally facing her again. 'I don't understand you at all, and it's as if you and Owen were of quite another race and another flesh. You make me feel very old-fashioned and simple and bad. But you must take me as I am, since you take so much else *with* me!' She spoke now with the drop of her resentment, with a dry and weary calm. 'It would have been better for me if I had never known you,' she pursued, 'and certainly better if I hadn't taken such an extraordinary fancy to you. But that too was inevitable: everything, I suppose, is inevitable. It was all my own doing – you didn't run after me: I pounced on you and caught you up. You're a stiff little beggar, in spite of your pretty manners: yes, you're hideously misleading. I hope you feel how handsome it is of me to recognize the independence of your character. It was your clever sympathy that did it – your extraordinary feeling for those accursed vanities. You were sharper about them than anyone I had ever known, and that was a thing I simply couldn't resist. Well,' the poor lady concluded after a pause, 'you see where it has landed us!'

'If you'll go for him yourself, I'll wait here,' said Fleda.

Mrs Gereth, holding her mantle together, appeared for a while to consider.

'To his club, do you mean?'

'Isn't it there, when he's in town, that he has a room? He has at present no other London address,' Fleda said: 'It's there one writes to him.'

'How do *I* know, with my wretched relations with him?' Mrs Gereth asked.

'Mine have not been quite so bad as that,' Fleda desperately smiled. Then she added: 'His silence, *her* silence, our hearing nothing at all – what are these but the very things on which, at Poynton and at Ricks, you rested your assurance that everything is at an end between them?'

Mrs Gereth looked dark and void. 'Yes, but I hadn't heard from you then that you could invent nothing better than, as you call it, to send him back to her.'

'Ah, but, on the other hand, you've learned from them what you didn't know – you've learned by Mrs Brigstock's visit that he cares for me.' Fleda found herself in the position of availing herself of optimistic arguments that she formerly had repudiated ; her refutation of her companion had completely changed its ground.

She was in a fever of ingenuity and painfully conscious, on behalf of her success, that her fever was visible. She could herself see the reflection of it glitter in Mrs Gereth's sombre eyes.

'You plunge me in stupefaction,' that lady answered, 'and at the same time you terrify me. Your account of Owen is inconceivable, and yet I don't know what to hold on by. He cares for you, it does appear, and yet in the same breath you inform me that nothing is more possible than that he's spending these days at Waterbath. Excuse me if I'm so dull as not to see my way in such darkness. If he's at Waterbath he doesn't care for you. If he cares for you he's not at Waterbath.'

'Then where is he?' poor Fleda helplessly wailed. She caught herself up, however ; she did her best to be brave and clear. Before Mrs Gereth could reply, with due obviousness, that this was a question for her not to ask, but to answer, she found an air of assurance to say : 'You simplify far too much. You always did and you always will. The tangle of life is much more intricate than you've ever, I think, felt it to be. You slash into it,' cried Fleda finely, 'with a great pair of shears, you nip at it as if you were one of the Fates! If Owen's at Waterbath he's there to wind everything up.'

Mrs Gereth shook her head with slow austerity. 'You don't believe a word you're saying. I've frightened you, as you've frightened me : you're whistling in the dark to keep up our courage. I do simplify, doubtless, if to simplify is to fail to comprehend the insanity of a passion that bewilders a young blockhead with bugaboo barriers, with hideous and monstrous

160

sacrifices. I can only repeat that you're beyond me. Your perversity's a thing to howl over. However,' the poor woman continued with a break in her voice, a long hesitation, and then the dry triumph of her will, 'I'll never mention it to you again! Owen I can just make out ; for Owen *is* a blockhead. Owen's a blockhead,' she repeated with a quiet, tragic finality, looking straight into Fleda's eyes. 'I don't know why you dress up so the fact that he's disgustingly weak.'

Fleda hesitated; at last, before her companion's, she lowered her look. 'Because I love him. It's because he's weak that he needs me,' she added.

'That was why his father, whom he exactly resembles, needed me. And I didn't fail his father,' said Mrs Gereth. She gave Fleda a moment to appreciate the remark ; after which she pursued: 'Mona Brigstock isn't weak ; she's stronger than you!'

'I never thought she was weak,' Fleda answered. She looked vaguely round the room with a new purpose: she had lost sight of her umbrella.

'I did tell you to let yourself go, but it's clear enough that you really haven't,' Mrs Gereth declared. 'If Mona has got him – '

Fleda had accomplished her search; her interlocutress paused. 'If Mona has got him?' the girl inquired, tightening the umbrella.

'Well,' said Mrs Gereth profoundly, 'it will be clear enough that Mona *has*.'

'Has let herself go?'

'Has let herself go.' Mrs Gereth spoke as if she saw it in every detail.

Fleda felt the tone and finished her preparation ; then she went and opened the door. 'We'll look for him together,' she said to her friend, who stood a moment taking in her face. 'They may know something about him at the Colonel's.'

'We'll go there.' Mrs Gereth had picked up her gloves and her purse. 'But the first thing,' she went on, 'will be to wire to Poynton.'

'Why not to Waterbath at once?' Fleda asked.

Her companion hesitated. 'In *your* name?'

'In my name. I noticed a place at the corner.'

While Fleda held the door open Mrs Gereth drew on her gloves. 'Forgive me,' she presently said. 'Kiss me,' she added.

Fleda, on the threshold, kissed her ; then they went out.

CHAPTER 19

IN the place at the corner, on the chance of its saving time, Fleda wrote her telegram – wrote it in silence under Mrs Gereth's eye and then in silence handed it to her. 'I send this to Waterbath, on the possibility of your being there, to ask you to come to me.' Mrs Gereth held it a moment, read it more than once ; then keeping it, and with her eyes on her companion, seemed to consider. There was the dawn of a kindness in her look ; Fleda perceived in it, as if as the reward of complete submission, a slight relaxation of her rigour.

'Wouldn't it perhaps after all be better,' she asked, 'before doing this, to see if we can make his whereabouts certain?'

'Why so? It will be always so much done,' said Fleda. 'Though I'm poor,' she added with a smile, 'I don't mind the shilling.'

'The shilling's *my* shilling,' said Mrs Gereth.

Fleda stayed her hand. 'No, no – I'm superstitious.'

'Superstitious?'

'To succeed, it must be all me!'

'Well, if that will make it succeed!' Mrs Gereth took back her shilling, but she still kept the telegram. 'As he's most probably not there – '

'If he shouldn't be there,' Fleda interrupted, 'there will be no harm done.'

'If he "shouldn't be" there!' Mrs Gereth ejaculated. 'Heaven help us, how you assume it!'

'I'm only prepared for the worst. The Brigstocks will simply send any telegram on.'

'Where will they send it?'

'Presumably to Poynton.'

'They'll read it first,' said Mrs Gereth.

'Read it?'

'Yes, Mona will. She'll open it under the pretext of having it repeated ; and then she'll probably do nothing. She'll keep it as a proof of your immodesty.'

163

'What of that?' asked Fleda.

'You don't mind her seeing it?'

Rather musingly and absently Fleda shook her head. 'I don't mind anything.'

'Well, then, that's all right,' said Mrs Gereth as if she had only wanted to feel that she had been irreproachably considerate. After this she was gentler still, but she had another point to clear up. 'Why have you given, for a reply, your sister's address?'

'Because if he *does* come to me he must come to me there. If that telegram goes,' said Fleda, 'I return to Maggie's tonight.'

Mrs Gereth seemed to wonder at this. 'You won't receive him here with me?'

'No, I won't receive him here with you. Only where I received him last – only there again.' She showed her companion that as to that she was firm.

But Mrs Gereth had obviously now had some practice in following queer movements prompted by queer feelings. She resigned herself, though she fingered the paper a moment longer. She appeared to hesitate; then she brought out: 'You couldn't then, if I release you, make your message a little stronger?'

Fleda gave her a faint smile. 'He'll come if he can.'

Mrs Gereth met fully what this conveyed; with decision she pushed in the telegram. But she laid her hand quickly upon another form and with still greater decision wrote another message. 'From *me*, this,' she said to Fleda when she had finished, 'to catch him possibly at Poynton. Will you read it?'

Fleda turned away. 'Thank you.'

'It's stronger than yours.'

'I don't care,' said Fleda, moving to the door. Mrs Gereth, having paid for the second missive, rejoined her, and they drove together to Owen's club, where the elder lady alone got out. Fleda, from the hansom, watched through the glass doors her brief conversation with the hall-porter and then met in silence her return with the news that he had not seen Owen for a fortnight and was keeping his letters till called for. These

164

had been the last orders; there were a dozen letters lying there. He had no more information to give, but they would see what they could find at Colonel Gereth's. To any connexion with this inquiry, however, Fleda now roused herself to object, and her friend had indeed to recognize that on second thoughts it couldn't be quite to the taste of either of them to advertise in the remoter reaches of the family that they had forfeited the confidence of the master of Poynton. The letters lying at the club proved effectively that he was not in London, and this was the question that immediately concerned them. Nothing could concern them further till the answers to their telegrams should have had time to arrive. Mrs Gereth had got back into the cab, and, still at the door of the club, they sat staring at their need of patience. Fleda's eyes rested, in the great hard street, on passing figures that struck her as puppets pulled by strings. After a little the driver challenged them through the hole in the top. 'Anywhere in particular, ladies?'

Fleda decided. 'Drive to Euston, please.'

'You won't wait for what we may hear?' Mrs Gereth asked.

'Whatever we hear, I must go.' As the cab went on she added: 'But I needn't drag *you* to the station.'

Mrs Gereth was silent a moment; then 'Nonsense!' she sharply replied.

In spite of this sharpness they were now almost equally and almost tremulously mild; though their mildness took mainly the form of an inevitable sense of nothing left to say. It was the unsaid that occupied them – the thing that for more than an hour had been going round and round without naming it. Much too early for Fleda's train, they encountered at the station a long half-hour to wait. Fleda made no further allusion to Mrs Gereth's leaving her; their dumbness, with the elapsing minutes, grew to be in itself a reconstituted bond. They slowly paced the great grey platform, and presently Mrs Gereth took the girl's arm and leaned on it with a hard demand for support. It seemed to Fleda not difficult for each to know of what the other was thinking – to know indeed that they had in common two alternating visions, one of which, at moments, brought them as by a common impulse to a pause.

This was the one that was fixed ; the other filled at times the whole space and then was shouldered away. Owen and Mona glared together out of the gloom and disappeared, but the replenishment of Poynton made a shining, steady light. The old splendour was there again, the old things were in their places. Our friends looked at them with an equal yearning; face to face, on the platform, they counted them in each other's eyes. Fleda had come back to them by a road as strange as the road they themselves had followed. The wonder of their great journeys, the prodigy of this second one, was the question that made her occasionally stop. Several times she uttered it, asked how this and that difficulty had been met. Mrs Gereth replied with pale lucidity – was naturally the person most familiar with the truth that what she undertook was always somehow achieved. To do it was to do it – she had more than one kind of magnificence. She confessed there, audaciously enough, to a sort of arrogance of energy, and Fleda, going on again, her inquiry more than answered and her arm rendering service, flushed in her diminished identity, with the sense that such a woman was great.

'You do mean literally everything, to the last little miniature on the last little screen?'

'I mean literally everything. Go over them with the catalogue!'

Fleda went over them while they walked again ; she had no need of the catalogue. At last she spoke once more: 'Even the Maltese cross?'

'Even the Maltese cross. Why not that as well as everything else? – especially as I remembered how you like it.'

Finally, after an interval, the girl exclaimed: 'But the mere fatigue of it, the exhaustion of such a feat! I drag you to and fro here while you must be ready to drop.'

'I'm very, very tired.' Mrs Gereth's slow head-shake was tragic. 'I couldn't do it again.'

'I doubt if they'd bear it again!'

'That's another matter: they'd bear it if I could. There won't have been, this time either, a shake or a scratch. But I'm too tired – I very nearly don't care.'

'You must sit down, then, till I go,' said Fleda. 'We must find a bench.'

'No. I'm tired of *them*: I'm not tired of you. This is the way for you to feel most how much I rest on you.' Fleda had a compunction, wondering as they continued to stroll whether it was right after all to leave her. She believed, however, that if the flame might for the moment burn low, it was far from dying out ; an impression presently confirmed by the way Mrs Gereth went on: 'But one's fatigue is nothing. The idea under which one worked kept one up. For you I *could* – I can still. Nothing will have mattered if *she's* not there.'

There was a question that this imposed, but Fleda at first found no voice to utter it: it was the thing that, between them, since her arrival, had been so consciously and vividly unsaid. Finally she was able to breathe: 'And if she *is* there – if she's there already?'

Mrs Gereth's rejoinder too hung back ; then when it came – from sad eyes as well as from lips barely moved – it was unexpectedly merciful. 'It will be very hard.' That was all, now ; and it was poignantly simple. The train Fleda was to take had drawn up ; the girl kissed her as if in farewell. Mrs Gereth submitted, then after a little brought out: 'If we *have* lost – '

'If we have lost?' Fleda repeated as she paused again.

'You'll all the same come abroad with me?'

'It will seem very strange to me if you want me. But whatever you ask, whatever you need, that I will always do.'

'I shall need your company,' said Mrs Gereth. Fleda wondered an instant if this were not practically a demand for penal submission – for a surrender that, in its complete humility, would be a long expiation. But there was none of the latent chill of the vindictive in the way Mrs Gereth pursued: 'We can always, as time goes on, talk of them together.'

'Of the old things?' Fleda had selected a third-class compartment: she stood a moment looking into it and at a fat woman with a basket who had already taken possession. 'Always?' she said, turning again to her companion. 'Never!'

she exclaimed. She got into the carriage, and two men with bags and boxes immediately followed, blocking up door and window so long that when she was able to look out again Mrs Gereth had gone.

CHAPTER 20

THERE came to her at her sister's no telegram in answer to her own: the rest of that day and the whole of the next elapsed without a word either from Owen or from his mother. She was free, however, to her infinite relief, from any direct dealing with suspense, and conscious, to her surprise, of nothing that could show her, or could show Maggie and her brother-in-law, that she was excited. Her excitement was composed of pulses as swift and fine as the revolutions of a spinning top: she supposed she was going round, but she went round so fast that she couldn't even feel herself move. Her emotion occupied some quarter of her soul that had closed its doors for the day and shut out even her own sense of it ; she might perhaps have heard something if she had pressed her ear to a partition. Instead of that she sat with her patience in a cold, still chamber from which she could look out in quite another direction. This was to have achieved an equilibrium to which she couldn't have given a name: indifference, resignation, despair were the terms of a forgotten tongue. The time even seemed not long, for the stages of the journey were the items of Mrs Gereth's surrender. The detail of that performance, which filled the scene, was what Fleda had now before her eyes. The part of her loss that she could think of was the reconstituted splendour of Poynton. It was the beauty she was most touched by that, in tons, she had lost – the beauty that, charged upon big wagons, had safely crept back to its home. But the loss was a gain to memory and love ; it was to her too, at last, that, in condonation of her treachery, the old things had crept back. She greeted them with open arms ; she thought of them hour after hour ; they made a company with which solitude was warm and a picture that, at this crisis, overlaid poor Maggie's scant mahogany. It was really her obliterated passion that had revived, and with it an immense assent to Mrs Gereth's early judgement of her. She too, she felt, was of the religion, and like any other of the passionately pious she could worship now even in the desert. Yes, it was all for her ; far round as she had gone she had been strong enough : her love had gathered in the spoils. She wanted indeed no catalogue to count them over ; the array of them, miles away, was complete ; each piece, in its turn, was perfect to her ; she could have drawn up a catalogue from memory. Thus again she lived with them, and she thought of them without a question of any personal right. That they might have been, that they might still be hers, that they were perhaps already another's, were ideas that had too little to say to her. They were nobody's at all – too proud, unlike base animals and humans, to be reducible to anything so narrow. It was Poynton that was theirs ; they had simply recovered their own. The joy of that for them was the source of the strange peace in which the girl found herself floating.

It was broken on the third day by a telegram from Mrs Gereth. 'Shall be with you at 11.30 – don't meet me at station.' Fleda turned this over, but was sufficiently expert not to disobey the injunction. She had only an hour to take in its meaning, but that hour was longer than all the previous time. If Maggie had studied her convenience the day Owen came, Maggie was also at the present juncture a miracle of refinement. Increasingly and resentfully mystified, in spite of all reassurance, by the impression that Fleda suffered more than she gained from the grandeur of the Gereths, she had it at heart to exemplify the perhaps truer distinction of nature that characterized the house of Vetch. She was not, like poor Fleda, at everyone's beck, and the visitor was to see no more of her than what the arrangement of luncheon might tantalizingly show. Maggie described herself to her sister as intending for a just provocation even the understanding she had had with her husband that he also should remain invisible. Fleda accordingly awaited alone the subject of so many manoeuvres – a period that was slightly prolonged even after the drawing-room door, at 11.30, was thrown open. Mrs Gereth stood there with a face that spoke plain, but no sound fell from her till the withdrawal of the maid, whose attention had immediately attached itself to the rearrangement of a window-blind and who seemed, while she bustled at it, to contribute to the pregnant silence; before the duration of which, however, she retreated with a sudden stare.

'He has done it,' said Mrs Gereth, turning her eyes avoidingly but not unperceivingly about her and in spite of herself dropping an opinion upon the few objects in the room. Fleda, on her side, in her silence, observed how characteristically she looked at Maggie's possessions before looking at Maggie's sister. The girl understood and at first had nothing to say; she was still dumb while Mrs Gereth selected, with hesitation, a seat less distasteful than the one that happened to be nearest. On the sofa near the window the poor woman finally showed what the two past days had done for the age of her face. Her eyes at last met Fleda's. 'It's the end.'

'They're married?'

'They're married.'

Fleda came to the sofa in obedience to the impulse to sit down by her; then paused before her while Mrs Gereth turned up a dead grey mask. A tired old woman sat there with empty hands in her lap. 'I've heard nothing,' said Fleda. 'No answer came.'

'That's the only answer. It's the answer to everything.' So Fleda saw; for a minute she looked over her companion's head and far away. 'He wasn't at Waterbath; Mrs Brigstock must have read your telegram and kept it. But mine, the one to Poynton, brought something. "We are here – what do you want?"' Mrs Gereth stopped as if with a failure of voice; on which Fleda sank upon the sofa and made a movement to take her hand. It met no response; there could be no attenuation. Fleda waited; they sat facing each other like strangers. 'I wanted to go down,' Mrs Gereth presently continued. 'Well, I went.'

All the girl's effort tended for the time to a single aim – that of taking the thing with outward detachment, speaking of it as having happened to Owen and to his mother and not in any degree to herself. Something at least of this was in the encouraging way she said: 'Yesterday morning?'

'Yesterday morning. I saw him.'

Fleda hesitated. 'Did you see her?'

'Thank God, no!'

171

Fleda laid on her arm a hand of vague comfort, of which Mrs Gereth took no notice. 'You've been capable, just to tell me, of this wretched journey, of this consideration that I don't deserve?'

'We're together, we're together,' said Mrs Gereth. She looked helpless as she sat there, her eyes, unseeingly enough, on a tall Dutch clock, old but rather poor, that Maggie had had as a wedding-gift and that eked out the bareness of the room.

To Fleda, in the face of the event, it appeared that this was exactly what they were not: the last inch of common ground, the ground of their past intercourse, had fallen from under them. Yet what was still there was the grand style of her companion's treatment of her. Mrs Gereth couldn't stand upon small questions, couldn't, in conduct, make small differences. 'You're magnificent!' her young friend exclaimed. 'There's a rare greatness in your generosity.'

'We're together, we're together,' Mrs Gereth lifelessly repeated. 'That's all we *are* now; it's all we have.' The words brought to Fleda a sudden vision of the empty little house at Ricks; such a vision might also have been what her companion found in the face of the stopped Dutch clock. Yet with this it was clear that she would now show no bitterness: she had done with that, had given the last drop to those horrible hours in London. No passion even was left to her, and her forbearance only added to the force with which she represented the final vanity of everything.

Fleda was so far from a wish to triumph that she was absolutely ashamed of having anything to say for herself; but there was one thing, all the same, that not to say was impossible. 'That he has done it, that he couldn't *not* do it, shows how right I was.' It settled forever her attitude, and she spoke as if for her own mind; then after a little she added very gently, for Mrs Gereth's: 'That's to say, it shows that he was bound to her by an obligation that, however much he may have wanted to, he couldn't in any sort of honour break.'

Blanched and bleak, Mrs Gereth looked at her. 'What sort of an obligation do you call that? No such obligation exists for an hour between any man and any woman who have hatred on one side. He had ended by hating her, and now he hates her more than ever.'

'Did he tell you so?' Fleda asked.

'No. He told me nothing but the great gawk of a fact. I saw him but for three minutes.' She was silent again, and Fleda, as before some lurid image of this interview, sat without speaking. 'Do you wish to appear as if you don't care?' Mrs Gereth presently demanded.

'I'm trying not to think of myself.'

'Then if you're thinking of Owen, how can you *bear* to think?'

Sadly and submissively Fleda shook her head; the slow tears had come into her eyes. 'I can't. I don't understand – I don't understand!' she broke out.

'*I* do, then.' Mrs Gereth looked hard at the floor. 'There was no obligation at the time you saw him last – when you sent him, hating her as he did, back to her.'

'If he went,' Fleda asked, 'doesn't that exactly prove that he recognized one?'

'He recognized rot! You know what *I* think of him.' Fleda knew; she had no wish to challenge a fresh statement. Mrs Gereth made one – it was her sole, faint flicker of passion – to the extent of declaring that he was too abjectly weak to deserve the name of a man. For all Fleda cared! – it was his weakness she loved in him. 'He took strange ways of pleasing you!' her friend went on. 'There was no obligation till suddenly, the other day, the situation changed.'

Fleda wondered. 'The other day?'

'It came to Mona's knowledge – I can't tell you how, but it came – that the things I was sending back had begun to arrive at Poynton. I had sent them for you, but it was *her* I touched.' Mrs Gereth paused; Fleda was too absorbed in her explanation to do anything but take blankly the full, cold breath of this. 'They were there, and that determined her.'

'Determined her to what?'

'To act, to take means.'

'To take means?' Fleda repeated.

'I can't tell you what they were, but they were powerful. She knew how,' said Mrs Gereth.

Fleda received with the same stoicism the quiet immensity of this allusion to the person who had not known how. But it made her think a little, and the thought found utterance, with unconscious irony, in the simple interrogation: 'Mona?'

'Why not? She's a brute.'

'But if he knew that so well, what chance was there in it for her?'

'How can I tell you? How can I talk of such horrors? I can only give you, of the situation, what I see. He knew it, yes. But as she couldn't make him forget it, she tried to make him like it. She tried and she succeeded: that's what she did. She's after all so much less of a fool than he. And what *else* had he originally liked?' Mrs Gereth shrugged her shoulders. 'She did what you wouldn't!' Fleda's face had grown dark with her wonder, but her friend's empty hands offered no balm to the pain in it. 'It was that if it was anything. Nothing else meets the misery of it. Then there was quick work. Before he could turn round he was married.'

Fleda, as if she had been holding her breath, gave the sigh of a listening child. 'At that place you spoke of in town?'

'At the Registrar's, like a pair of low atheists.'

The girl hesitated. 'What do people say of that? I mean the "world".'

'Nothing, because nobody knows. They're to be married on the 17th, at Waterbath church. If anything else comes out, everybody is a little prepared. It will pass for some stroke of diplomacy, some move in the game, some outwitting of *me*. It's known there has been a row with me.'

Fleda was mystified. 'People surely knew at Poynton,' she objected, 'if, as you say, she's there.'

'She was there, day before yesterday, only for a few hours. She met him in London and went down to see the things.'

Fleda remembered that she had seen them only once. 'Did *you* see them?' she then ventured to ask.

'Everything.'

'Are they right?'

'Quite right. There's nothing like them,' said Mrs Gereth. At this her companion took up one of her hands again and kissed it as she had done in London. 'Mona went back that night; she was not there yesterday. Owen stayed on,' she added.

Fleda stared. 'Then she's not to live there?'

'Rather! But not till after the public marriage.' Mrs Gereth seemed to muse; then she brought out: 'She'll live there alone.'

'Alone?'

'She'll have it to herself.'

'He won't live with her?'

'Never! But she's none the less his wife, and you're not,' said Mrs Gereth, getting up. 'Our only chance is the chance she may die.'

Fleda appeared to consider: she appreciated her visitor's magnanimous use of the plural. 'Mona won't die,' she replied.

'Well, *I* shall, thank God! Till then' – and with this, for the first time, Mrs Gereth put out her hand – 'don't desert me.'

Fleda took her hand, and her clasp of it was a reiteration of a promise already given. She said nothing, but her silence was an acceptance as responsible as the vow of a nun. The next moment something occurred to her. 'I musn't put myself in your son's way.'

Mrs Gereth gave a dry, flat laugh. 'You're prodigious! But how shall you possibly be more out of it? Owen and I – ' She didn't finish her sentence.

'That's your great feeling about *him*,' Fleda said: 'but how, after what has happened, can it be his about you?'

Mrs Gereth hesitated. 'How do you know what has happened? You don't know what I said to him.'

'Yesterday?'

'Yesterday.'

They looked at each other with a long, deep gaze. Then as Mrs Gereth seemed again about to speak, the girl, closing her eyes, made a gesture of strong prohibition. 'Don't tell me!'

'Merciful powers, how you worship him!' Mrs Gereth wonderingly moaned. It was, for Fleda, the shake that made the cup overflow. She had a pause, that of the child who takes time to know that he responds to an accident with pain; then,

175

dropping again on the sofa, she broke into tears. They were beyond control, they came in long sobs, which for a moment Mrs Gereth, almost with an air of indifference, stood hearing and watching. At last Mrs Gereth too sank down again. Mrs Gereth soundlessly, wearily wept.

CHAPTER 21

'IT looks just like Waterbath; but, after all, we bore *that* together': these words formed part of a letter in which, before the 17th, Mrs Gereth, writing from disfigured Ricks, named to Fleda the day on which she would be expected to arrive there on a second visit. 'I sha'n't, for a long time to come,' the missive continued, 'be able to receive anyone who may *like* it, who would try to smooth it down, and me with it ; but there are always things you and I can comfortably hate together, for you're the only person who comfortably understands. You don't understand quite everything, but of all my acquaintance you're far away the least stupid. For action you're no good at all ; but action is over, for me, for ever, and you will have the great merit of knowing, when I'm brutally silent, what I shall be thinking about. Without setting myself up for your equal, I dare say I shall also know what are your own thoughts. Moreover, with nothing else but my four walls, you'll at any rate be a bit of furniture. For that, you know, a little, I've always taken you – quite one of my best finds. So come, if possible, on the 15th.'

The position of a bit of furniture was one that Fleda could conscientiously accept, and she by no means insisted on so high a place in the list. This communication made her easier, if only by its acknowledgement that her friend had something left: it still implied recognition of the principle of property. Something to hate, and to hate 'comfortably', was at least not the utter destitution to which, after their last interview, she had helplessly seemed to see Mrs Gereth go forth. She remembered indeed that, in the state in which they first saw it, she herself had 'liked' the blessed refuge of Ricks ; and she now wondered if the tact for which she was commended had then operated to make her keep her kindness out of sight. She was at present ashamed of such obliquity, and made up her mind that if this happy impression, quenched in the spoils of Poynton, should revive on the spot, she would utter it to her companion without reserve. Yes, she was capable of as much 'action' as that: all the more that the spirit of her hostess seemed, for the time at least, wholly to have failed. Mrs Gereth's three minutes with Owen had been a blow to all talk of travel, and after her woeful hour at Maggie's she had, like some great moaning, wounded bird, made her way, with wings of anguish, back to the nest she knew she should find empty. Fleda, on that dire day, could neither keep her nor give her up; she had pressingly offered to return with her, but Mrs Gereth, in spite of the theory that their common grief was a bond, had even declined all escort to the station, conscious apparently of something abject in her collapse and almost fiercely eager, as with a personal shame, to be unwatched. All she had said to Fleda was that she would go back to Ricks that night, and the girl had lived for days after with a dreadful image of her position and her misery there. She had had a vision of her now lying prone on some unmade bed, now pacing a bare floor like a lioness deprived of her cubs. There had been moments when her mind's ear was strained to listen for some sound of grief wild enough to be wafted from afar. But the first sound, at the end of a week, had been a note announcing, without reflections, that the plan of going abroad had been abandoned. 'It has come to me indirectly, but with much appearance of truth, that *they* are going – for an indefinite time. That quite settles it; I shall stay where I am, and as soon as I've turned round again I shall look for you.' The second letter had come a week later, and on the 15th Fleda was on her way to Ricks.

Her arrival took the form of a surprise very nearly as violent as that of the other time. The elements were different, but the effect, like the other, arrested her on the threshold: she stood there stupified and delighted at the magic of a passion of which such a picture represented the low-water mark. Wound up but sincere, and passing quickly from room to room, Fleda broke out before she even sat down. 'If you turn me out of the house for it, my dear, there isn't a woman in England for whom it wouldn't be a privilege to live here.' Mrs Gereth was as honestly bewildered as she had of old been falsely calm. She looked about at the few sticks that, as she afterwards phrased it, she had gathered in, and then hard at her guest, as if to protect herself against a joke sufficiently cruel. The girl's heart gave a leap, for this stare was the sign of an opportunity. Mrs Gereth was all unwitting ; she didn't in the least know what she had done, and as Fleda could tell her Fleda suddenly became the one who knew most. That counted for the moment as a magnificent position ; it almost made all the difference. Yet what contradicted it was the vivid presence of the artist's idea. 'Where on earth did you put your hand on such beautiful things?'

'Beautiful things?' Mrs Gereth turned again to the little worn, bleached stuffs and the sweet spindle-legs. 'They're the wretched things that were here – that stupid starved old woman's.'

'The maiden aunt's, the nicest, the dearest old woman that ever lived? I thought you had got rid of the maiden aunt.'

'She was stored in an empty barn – stuck away for a sale ; a matter that, fortunately, I've had neither time nor freedom of mind to arrange. I've simply, in my extremity, fished her out again.'

'You've simply, in your extremity, made a delight of her.' Fleda took the highest line and the upper hand, and as Mrs Gereth challenging her cheerfulness turned again a lustreless eye over the contents of the place, she broke into a rapture that was unforced but that she was conscious of an advantage in being able to feel. She moved, as she had done on the previous occasion, from one piece to another, with looks of recognition and hands that lightly lingered, but she was as feverishly jubilant now as she had formerly been anxious and mute. 'Ah, the little melancholy, tender, tell-tale things: how can they *not* speak to you and find a way to your heart? It's not the great chorus of Poynton ; but you're not, I'm sure, either so proud or so broken as to be reached by nothing but that. This is a voice so gentle, so human, so feminine – a faint, far-away voice with the little quaver of a heart-break. You've listened to it unawares ; for the arrangement and effect of everything – when I compare them with what we found the first day we came down – shows, even if mechanically and disdainfully exercised, your admirable, infallible hand. It's your extraordinary genius; you make things "compose" in spite of yourself. You've only to be a day or two in a place with four sticks for something to come of it!'

'Then if anything has come of it here, it has come precisely of just four. That's literally, by the inventory, all there are!' said Mrs Gereth.

'If there were more there would be too many to convey the impression in which half the beauty resides – the impression, somehow, of something dreamed and missed, something reduced, relinquished, resigned: the poetry, as it were, of something sensibly *gone*.' Fleda ingeniously and triumphantly worked it out. 'Ah, there's something here that will never be in the inventory!'

'Does it happen to be in your power to give it a name?' Mrs Gereth's face showed the dim dawn of an amusement at finding herself seated at the feet of her pupil.

'I can give it a dozen. It's a kind of fourth dimension. It's a presence, a perfume, a touch. It's a soul, a story, a life. There's ever so much more here than you and I. We're in fact just three!'

'Oh, if you count the ghosts!'

'Of course I count the ghosts. It seems to me ghosts count double – for what they were and for what they are. Somehow there were no ghosts at Poynton,' Fleda went on. 'That was the only fault.'

Mrs Gereth, considering, appeared to fall in with the girl's fine humour. 'Poynton was too splendidly happy.'

'Poynton was too splendidly happy,' Fleda promptly echoed.

'But it's cured of that now,' her companion added.

'Yes, henceforth there'll be a ghost or two.'

Mrs Gereth thought again: she found her young friend suggestive. 'Only *she* won't see them.'

'No, "she" won't see them.' Then Fleda said, 'What I mean is, for this dear one of ours, that if she had (as I *know* she did; it's in the very taste of the air!) a great accepted pain –'

She had paused an instant, and Mrs Gereth took her up. 'Well, if she had?'

Fleda still hesitated. 'Why, it was worse than yours.'

Mrs Gereth reflected. 'Very likely.' Then she too hesitated. 'The question is if it was worse than yours.'

'Mine?' Fleda looked vague.

'Precisely. Yours.'

At this our young lady smiled. 'Yes, because it was a disappointment. She had been so sure.'

'I see. And you were never sure.'

'Never. Besides, I'm happy,' said Fleda.

Mrs Gereth met her eyes awhile. 'Goose!' she quietly remarked as she turned away. There was a curtness in it ; nevertheless it represented a considerable part of the basis of their new life.

On the 18th the *Morning Post* had at last its clear message, a brief account of the marriage, from the residence of the bride's mother, of Mr Owen Gereth of Poynton Park to Miss Mona Brigstock of Waterbath. There were two ecclesiastics and six bridesmaids and, as Mrs Gereth subsequently said, a hundred frumps, as well as a special train from town: the scale of the affair sufficiently showed that the preparations had been complete for weeks. The happy pair were described as having taken their departure for Mr Gereth's own seat, famous for its unique collection of artistic curiosities. The newspapers and letters, the fruits of the first London post, had been brought to the mistress of Ricks in the garden ; and she lingered there alone a long time after receiving them. Fleda kept at a distance ; she knew what must have happened, for from one of the windows she saw her rigid in a chair, her eyes strange and fixed, the newspaper open on the ground and the letters untouched in her lap. Before the morning's end she had disappeared, and the rest of that day she remained in her room: it recalled to Fleda, who had picked up the newspaper, the day, months before, on which Owen had come down to Poynton to make his engagement known. The hush of the house was at least the same, and the girl's own waiting, her soft wandering, through the hours: there was a difference indeed sufficiently great, of which her companion's absence might in some degree have represented a considerate recognition. That was at any rate the meaning Fleda, devoutly glad to be alone, attached to her opportunity. Mrs Gereth's sole allusion, the next day, to the subject of their thoughts, has already been mentioned: it was a dazzled glance at the fact that Mona's quiet pace had really never slackened.

Fleda fully assented. 'I said of our disembodied friend here that she had suffered in proportion as she had been sure. But that's not always a source of suffering. It's Mona who must have been sure!'

'She was sure of *you*!' Mrs Gereth returned. But this didn't diminish the satisfaction taken by Fleda in showing how serenely and lucidly she could talk.

CHAPTER 22

HER relation with her wonderful friend had, however, in becoming a new one, begun to shape itself almost wholly on breaches and omission. Something had dropped out altogether, and the question between them, which time would answer, was whether the change had made them strangers or yokefellows. It was as if at last, for better or worse, they were, in a clearer, cruder air, really to know each other. Fleda wondered how Mrs Gereth had escaped hating her: there were hours when it seemed that such a feat might leave after all a scant margin for future accidents. The thing indeed that now came out in its simplicity was that even in her shrunken state the lady of Ricks was larger than her wrongs. As for the girl herself, she had made up her mind that her feelings had no connexion with the case. It was her pretension that they had never yet emerged from the seclusion into which, after her friend's visit to her at her sister's, we saw them precipitately retire: if she should suddenly meet them in straggling procession on the road it would be time enough to deal with them. They were all bundled there together, likes with dislikes and memories with fears; and she had for not thinking of them the excellent reason that she was too occupied with the actual. The actual was not that Owen Gereth had seen his necessity where she had pointed it out; it was that his mother's bare spaces demanded all the tapestry that the recipient of her bounty could furnish. There were moments during the month that followed when Mrs Gereth struck her as still older and feebler, and as likely to become quite easily amused.

At the end of it, one day, the London paper had another piece of news: 'Mr and Mrs Owen Gereth, who arrived in town last week, proceed this morning to Paris.' They exchanged no word about it till the evening, and none indeed would then have been uttered had not Mrs Gereth irrelevantly broken out: 'I dare say you wonder why I declared the other day with such

183

assurance that he wouldn't live with her. He apparently *is* living with her.'

'Surely it's the only proper thing for him to do.'

'They're beyond me – I give it up,' said Mrs Gereth.

'I don't give it up – I never did,' Fleda returned.

'Then what do you make of his aversion to her?'

'Oh, she has dispelled it.'

Mrs Gereth said nothing for a minute. 'You're prodigious in your choice of terms!' she then simply ejaculated.

But Fleda went luminously on; she once more enjoyed her great command of her subject: 'I think that when you came to see me at Maggie's you saw too many things, you had too many ideas.'

'You had none,' said Mrs Gereth: 'you were completely bewildered.'

'Yes, I didn't quite understand – but I think I understand now. The case is simple and logical enough. She's a person who's upset by failure and who blooms and expands with success. There was something she had set her heart upon, set her teeth about – the house exactly as she had seen it.'

'She never saw it at all, she never looked at it!' cried Mrs Gereth.

'She doesn't look with her eyes; she looks with her ears. In her own way she had taken it in; she knew, she felt when it had been touched. That probably made her take an attitude that was extremely disagreeable. But the attitude lasted only while the reason for it lasted.'

'Go on – I can bear it now,' said Mrs Gereth. Her companion had just perceptibly paused.

'I know you can, or I shouldn't dream of speaking. When the pressure was removed she came up again. From the moment the house was once more what it had to be, her natural charm reasserted itself.'

'Her natural charm!' Mrs Gereth could barely articulate.

'It's very great; everybody thinks so; there must be something in it. It operated as it had operated before. There's no need of imagining anything very monstrous. Her restored good humour, her splendid beauty, and Mr Owen's impressibility

184

and generosity sufficiently cover the ground. His great bright sun came out!'

'And his great bright passion for another person went in. Your explanation would doubtless be perfection if he didn't love you.'

Fleda was silent a little. 'What do you know about his "loving me?"'

'I know what Mrs Brigstock herself told me.'

'You never in your life took her word for any other matter.'

'Then won't yours do?' Mrs Gereth demanded. 'Haven't I had it from your own mouth that he cares for you?'

Fleda turned pale, but she faced her companion and smiled. 'You confound, Mrs Gereth, you mix things up. You've only had it from my own mouth that I care for *him*!'

It was doubtless in contradictious allusion to this (which at the time had made her simply drop her head as in a strange, vain reverie) that Mrs Gereth, a day or two later, said to Fleda: 'Don't think I shall be a bit affected if I'm here to see it when he comes again to make up to you.'

'He won't do that,' the girl replied. Then she added, smiling: 'But if he should be guilty of such bad taste, it wouldn't be nice of you not to be disgusted.'

'I'm not talking of disgust; I'm talking of its opposite,' said Mrs Gereth.

'Of its opposite?'

'Why, of any reviving pleasure that one might feel in such an exhibition. I shall feel none at all. You may personally take it as you like; but what conceivable good will it do?'

Fleda wondered. 'To me, do you mean?'

'Deuce take you, no! To what we don't, you know, by your wish, ever talk about.'

'The old things?' Fleda considered again. 'It will do no good of any sort to anything or anyone. That's another question I would rather we shouldn't discuss, please,' she gently added.

Mrs Gereth shrugged her shoulders.

'It certainly isn't worth it!'

Something in her manner prompted her companion, with a certain inconsequence, to speak again. 'That was partly why I came back to you, you know – that there should be the less possibility of anything painful.'

'Painful?' Mrs Gereth stared. 'What pain can I ever feel again?'

'I meant painful to myself,' Fleda, with a slight impatience, explained.

'Oh, I see.' Her friend was silent a minute. 'You use sometimes such odd expressions. Well, I shall last a little, but I sha'n't last forever.'

'You'll last quite as long – ' Here Fleda suddenly hesitated.

Mrs Gereth took her up with a cold smile that seemed the warning of experience against hyperbole. 'As long as what, please?'

The girl thought an instant ; then met the difficulty by adopting, as an amendment, the same tone. 'As any danger of the ridiculous.'

That did for the time, and she had moreover, as the months went on, the protection of suspended allusions. This protection was marked when, in the following November, she received a letter directed in a hand at which a quick glance sufficed to make her hesitate to open it. She said nothing, then or afterwards ; but she opened it, for reasons that had come to her, on the morrow. It consisted of a page and a half from Owen Gereth, dated from Florence, but with no other preliminary. She knew that during the summer he had returned to England with his wife, and that after a couple of months they had again gone abroad. She also knew, without communication, that Mrs Gereth, round whom Ricks had grown submissively and indescribably sweet, had her own interpretation of her daughter-in-law's share in this second migration. It was a piece of calculated insolence – a stroke odiously directed at showing whom it might concern that now she had Poynton fast she was perfectly indifferent to living there. The *Morning Post*, at Ricks, had again been a resource: it was stated in that journal that Mr and Mrs Owen Gereth proposed to spend the winter in India. There was a person to whom it was clear that she led her wretched husband by the nose. Such was the light in which contemporary history was offered to Fleda until, in her own room, late at night, she broke the seal of her letter.

I want you, inexpressibly, to have, as a remembrance, something of mine – something of real value. Something from Poynton is what I mean and what I should prefer. You know everything there, and far better than I what's best and what isn't. There are a lot of differences, but are'nt some of the smaller things the most remarkable? I mean for judges, and for what they'd bring. What I want you to take from me, and to choose for yourself, is the thing in the whole house that's most beautiful and precious, I mean the "gem of the collection", don't you know? If it happens to be of such a sort that you can take immediate possession of it – carry it right away with you – so much the better. You're to have it on the spot, whatever it is. I humbly beg of you to go down there and see. The people have complete instructions: they'll act for you in every possible way and put the whole place at your service. There's a thing mamma used to call the Maltese cross and that I think I've heard her say is very wonderful. Is *that* the gem of the collection? Perhaps you would take it, or anything equally convenient. Only I do want you awfully to let it be the very pick of the place. Let me feel that I can trust you for this. You won't refuse if you will think a little what it must be that makes me ask.

Fleda read that last sentence over more times even than the rest; she was baffled – she couldn't think at all of what it might be. This was indeed because it might be one of so many things. She made for the present no answer; she merely, little by little, fashioned for herself the form that her answer should eventually wear. There was only one form that was possible – the form of doing, at her time, what he wished. She would go down to Poynton as a pilgrim might go to a shrine, and as to this she must look out for her chance. She lived with her letter, before any chance came, a month, and even after a month it had mysteries for her that she couldn't meet. What did it mean, what did it represent, to what did it correspond in his imagination or his soul? What was behind it, what was beyond it, what was in the deepest depth, within it? She said to herself that with these questions she was under no obligation to deal. There was an explanation of them that, for practical purposes, would do as well as another: he had found in his marriage a happiness so much greater than, in the distress of his dilemma, he had been able to take heart to believe, that he now felt he owed her a token of gratitude for having kept him in the straight path. That explanation, I say, she could throw off ; but no explanation in the least mattered: what determined her was the simple strength of her impulse to respond. The passion for which what had happened had made no difference, the passion that had taken this into account before as well as after, found here an issue that there was nothing whatever to choke. It found even a relief to which her imagination immensely contributed. Would she act upon his offer? She would act with secret rapture. To have as her own something splendid that he had given her, of which the gift had been his signed desire, would be a greater joy than the greatest she had supposed to be left to her, and she felt that till the sense of this came home she had even herself not known what burned in her successful stillness. It was an hour to dream of and watch for ; to be patient was to draw out the sweetness. She was capable of feeling it as an hour of triumph, the triumph of everything in her recent life that had not held up its head. She moved there in thought – in the great rooms she knew ; she should be able to say to herself that, for once at least, her possesion was as complete as that of either of the others whom it had filled only with bitterness. And a thousand times yes – her choice should know no scruple: the thing she should go down to take would be up to the height of her privilege. The whole place was in her eyes, and she spent for weeks her private hours in a luxury of comparison and debate. It should be one of the smallest things because it should be one she could have close to her ; and it should be one of the finest because it was in the finest he saw his symbol. She said to herself that of what it would symbolize she was content to know nothing more than just what her having it would tell her. At bottom she inclined to the Maltese cross – with the added reason that he had named it. But she would look again and judge afresh ; she would on the spot so handle and ponder that there shouldn't be the shade of a mistake.

Before Christmas she had a natural opportunity to go to London ; there was her periodical call upon her father to pay as well as a promise to Maggie to redeem. She spent her first night in West Kensington, with the idea of carrying out on the morrow the purpose that had most of a motive. Her father's affection was not inquisitive, but when she mentioned to him that she had business in the country that would oblige her to catch an early train, he deprecated her excursion in view of the menace of the weather. It was spoiling for a storm ; all the signs of a winter gale were in the air. She replied that she would see what the morning might bring ; and it brought, in fact, what seemed in London an amendment. She was to go to Maggie the next day, and now that she had started her eagerness had become suddenly a pain. She pictured her return that evening with her trophy under her cloak ; so that after looking, from the doorstep, up and down the dark street, she decided, with a new nervousness, and sallied forth to the nearest place of access to the 'Underground'. The December dawn was dolorous, but there was neither rain nor snow ; it was not even cold, and the atmosphere of West Kensington, purified by the wind, was like a dirty old coat that had been bettered by a dirty brush. At the end of almost an hour, in the larger station, she had taken her place in a third-class compartment ; the prospect before her was the run of eighty minutes to Poynton. The train was a fast one, and she was familiar with the moderate measure of the walk to the park from the spot at which it would drop her.

Once in the country, indeed, she saw that her father was right : the breath of December was abroad with a force from which the London labyrinth had protected her. The green fields were black, the sky was all alive with the wind ; she had, in her anxious sense of the elements, her wonder at what might happen, a reminder of the surmises, in the old days of going to the Continent, that used to worry her on the way, at night, to the horrid cheap crossings by long sea. Something, in a dire degree, at this last hour, had begun to press on her heart : it was the sudden imagination of a disaster, or at least of a check, before her errand was achieved. When she said to herself that something might happen she wanted to go faster than the train. But nothing could happen save a dismayed discovery that, by some altogether unlikely chance, the master and mistress of the house had already come back. In that case she must have had a warning, and the fear was but the excess of her hope. It was everyone's being exactly where everyone was that lent the quality to her visit. Beyond lands and seas and alienated forever, they in their different ways gave her the impression to take as she had never taken it. At last it was already there, though the darkness of the day had deepened; they had whizzed past Chater – Chater, which was the station before the right one. Off in that quarter was an air of wild rain, but there shimmered straight across it a brightness that was the colour of the great interior she had been haunting. That vision settled before her – in the house the house was all ; and as the train drew up she rose, in her mean compartment, quite proudly erect with the thought that all for Fleda Vetch then the house was standing there.

But with the opening of the door she encountered a shock, though for an instant she couldn't have named it ; the next moment she saw it was given her by the face of the man advancing to let her out, an old lame porter of the station, who had been there in Mrs Gereth's time and who now recognized her. He looked up at her so hard that she took an alarm and before alighting broke out to him: 'They've come back?' She had a confused, absurd sense that even he would know that in this case she mustn't be there. He hesitated, and in the few seconds her alarm had completely changed its ground: it seemed to leap, with her quick jump from the carriage, to the ground that was that of his stare at her. 'Smoke?' She was on the platform with her frightened sniff: it had taken her a minute to become aware of an extraordinary smell. The air was full of it, and there were already heads at the windows of the train, looking out at something she couldn't see. Someone, the only other passenger, had got out of another carriage, and the old porter hobbled off to close his door. The smoke was in her eyes, but she saw the station-master, from the end of the platform, recognize her too and come straight to her. He brought her a finer shade of surprise than the porter, and while he was coming she heard a voice at the window of the train say that something was 'a good bit off – a mile from the town'. That was just what Poynton was. Then her heart stood still at the white wonder in the station-master's face.

'You've come down to it, miss, already?'

At this she knew. 'Poynton's on fire?'

'Gone, miss – with this awful gale. You weren't wired?

190

Look out!' he cried in the next breath, seizing her; the train was going on, and she had given a lurch that almost made it catch her as it passed. When it had drawn away she became more conscious of the pervading smoke, which the wind seemed to hurl in her face.

'*Gone?*' She was in the man's hands; she clung to him.

'Burning still, miss. Ain't it quite too dreadful? Took early this morning – the whole place is up there.'

In her bewildered horror she tried to think. 'Have they come back?'

'Back? They'll be there all day!'

'Not Mr Gereth, I mean – nor his wife?'

'Nor his mother, miss – not a soul of *them* back. A pack o' servants in charge – not the old lady's lot, eh? A nice job for caretakers! Some rotten chimley or one of them portable lamps set down in the wrong place. What has done it is this cruel, cruel night.' Then as a great wave of smoke half choked them, he drew her with force to the little waiting-room. 'Awkward for you, miss – I see!'

She felt sick; she sank upon a seat, staring up at him. 'Do you mean that great house is *lost*?'

'It was near it, I was told, an hour ago – the fury of the flames had got such a start. I was there myself at six, the very first I heard of it. They were fighting it then, but you couldn't quite say they had got it down.'

Fleda jerked herself up. 'Were they saving the things?'

'That's just where it was, miss – to get *at* the blessed things. And the want of right help – it maddened me to stand and see 'em muff it. This ain't a place, like, for anything organized. They don't come up to a *reel* emergency.'

She passed out of the door that opened towards the village and met a great acrid gust. She heard a far-off windy roar which, in her dismay, she took for that of flames a mile away, and which, the first instant, acted upon her as a wild solicitation. 'I must go there.' She had scarcely spoken before the same omen had changed into an appalling check.

Her vivid friend, moreover, had got before her; he clearly suffered from the nature of the control he had to exercise. 'Don't do that, miss – you won't care for it at all.' Then as she waveringly stood her ground, 'It's not a place for a young lady, nor if you'll believe me, a sight for them as are in any way affected.'

Fleda by this time knew in what way she was affected: she became limp and weak again; she felt herself give everything up. Mixed with the horror, with the kindness of the station-master, with the smell of cinders and the riot of sound, was the raw bitterness of a hope that she might never again in life have to give up so much at such short notice. She heard herself repeat mechanically, yet as if asking it for the first time: 'Poynton's *gone*?'

The man hesitated. 'What can you call it, miss, if it ain't really saved?'

A minute later she had returned with him to the waiting-room, where, in the thick swim of things, she saw something like the disk of a clock. 'Is there an up-train?' she asked.

'In seven minutes.'

She came out on the platform: everywhere she met the smoke. She covered her face with her hands. 'I'll go back.'